YOUNG AND DUMB

DUMB

Year of Years

Thomas Louis Carroll

Cover by 100Covers

ISBN: 978-1-7366339-1-5

To contact the author about speaking appearances or signed copies, go to www.ThomasLouisCarroll.com

ALMANOR
& LORAQUE
PRESS

Almanor & Loraque Press
300 Central Avenue SW
Suite 2000 East
Albuquerque, NM 87102

This book is dedicated to the late Jennifer Carroll Wilson

This is a true story.
Well, most of it is true, or some of it anyway, or—oh, to hell
with it, who cares, just read the damned book . . .

Contents

Chapter One
Ten Thousand Miles to Go

"*Thomas!* Come in here."

Thomas? Who the hell was she calling Thomas? No one called me Thomas. Never. It was Tommy, Tommy, always Tommy, even from her. And if my mother was calling me Thomas, something was up. And probably nothing good.

"I'm late," I yelled, heading for the elevator of my Fifth Avenue apartment. Had to split.

"Come in here," she yelled from the library.

"I have dancing school. Can't be late." I stood in front of the elevator, but she caught me.

"Come in here for a moment."

A summons! I hated a summons. It's never good. And here I was, dressed in the wardrobe of the Pierre Hotel Dancing School—grey flannels, blue blazer, white shirt, striped tie, always the striped tie, Gucci shoes, white gloves. You know, the usual. And I didn't want to be late to my ballroom class, because if you were late, Mrs. Tambien made you dance the foxtrot with Alice

Fourgatt, God forbid, who had hair that hadn't been washed since Geo W. cut down the cherry tree. But Mother was calling. What choice did I have? I went into the book-lined library.

"I can't be late," I said, standing before her.

"Yes, yes, sit down," she said. I sat, but not without hesitation. Sitting meant staying. She looked me over in a way that made me very uncomfortable.

"Yes," she said, "I've made the right decision."

"What is it, Mother? I have to be—"

"Yes, I just wanted to be sure, and now I am."

"Sure of what?"

"What I have done," she said. "Tommy, I have a letter here."

At least it was back to Tommy. "And what does it have to do with me?" I grumbled.

"A great deal, a very great deal, I'm afraid."

I considered bolting. Just taking off and never looking back, because whenever my mother said, "a very great deal," it was a very great deal.

"You have been admitted to Bashford."

"Bashford?"

"Yes, that august institution. Bashford School."

"That's a boarding school."

"Yes, the one your father went to, and his father, and his father before him."

"I think I've heard of it," I said, knowing that I'd heard of it a thousand times. "And why would I be admitted?"

"Because you are going there."

"That's ridiculous. I'm not going there."

"It's settled," she said.

"Can I remind you that I start my senior year next week, and that I'm already in school right here in New York City?"

"I withdrew you."

"You did WHAT?"

"I just got off the phone with Mr. Lacklan, and he fully understood."

"Understood what?"

"That you are going to spend your senior year at Bashford."

"Mother, you've been hitting the highballs again."

It was a common phrase in my house, "you've been hitting the highballs," and it meant exactly what it sounded like, *you're drunk.*

"Mom," I said, changing strategy on the fly, with an infinitely softer tone, "let's think about this. I'm here. It's my senior year. I have my friends. Why don't I just finish up here?"

"You're going to Bashford," she said. She said it with finality I didn't like. Change of strategy again. "I'm not going."

"Look, Tommy, I've done you a grave disservice."

"You have? I feel my service has been just fine."

"Yes. Look at you. You're seventeen years old. And you're dressed like an old man, with your grey flannels and blue blazer. I wasn't always like this, you know. I was young and wild and active if you know what I mean. Don't tell your father."

"This is not reassuring me, Mother."

"And you, son, need to live a little. Get out. Be free."

"I am free just the way I am."

"Here's the skinny, son," she said. "The world is changing. It's not all yacht clubs and Rolls Royces and trips to Lyford Cay—"

"It isn't? Well, hell, someone should have told me," I said, thinking a little levity might work.

She went on, "They're rioting out there about the Vietnam War. There's drugs and the pill and hippies in San Francisco. I know, I see it all on TV."

"Mom, everything is fine."

"You're just lucky I saw it now and not after it was too late."

"Mom," I said, "let's be sensible. I'm not going to any stupid boarding school."

"Go pack," she said forcefully, and it was then I knew the gig was up.

I presented myself next morning at eight o'clock (yes, that ungodly hour). Chauffeur Fritzy attempted to pack my steamer trunk into the Rolls Royce. It didn't quite fit.

"Thank God," I said, "guess I can't go."

"Force it, Fritzy," said my mother. He did.

"Isn't this a little rushed?" I insisted desperately, a last attempt.

"Get in the car, Tommy."

Fritzy floored it, as if I might jump out. And before you knew it, we were flying up the FDR Drive, headed to somewhere in the wilds of Connecticut.

"Don't kill us, Fritzy. Tommy here has his whole life ahead of him," said my mother.

"Yes, Ma'am," he said, slowing down a bit.

As we drove in silence for a while, I contemplated what jumping from a moving Rolls Royce would do to my Gucci shoes.

"Would you like some music?" asked Fritzy, fiddling with the radio while my mother stared out the window. James Taylor came on.

With ten miles behind me
And ten thousand more to go . . .

"Oh, turn that. I don't understand rock n' roll, Tommy, do you?"

"Oh, for God's sake, Mother, please."

Fritzy turned it to Broadway tunes.

"Ooooooklahommmma, where the wind comes sweeping down the plain."

"Much better," she said. "Now that's a score."

"I'm sure gonna miss this," I said. My mother shot me a look, but too bad for her—she was kicking me out.

New York City has a way of leaving you behind for no good reason, as if it doesn't care about you at all, and before long we were crossing bridges, whizzing through toll booths, finding our way to I-95 and into that vast wasteland we call the country. We zoomed by Greenwich, Stanford, Westport, New Haven, then turned north to Hartford and some nightmarish small town called Windsor, with an orange-roofed thing called Howard Johnson's.

"Mother, they don't have a Ritz Carlton here, you know."

"Hmm," she quipped dryly. "Very funny."

Chapter Two
Tied to the Whipping Post

At about noon, we arrived at Bashford, pulling up to the front of Founder's Hall, with a shocking amount of brick, like brick everywhere. Like what's the deal with brick?

"Oh, look, it's right out of Dickens," I said. "Can I have some *more*?"

"Oh, stop it, Tommy."

"I'm sure someone will be here soon to flog me."

"Oh, quiet."

Jumping out, Fritzy wrestled my steamer trunk to the sidewalk, and my mother glanced around at the august hall in front of her, and the dorms on both sides, with boys popping their heads out, and the Headmaster's house in front. All very satisfactory, at least for her.

"Aren't you getting out?" she inquired.

"No."

"Tommy, please." Several more boys stuck their heads out from the windows—smelling the blood of a new student, I imagined.

"Look, an eager new boy ready to be buggered," I said.

"Tommy, please get out."

"I'm not getting out. This is all a terrible mistake. And we can rectify it by getting back in the car and going back to the city."

I heard some laughter coming from the windows. It was a mild September evening, and all the dorm windows now flew open onto the scene.

"Tommy, just come out and—"

"I'm not going here, Mother, and that's final."

A long pause, during which I cocked my head quizzically and wondered what was going on.

"Fritzy," I heard my mother order, "proceed."

Fritzy climbed into the back seat, grabbed me around the waist, and pulled. Taking hold of the head rest of the front seat, I held on for dear life.

"Let go," said my mother.

"No."

"You have to, Tommy—"

"No. I said no."

As gales of laughter came from the dorm windows, I came to the realization that any chance I had at this school was now totally blown.

"Grab his legs."

Fritzy got a hold of my legs, and as he ripped the headrest from my hands, I fell on my ass in the back seat. Quickly, he pulled me out of the car, and I landed with a thud on the asphalt. This caused a giant laugh from the windows. I picked myself up, dusted myself off, regained my dignity, and bolted back for the car. Fritzy headed me off.

"I thought you were my friend, Fritzy," I said indignantly.

"Sorry—you know, my job."

Now every window filled with boys. And it was me they were laughing at.

"See what you've done."

"All right, boys, back inside," yelled a commanding, towering voice. And the moment was rescued by the arrival of Mr. Grover Howe, a teacher, or was he a master? I mean, it was 1972. Did they still call them masters? Who the hell knew?

"Hello, I'm Mr. Howe"—he introduced himself to my mother.

"Nice to meet you," she said, meaning it, relief in her tone.

"And this must be Tommy Stafford himself, our new senior."

"Yes, I'm Tommy," I said. "Could I talk to you a second?"

He consented to be pulled aside by me and I lost sight of my mother. "You see, Mr. Howe, this is all a very big mistake," I said. "I mean, I'd very much like to try your school, but I'm afraid they're expecting me back at my school in New York City."

He deadpanned, "Should I call you a cab, then?"

"A cab?"

"Yes, to get to the train station?"

"The train station?"

"Yes, because your mother just took off in the car."

I looked up. Fritzy was making high speed, receding into the distance down the tree-lined road. I did the only dignified thing I could think of—I galloped after the car, waving my arms.

"Come back, come back," I yelled. "Please come back."

No dice. Fritzy kept his foot on the gas. To my horror the car got to the end of the road and turned, never to be seen again. Or at least till Thanksgiving. I made my way back to my steamer trunk and Mr. Howe.

"I can drive you to the station," said Mr. Howe. "Or you could give it a try."

"Oh, hell," I said. "Lead on."

He picked up one side of the steamer trunk, I picked up the other. And we entered the world of brick, vast amounts of brick, a shocking amount of brick, and windows and boys everywhere. Just boys. I got a sinking feeling. I turned to Mr. Howe.

"This is coeducational school, isn't it?"

"All boys," he said.

"Oh, great. Just great."

"But we have dances with the local girls' school, Chalmers. It's just down the road."

"Well, that's something."

As we walked, an Allman Bros. song floated out of the dorm window.

> *Tied to the whipping post*
> *Tied to the whipping post*
> *Good, lord, I feel like I'm dying . . .*

And good lord, I thought, was I tied to the whipping post!

Chapter Three
A Prayer for Tommy

Mr. Howe took me back to his dorm, rattling on all the way about "This is the dining hall . . . This is the science lab," and "This is the library," as if I couldn't tell what was a dining hall or a library.

"And this is your dorm," he said, arriving at the front door. It was classic whatever architecture they called it, you know, brick and ivy crawling up it, with wooden windows and some kind of metal roof and balconies on the upper floors, where at the moment snippy upper classmen were languidly hanging over the balcony, acting like God had chosen them for this assignment.

Mr. Howe turned to me. "You're a senior, and I thought I'd put you with a really good kid, Ben Warden, who can see that you get off on the right foot, if you are okay with that. He's a real Bashford man."

I wasn't sure just what a Bashford man was, and I wasn't sure I cared. So I just nodded. What choice did I have? I was a prisoner of fate. We clunked the trunk up the stairs to the second floor and into the first room on the right, where three boys were playing cards on the bed. One of them, a skinny boy with bad skin and a face like a bird of prey, briefly eyed me but did not get up.

"Ben Warden, meet Tommy Stafford, the new boy." Mr. Howe waved his hand in my direction. "He'll be in here with you."

"Hello," I said.

Ben looked at me as if I were some species of insect, before going back to the game.

"What are you playing?" I asked. "Gin?"

They rolled their eyes at me. Literally rolled their eyes. I thought that only happened in bad movies.

"I can play backgammon if you have a board," I said, warming up. They didn't respond to that either.

"Well, I'll let you get acquainted," said Mr. Howe, backing towards the door. "Warden, take care of him or I'll have you working in the kitchen for the year."

"Yes, Mr. Howe," said Warden.

I didn't like the fact that he had to threaten Warden to be nice to me, but I let it go and, opening my trunk, took out my tennis sweaters.

"Do you play?" asked a boy.

"Sure." I said it like, *doesn't everybody?*

"Do you play football?" asked Warden, with a sudden spark of interest.

"No, not football."

"We all are on the football team," said Warden.

"Hey, Warden, call."

"Okay, two pair." Warden flipped over his cards.

"No way," said the kid, and he threw his cards down.

"Play poker?" Warden said to me.

"Sure," I lied.

"Got any money?"

"A little."

"Let's see it," said Warden. "Give him some chips."

A moment later a stack of white, red and blue chips sat in front of me. I wasn't sure how much they were worth, but he dealt out the cards, and if someone threw in a blue, I threw in a blue, and so on. At this point, I had to admit I didn't really play poker, and they didn't care 'cause they managed to take the ten bucks off me in about ten minutes. Then without so much as a goodbye they left. Promising start, I thought.

I unpacked and sat there, staring at the wall. I knew there might be something going on, like some nonsensical orientation session I should attend, or tryouts for male cheerleading, or the glee club or whatever, but I must admit it didn't interest me. So I just sat there staring at my furniture, a wooden desk, a steel chair, a bed with a mattress about as thick as a quarter pounder. Fun times, I thought. The door flew open and Warden stuck his head in.

"Want to go with us to town?" he asked.

"Uh, sure." I got up to go with him.

"No, not yet. Meet us at Building and Grounds in half an hour."

"I don't know where that is."

"You'll find it. See you there."

"I could just go with you—"

But he was gone. I threw on a pair of grey flannel slacks and a V-neck tennis sweater, what I thought to be the right outfit, and walked out onto the Quad, the Grand Central Station for students, about a hundred yards long and half as wide, filled with hundreds of boys and, I'm glad to say, a few Chalmers girls. It was then I realized I might not be dressed as appropriately as I thought, as everyone seemed to be in jeans with T-shirts and jean shirts and sandals, and everything seemed ripped—ripped jeans, ripped shirts, even ripped bandanas. And the hair. Mine was short, but theirs was longish, or actually long, and for the most part scraggily uncombed.

I had a walk around campus. Besides the brick, there were walkways—you know, dirt walkways, cobblestone walkways, asphalt walkways. The Quad had seven dormitories around it, each with a pedestrian name like Foster, Martin, Donner, with walkways between them and spaces between buildings to exit the Quad every thirty yards or so. Each dorm had a very imposing door at the front, as if to say, *This is a dorm, duncehead, in case you didn't know.* The dining hall, with its row of white windows, was at one end of the Quad; at the other end was Founder's Hall, the nerve center of it all, with the Dean's Office, the classrooms on the top floor, and the chapel, which I hoped to spend as little time in as possible.

I walked through Founder's and came out facing a river. Or I thought it was a river. It looked like a river, but hell, what did I know about rivers? If it wasn't the Hudson or the East River, it was a stream, wasn't it? An inconsequential waterway on the way to nowhere. Next to this waterway were a series of playing fields, football, soccer, lacrosse, track and field—you know, the fields for any school that wanted to grow real men. Not sure where that left me, however. The tree-lined road leading in and out of school ran to the east, and I took it, and probably would have walked all the way to Hartford, except an earnest-looking young man came towards me on the road.

"Excuse me, can you tell me where Building and Grounds is?" He eyed me suspiciously. "I'm new," I explained.

"Go that way," he said, pointing towards the lacrosse field. "Jump the guardrail, go down the hill, and you'll see a dirt road. Follow it till you see a big red building. That's B&G."

"Right, B&G," I replied, not knowing what the hell was a B&G. I walked on till I saw the guardrail, jumped it, went down the hill, and came across the building called Building and Grounds. Oh, B&G . . . No one was there, so I waited. And waited. And waited. About an hour later a car drove by, and Warden stuck his head out and yelled, "Fucking whuss," and they kept going. I got the message. I walked slowly back to my dorm, wondering if one could get a good Waldorf salad anywhere nearby, then sat in my dorm room, ruminating about dancing school and how I wouldn't mind dancing with Alice Fourgatt after all.

Warden returned a few hours later. "We looked for you," he said.

I wasn't playing this game, so I said, "I decided not to go."

"Well, you should have told us."

"Sorry."

Warden let me accompany him to dinner, in a giant rectangular room, with high ceilings, maybe twenty feet high, and dozens of round wooden tables with cracks in the wooden tops and with food stuck down in the crevices, with a layer of grease on top.

"Sit with us," said Warden, "after you get your food." He pointed to the line.

I stood in line and got my Turkey Surprise, which seemed somewhat devoid of turkey, instant mashed potatoes you could form into a hockey puck, string beans that were more like pencils, and a roll you could play baseball with. Warden and his football-playing heathens motioned me to come sit with them in the corner of the room. There were seven of them at the table and eight chairs, so I went around to take my chair. They were all laughing. You know, that suppressed laugh that's not really suppressed at all, with heads down. I put my tray down and looked down at my chair.

"There's pudding on my chair," I said. It looked like rice pudding, but it could have been any variety of pudding, smeared all over the seat.

"I don't know how *that* got there," said Warden, busting a gut; they all joined in.

"Very funny," I said.

I walked away and found an empty table, sat down, and pulled out my disgusting silverware, noticing that if you looked closely at the knife, you could see grease stains that looked like a map of Eastern Europe. I ate my Turkey Surprise by myself. Occasionally, I snuck a look back at Warden and could see they were all still having a good laugh. I spotted Mr. Howe sitting not far off and thought, "Oh, no, he's going to come over," and sure enough, he got up and came over.

"Stafford," he said.

"Mr. Howe."

"Sitting by yourself?"

"Just this once," I responded. "It's all kind of overwhelming, so I wanted to be alone for a while."

"Okay, but just this once. Don't be a loner," said Mr. H.

"No, not me."

"Warden taking care of you?"

"Oh, he's taking care of me, all right," I said, with a little more truth than I intended.

"That's good. He's a good man."

"He's a real pip," I said. I wasn't quite sure what a pip was, but it sounded about right for a boarding school in the middle of frickin' nowhere with a bunch of football-playing psychos as roommates.

Mr. Howe retreated to his seat, and I settled back in, enjoying my instant rice pudding as if it were my only lifeboat to sanity. It wasn't bad, actually. After dinner I wandered around and ended up in the library, where the librarian, Mrs. Sanders, found me a book on leaf fossils, and I actually read it and kind of liked it. I thanked her as I headed back to my dorm. Perhaps that was my destiny, studying leaf fossils. *Au revoir*, New York New York.

In record time, I fell asleep, since being asleep seemed far better than awake at this point, and I would have slept a good ten hours except for being awoken by a flurry of arms and fists and elbows and lots of yelling by Warden and his boys, "Get him. Hit him, hard." I wrapped my arms around my head to protect me from the blows, which kept coming.

"Hit him," Warden yelled over the din. "Hard."

I managed to free myself and jump up and hit back after several seconds. The boys shrieked with laughter, running out of the room. I turned on the light. Warden's bed was empty. I went to the mirror. It hurt but wasn't so bad, just a mere saber wound, as my father would say, so I rubbed my head a bit, locked the door, and got back into bed. Waking me up, Warden pounded on the door a while later. I got up in my Bloomindales pajamas and opened the door.

"What did you lock it for?" he asked.

"Fuck you," I said, getting back into bed. I said a prayer. 'Cause it had been quite a first day, a real corker, and I wanted to thank God that I was fortunate enough to attend such an elite boarding school with such great examples of humanity, and how lucky I was to be alive!

Chapter Four
Polished Silver

Warden put the word out that no one was to speak to me—the silent treatment—and at first, I didn't know; I thought people here were just boring. But after a while I figured it out and resigned myself to exile. So getting along with people was something I didn't have to worry about, I said to myself.

"It's like West Point," I told my mother on my weekly phone call. "No one speaks to me."

"What did you do?"

"Mother, I didn't do anything. Except show up."

"Well, do your best."

Classes started a few days later. At least there was someone, if not to talk to, to listen to. My first class was in Founder's Hall, and I headed there in my best tennis sweater.

"How's it going?" asked Mr. Howe, passing me in the Quad.

"Going great, Mr. Howe," said I, and kept on walking. I should have said I was tired of getting beat up in the middle of the night by a bunch of low-IQ morons, and that I was going back to New York to file a class-action lawsuit against the school. But I didn't.

My English class was taught by a tall, pencil-thin thirty-year-old named Mr. Rock, whom I took an immediate dislike to, and halfway through the first class I said under my breath, "Those who can't do, teach."

"We have a new senior this year," said Mr. Rock soberly. "Thomas Stafford. From New York. Let's take a moment and see what you've learned in your previous school, Thomas."

"Tommy," I corrected.

"Have you read Chaucer?"

"No." I looked around at the other boys, like, *who the hell reads Chaucer?* But no one nodded back, so I looked back at Mr. Rock.

"Coleridge?"

"Who?"

"Yeats? Byron? Keats?"

"Uh, no."

"Who have you read, Mr. Stafford, if I may ask?"

"Red Badge of Courage," I said, with a sudden swagger in my voice.

"Nonsense," said Mr. Rock. "Pure American pulp. Garbage."

"You're pure American pulp," I muttered, but he couldn't make it out.

"What did you say?" He whirled around.

"Nothing."

"I don't care if you come from New York City or the moon. In my class you will read the classics and you will like them," intoned Mr. Rock. A voice from the back of the room yelled, "But they suck," and the room exploded in laughter. The kid who yelled out had long black hair parted in the middle and wore a jean shirt, with a red bandana around his neck; he had a wicked smile.

"Another thoughtful comment from you, I see, Mr. Burke," Rock said. "Thank you for that trenchant analysis, once again,"

"Well, they do," said George Burke.

"Yes, well, we won't dwell on your ignorance, will we?"

"Today's assignment was John Donne," he said. "Did you do your reading for today, Thomas?"

"Uh, no, I don't have the book."

"It was dropped off in your room a week ago."

I heard laughing from Warden in the back of the room. *Bastard.*

"I didn't get it. Sorry."

"Mr. Stafford, I'll tell you something. If you don't do the homework, you won't last here at Bashford. If you insist on ignoring my assignments, you can—"

"I didn't get the book," I insisted.

"Well, we'll see about that," he said, moving on to John Donne. I didn't know who Donne was and didn't really care, but when he got to the part about *No man is an island,* I muttered, "You got that fucking right."

"Another brilliant observation?" asked Mr. Rock, his eyebrows arching.

"No, sir."

As I left the class, I took a look back for George, but the chair was empty now. He was nowhere to be found. Ben Warden snickered at me and withdrew with his Neanderthal football players into the hall. But a few days later, Warden and his friends burst into my room and looked actually happy to see me.

"Come out for football," said Warden.

"I don't play football, and besides"—I was suspicious—"tryouts are over."

"We talked to Coach Turner, and he said it would be okay."

"Really?"

"Yeah, today after classes. Come on, Stafford, we really need you."

"You *need* me?"

"Tommy, we need you," he said.

"Oh, okay." If they needed me, it was my scholastic duty. Right?

I reported to the Cage—you know, that horrifying place where all athletic gear goes to die—after class.

And Socks, (his name was really Socks), the head of the Cage, looked me over. Socks appeared to have been born bald; he looked like he never grew hair ever, with a scar on his face obviously from a knife fight on board an aircraft carrier, and hands that seemed obviously a complete stranger to a bar of soap.

"You going out?" He was skeptical.

"Yes."

"Okay." So he piled me up, shoulder pads, football pants with plastic sliding pads inserted, a helmet with leather strap, cleats with old laces knotted together, a jersey with the number 87, and an old jock strap. I held up the jock strap as if to say, *really?*

"Just wear it," he said. "You'll be glad you did."

I suited up. It felt good to suit up. I had never suited up before. As I walked out of the locker room, my cleats clattering on the cement floor, I thought, *how hard could this be?* Especially with all this padding on. I might have even strutted. I don't know if I did, but I might have. From the window of a dorm came the song . . .

Born to be Wild
Born to be Wild

On the field, the whistle blew. "Sprints!" *Oh, my God, they aren't gonna make us run?* I asked myself. But sure enough, the whole herd of brown jerseys lumbered down the field towards the goal posts. I could only think of those massive herds of buffalo crossing the plains in the days of ole. "Run it again," yelled the coach. And off we went again.

"Okay, down set," yelled Coach Turner. The guys all knew what this meant. I had no idea. They lined up across from each other. Warden lined up against me. I wasn't sure what was going on. The whistle blew. The two lines rushed at each other, colliding with a fury of helmet hits. I just stood there, watching, wondering if ambulances were in the wings.

Warden rushed at me. At the last second, with no time to brace, I saw him. He flattened me.

Now when someone knocks the wind out of you, you may remember, you can't breathe for many seconds, and you roll around like you are dying and wondering when the lungs might work again. I flopped around like a fish on the dock. Coach Turner blew the whistle and came over.

"What's wrong with him?" he said in that gruff football tone.

"Just got the wind knocked out of him," said Warden as I regained consciousness. Coach Turner looked down at me.

"You want to play football, son?"

"Uh, I guess so."

"You guess so? What the hell kind of answer is that? If you don't want to play football, what the hell are you doing here?"

"You needed me."

"What in hell—"

"Warden said you needed players."

The whole squad broke out laughing.

"Where'd you play before?"

"I haven't," I said.

"Then what the hell are you doing out here?" he yelled. "Warden!"

"Sorry, Coach. He told me he played."

A tall, skinny boy, wearing number 56, walked out of the crowd and picked me up by the shoulder pads. "You okay?"

"Yeah," I said.

"Don't let 'em fuck with you," he said. "Come on." He walked me off the field and up the stairs to the locker room. "It's a trick they play on the new guys. Bring some guy who doesn't play and beat the crap out of him."

"Fun game."

"I gotta get back," he said, hotfooting it out of sight before I could get his name.

In the locker room I took off my pads, gave them back to Socks. "Don't worry," he said, "Happens to lots of kids."

"Socks, who's number 56?" I asked.

"Oh, that's O'Connor."

"Who?"

"Jamie O'Connor. From Virginia. Plays end. Why?"

"No reason." I dressed and headed back to civilization.

Weeks went by. Because no one would talk to me, I spent a lot of time at the library. Mrs. Sanders gave me a book on the national parks, and I drew maps and calculated how long it would take to drive from Yosemite to Acadia in Maine. From there I wandered back to my room. Giving up after a few nights, Warden set up his bed in another room, so I locked the door at night and kept the goons at bay. I put a sign on the door that said FUCK OFF, and each night they'd come, bang on the door, read the sign as if they had never seen it before, break out laughing and go away. It was a game to them.

Everyone at Bashford had a work job, a job around school to help keep things up, a way to learn discipline. Oh, and help the school fire half the workers. As if the tuition wasn't expensive enough, they had to make us work. I was assigned to the kitchen, dish duty, like, yes, washing *dishes*. I couldn't wait. A week after I arrived, I reported for my first night and found myself standing there at the kitchen door with a half-dozen men who looked as though they were escapees from the local correctional facility. And me. I'd been standing there for what seemed like an eternity, hoping I could just leave, when a man approached with the biggest arms I've ever seen, like massive biceps, a flattop haircut, a barrel chest, short legs, clean shaven, and weary eyes.

"You Stafford?" I nodded. Squinting at me, he gave me a look that did not inspire confidence. "Okay, I'll get you started."

He took me back into the kitchen to the conveyor belt where the dishes returned from the dining hall. "Here's what you do—pull 'em, scrape 'em, pile 'em, stack 'em," he said.

"You mean, touch them?" I said. He smirked and left me alone. The Salisbury steak and gravy sloshed over the side of the plates coming back on the conveyor belt.

"You pull 'em, you scrape 'em, you pile 'em, stack 'em." Wugs came back with a pair of work gloves.

"I assume I'm to put these on," I said.

"You bet your ass, unless you want to beat the crap out of your hands."

So I put on the gloves. "What do I call you, sir?" I asked.

"Sir? No one's ever called me sir, and I've been here twenty years. Call me Wugs."

"Wugs?"

"Yup." And he left me. A plate came by, and against my will I touched it, grabbed it, swiped the food into a garbage pail, and stacked the plate on a stainless-steel rack, then reached for the next one. Pull 'em, scrape 'em, pile 'em, stack 'em. The smells made me want to throw up at first but soon didn't bother me anymore. The plates came faster and faster. Before long, I was stacking three at a time, grabbing, swiping, stacking. My shirt got wet and my pants from the spray coming off the rinser. Wugs returned with an apron. "Wear this," he said.

"Thanks." He looked at the pile of plates, all wiped clean, stacked nicely, and then he looked again at me without a word, took the rack back to the dishwasher, and moved another rack into place. I put on the apron, tied tightly behind my back. Now I was into it. The plates came—two, four, six at a time—and I whipped them off, swiped them clean, racked them up, and when Wugs came in as the stack of dishes was at its height, a giant wobbly pile of dishes well over my head, and said, "Need another hand?" I waved him off, lunging for a half-eaten plate of Turkey Surprise.

When the ordeal was over, I loaded them into a massive gleaming dish washer, and when it was full, Wugs filled it with soap and closed it up and ran it. "You need a hat," he said, retrieving a Bashford baseball hat. I put it on, and he reached for it and turned it backwards on my head. "There," he said, "that's it."

The washer popped open a bit later, and the workers hoisted the silverware and spilled the knives, forks, and spoons onto great grey plastic trays with holes to let the water drip off into a drain. A heat lamp came on red hot, drying the silver but with marks still on it. I picked up one knife, wiping it with the clean part of my apron.

"No time for that," said Wugs, walking by. So I let it all go. It got put back into the silverware bins for breakfast.

"Okay, you can leave," Wugs told me, taking off his apron.

I was disappointed. I didn't want to go. At least not back to my room. Here for once someone talked to me. But I hung up my apron, and Wugs wrote my name on a piece of tape, "Stafford," and put it above my apron. I nodded and left.

"Mr. Howe," I said, running into him in the Quad the next day, "I started my work job."

"Good, how did it go?"

"Who's Wugs?"

"Oh, don't mind him. He's been here twenty years. He runs the kitchen. Did he bother you?"

"Uh, no. I was just wondering."

"He was in prison," said Mr. Howe.

"Prison?"

"Yeah, many years ago."

"For what?"

"Ask him," said Mr. Howe. "He'll tell ya."

My work job was three times a week: Tuesday, Thursday, Saturday. So I had to wait another day to go back, and this time for lunch. I showed up, went straight to the scraper station, and worked the whole lunch without seeing Wugs. Finally, I asked someone.

"Where's Wugs?"

"He's off." That was all. I realized that asking wouldn't yield anything, so I went back to scraping. But when the silverware came out, this time I laid it all on the grey plastic trays, set up a towel system, and before putting each piece back in the bin I shined it. I left hundreds of shiny knives, forks, and spoons gleaming under the fluorescent lights of the dining hall. And by God, I may not make it at Bashford and be a Bashford man, but I would have the shiniest silver in New England, or die trying anyway.

In English class we were reading Dickens, a writer I'd actually read. So I raised my hand.

"Stafford, you want to say something?" Mr. Rock seemed genuinely surprised.

"I read the book."

"Well, that's an improvement," he said. "What does our New York friend think about it?"

"Well, the characters in Dickens are a lot like the characters around here," I said.

"Is that right?"

"Yeah. Ben Warden reminds me of Fagin." The room bust a gut.

"Mr. Howe reminds me of Mr. Pickwick."

Another laugh.

"And just who do I remind you of?" asked Mr. Rock.

"Uriah Heap," I said.

"Right the fuck on," said George.

"Well, I don't particularly like the reference," said Mr. Rock. "But at least you are reading the books."

I called my mother that night from the pay phone in the hall.

"How are you?" she wanted to know.

"Fine."

"Do you like it there?"

"No."

"Give it time, Tommy. It will be all right."

"No, it won't. I hate it here."

"You've always done well at school."

"I don't like the other boys. They don't like me."

"You're not popular?"

"No, Mother. I'm not popular."

"It's only a year, son. Then you'll go to Yale."

"A year is a long time, Mother."

Chapter Five
Change in New Haven

I set my alarm for two. Like two a.m. It looked so strange on the alarm clock. I mean, two o'clock in the morning. Who gets up then? Switching on my desk lamp created a ring of light. Out the window was impenetrable darkness. My bags were packed and ready. I pushed my bologna sandwich I had stolen from the dining hall into my sack. I dressed quickly, zippering my coat all the way up, slipping on my Gucci loafers. I mean, what else do you wear when running away from school? Ben would come back later for his clothes, but he wouldn't notice me gone. So I knew I had time. If I could get away clean.

I let myself out into the hallway. The red exit sign blazed at the end of the hall. I walked down, stepping lightly, and pressed my shoulder against the door. When it opened, the frigid two-in-the-morning November air surged over me. I let myself out. In the Quad, a few security lights blazed in the night sky. I started walking.

It was against the rules not to be in your dorm after lights out, so getting caught at two in the a.m. would get me in a lot of trouble, but I didn't care. Hell, I wanted to be thrown out. Crossing the Quad, I noticed the light in the security office. It was on. So I ducked down and passed it without incident. At Founder's, I found myself on the perimeter of the campus, about to take that fateful step. Being caught out here after lights out was an offense but being caught off campus after lights out was grounds for expulsion. I was taking my new life into my hands. So I took the step. I crossed the line. I was free. Well, actually I was walking in subzero temperatures, holding a small backpack, twenty miles from my destination, the train station in Hartford. So I wasn't really free at all. In fact, I was unbelievably fucking cold.

The road to town led straight down the tree-lined street. I hurried. My breath made white clouds in the moonlight in front of me. I saw no one. No one tried to stop me as I found my way to the main road. A few cars went by. Who the hell was out at this time? Slinging my pack over my shoulder, I started walking south towards Hartford. After about two blocks, a car slowed down and stopped. A man looked out.

"Need a ride?"

I hadn't thought of hitching at that hour, but—.

"Sure." I jumped in. The man had short curly hair. His hands were rough, his nails bitten to the bloody skin. But the car was warm.

"Where you going?" he asked.

"Train station."

"They running trains at this time of night?" I could detect suspicion in his voice.

"I'm catching the train to New York in the morning."

"Okay."

He started his Pinto, and we rode for a while without talking. He lit a cigarette and smoked it, then used it to light another. The car filled up with smoke.

"Want to make some money?" he asked.

"Money?"

"Yeah, want to make some?"

"Doing what?"

"Whatever you want."

Now, that's something you don't hear every day—making money doing whatever you want. But it seemed a little creepy. Really creepy.

"Yeah, whatever you want," he repeated.

"I'll get out here." Okay, so I wasn't at the Ritz-Carlton anymore. I wasn't at the Pierre Hotel. I wasn't at the Gucci store, getting the latest gold-buckled loafer. I was in some weird guy's car, at two-thirty in the morning, and this guy was hitting on me. How the mighty have fallen.

"Don't get mad at me," he said. "I was just trying to get you some work."

"I don't want any work. Now, let me out."

"I'll drive you to the station. It's just over two blocks."

I didn't say goodbye when he let me out, and he didn't say it either, but no harm done. I was glad to walk into a warm, well-lit place, the train station. It was a massive brick (what else?) building with large windows facing the street. It had long wooden benches, and the place was empty. I put my pack down. I sat down, and despite saying to myself, "Don't fall asleep," I fell asleep. The bustle of the train station woke me at about six. The New Haven train ran at 7:20, so I went to the window to buy a ticket.

"Grand Central."

"Change in New Haven," said the gruff ticket agent, throwing my change back at me.

The route started there in Hartford, so the train was already waiting. I got on early and chose a seat next to the window, eating my bologna sandwich even though it wasn't seven o'clock yet. A lurch came right at 7:20, and off we went, with the car filling up with commuters at the stations along the way. At New Haven I made the change to the New Haven Line south.

"Westport!" "Stanford!" "Greenwich!" "Harlem One Hundred Twenty-fifth Street," called out the conductor.

The train slowed through Harlem and slowed even more as it entered the tunnel under Manhattan to Grand Central Station. As it stopped a few times I could see the rats scurrying around inside the tunnel, disappearing into holes. When the train stopped at its final resting place at GCS, the station was lit up like a lighthouse, the bagel shop was full, the hot dog guy was setting up and the line for coffee was long. I went by them all and let myself out onto Forty-second Street. I didn't have enough money left for a cab, and there was no limo waiting (egad!), so I walked uptown to my street and over to Madison and then to Fifth Avenue and into my building. The doorman held the door.

"Tommy, you're back."

"I am," I said.

"Your parents aren't here, you know."

"They're not?" I stopped. He could see it came as a shock.

"They left yesterday—for the Bahamas, I think."

"Oh."

"Go on up. Agnes is there."

The elevator let me out on the fifth floor, and I went in. Agnes wasn't up yet, so I made myself toast for breakfast and drank a coke from the pantry. Agnes came in as I was finishing. Agnes was the maid. She was Irish, you know, American but Irish, from Staten Island. She was more of a friend than a maid, at least to me, but she needed this job.

"What are you doing here?" she snapped. Something, or I should say someone, moved behind her. A man. In our house. She tried to block my view, but she knew I saw. While the cat's away . . . I smiled, like it was okay, and she relaxed a bit. Having a lover in the house overnight could get her fired. But I wasn't going to tell. The man disappeared down the hall and out of sight.

"Where's Mom?" I asked.

"They left for Lyford Cay yesterday."

"When are they coming back?"

"Two weeks."

"Oh."

Two weeks? What was I going to do for two weeks? I needed my mother here to have it out with her, get back into my old school, and forget the whole thing ever happened. But she wasn't here. She was in the frickin' Bahamas. Now what?

"You look tired," commiserated Agnes.

"Yeah, maybe I'll sleep for a while."

"You can't sleep in your room," she said.

"Why not?"

"Your mother turned it into a study."

"Already? I just left."

"Sleep in the guest room," she said sweetly.

"Okay."

I woke up thinking this sucked. I was not at school. And not welcome here. My room was gone. My parents gone. I was out of money. I could stay here, I guessed, but what would I do? I wanted a showdown with my mother. I wanted closure. I wanted my life back.

I went to my mother's china pot, opened it, finding a wallet but no money. I hunted through her desk. Nothing. Empty desk drawers too. I found some money in her bathroom, under her pills, two twenty-dollar bills. I packed my bag again. Without saying goodbye to Agnes, I went down in the elevator to the street—the doorman nowhere to be seen. After footing it to Grand Central, I bought a ticket, had enough for a hot dog and a coke, got on the train, changed in New Haven, and made the return trip in two hours and a half. A sophomore kid from Bashford was there with his father, catching a cab, so they gave me a ride. Either the kid didn't know he wasn't supposed to talk to me, or he didn't care. Either way I got a ride. I got back about five. I threw my bag on my bed.

"Where were you?" said Warden, getting a change of clothes.

"None of your fucking business," I said. And for once he shut up.

Chapter Six
Born to be Wild

Weeks went by, and each day the sun set earlier. As the darkness started getting to me, I thought maybe I should just lie down on the railroad tracks that ran by the school and wait for the 7:15 to New Haven, the particularly fast express. Quick and easy. How nice to just end all this. Then I thought maybe I should just tie Ben Warden to the tracks and let him feel the undercarriage of the 7:15. What the fuck.

I wandered through life. If you've ever done that, you know it means just floating, never sticking to one place, trying not to think at all about your next encounter or where you'll be in the next hour. You just drift. You just get by. That's what I did. I got by. I hardly spoke to anyone. I barely looked anyone in the eye. The only thing I looked forward to was my work study job. Shining silverware.

Wugs came out of his kitchen to watch me shine. He didn't acknowledge me, or even look at me, but he watched me, with heavy eyes and great concentration. After several minutes, he took a few steps forward. Grabbing the knife, he held it up. I caught my breath. He slowly nodded, looking at me. I looked at him, like *okay?* He put the knife down and went back to his kitchen, yelling along the way about the Salisbury Steak. After my shift ended, I went to where he was smoking a cigarette in his tiny office, with loads of notebooks piled high on the one shelf behind him.

"Wugs," I said.

"Yeah?"

I didn't say anything. I couldn't. It didn't take him long to figure it all out.

"You having a rough time?" he asked.

"I'm on silence," I said. He knew about silence. The silent treatment. I wasn't the first, and he'd been there twenty years.

"Look, kid," he said. "Everybody knows I been in prison, right?" I nodded. "So listen to me. It could always get worse. Who put you there?"

"Warden."

"Oh, that guy?" He laughed softly, the kind of chuckle you make when you don't like somebody. I felt better.

"I'm going to put you on the line," he said.

"The line?" He said *the line*. Now, the line was the cooking, and nobody got on the line except Wugs himself, plus two of his cooks, who also had obviously been to prison if judging by their command of the English language. No one, no student that is, had ever worked the line. And he was asking me to work the line.

"You'll have to come in early," he said.

"I'll come in," I said. "Anytime."

"Good, start tonight. You can make the mashed."

And so my family became Wugs and his guys, which I kinda liked. I got to hang my apron up with his guys (no other students got to do that either) and wore my Bashford cap on backwards like Wugs told me to do and make mashed potatoes and then some creamed corn another night and French toast for breakfast. And soon the other students were making fun of me, calling me Son of Wugs and that kind of thing, but I didn't care.

After work, I'd wander over to the library. While the librarian was polite, even the adults figure out who's on silence. No one wants to talk to an outcast, so she kept her distance too. I mean, even the librarian wouldn't talk to me. I stopped calling home, no reason really, and my mother stopped calling me, figuring there wasn't much to be done anyway.

It was a weekend, either Saturday or Sunday, when I was sitting on my bed after my kitchen shift, when Warden stuck his head in the room.

"Hey, we're going down by the river. Want to go?"

"Fuck you, Warden," I replied.

"Look, I'm sorry," he said. "I've been rough on you, so I want to make it up to you."

"Make it up?"

"Yeah. I shouldn't have been such a jerk to you and put you on silence. I know that now. So me and the guys are going down by the river, and we wanted to know if you'd like to come along."

Warden never wanted me to go anywhere without some reason, but I was kind of desperate. And eager to get off silence.

"Okay," I said. "Why not?"

"Excellent," he said, very convincingly.

It was a cold November day, dreary like you've never seen dreary. After I threw on my Bashford sweatshirt and my Gucci loafers, we headed out on the damp, wet ground, with the sky overcast like the clouds were made of lead. We walked through the Quad, past the dorms, over the road; jumped the guardrail, slid down the hill, went into the woods, past the B&G building, and down a dirt road. Several others joined us, wearing their football jerseys, the football goons.

"It's Son of Wugs," said one, but it seemed good-natured.

We arrived at a squat brick building, with an old smokestack, abandoned now, but once a workhorse for the school, probably used as a heating plant back in the day. It had a small clearing in front of it and a stream behind it, and woods all around. We stopped there. The cornerstone plaque read 1905. We were facing a mass of small-paned windows, like forty panes across and fifteen panes down. Warden picked up a rock.

"Third row, fifth window," said Warden. He threw. Glass shattered. "Fuck," he said. He had hit a window, but not third row fifth window from the left. Another guy picked up a rock.

"Eighth row, second window," he said and threw. Glass shattered. "Fuck," he said.

Another guy picked up a massive rock. "Third, tenth," he said and let fly. "Right on," he said as glass shattered on the window in the third row, tenth from the left. "Right the fuck on."

"You try," said Warden.

Now, I really didn't see the point of breaking windows like this, but since this was the only human interaction I'd had in the past month and I was off silence, I said why not, and picked up a rock.

"Fourth row, fifth one over," said I, and let fly. And amazingly, it hit the window in the fourth row, fifth from the left.

"All right," I said.

I turned to celebrate, but the guys were gone. Gone. Like nowhere to be seen. All of them. I looked back and saw a security jeep speeding up down the dirt road. *I was being set up again.* So I ran. Into the woods, behind a tree. The jeep stopped, and two security cops got out and, looking for me. I could see their boots as they walked in my general direction, but that's about it. Cop boots.

"Come out," the officer yelled. "We know you're there."

That wasn't going to happen.

"Come out," yelled the other officer. "We saw you."

I took off. I had the good sense to cover my face with my Bashford sweatshirt as I ran.

"Stop," yelled the security guard, bolting after me. "Stop."

I did not stop. I ran with everything I had, letting the mud splatter up over my Gucci loafers, getting into those little gold buckles. I could hear the officers running after me. I was a good runner. And I ran. Then I heard the jeep start up, so I knew they had doubled back. Now it was a race between man and machine. I crossed the stream, knowing they would have to drive down to the bridge about a quarter mile away. I came up on the other side and onto the lacrosse field. I crossed it, moving away from the campus, as I knew they would be watching the road back to school. As I ran along the wooded edge of the field, I could see my breath as I ran.

Near the river the field came to an end, so I turned and ran along the water's edge. When the jeep burst out onto the field, I dashed into the woods and ran straight in. The trees overhead blotted out the sun as I got deeper and deeper into the woods. The woods got thicker, with old rotting logs to jump over, poison ivy, fallen leaves in great puddles of rainwater, moss on rocks, little streams to cross. My plan was to go as far as I could and then double back to the campus, hoping they'd given up. I stopped running after a while and listened. Nothing. But not wanting to take any chances, I walked deeper and deeper into the woods. After a while through the trees I saw something. It came in and out of view as I got closer until I was standing in front of a cabin, a small cabin, a dirty grungy cabin with the roof falling in, a wooden door, a cinderblock front, peeling paint, and a small tin pipe on top of the roof. Smoke trailed upward.

Someone was inside. But who? Where was I? I was cold. I had muddy feet. I was tired. But go in?

"You lost 'em," said a husky voice behind me. "It was close, but you lost 'em."

I whipped around. It was that kid from my English class, George Burke, the one who shouted out stuff from the back of the room at Mr. Rock. The kid with the long, very long, black hair parted in the middle and tucked behind his ears. He had a thin face, like a fine bird of prey, and wire-rimmed glasses.

"You saw?"

"I saw the whole thing," he said. "It was fucking awesome. Why were they chasing you?"

"I was throwing rocks at the old B&G building."

"Warden, right?" he said.

"What?"

"It's an old jock trick. Take someone you want to fuck over to the building and then split when security shows up."

"How would they know?"

"They tip 'em off."

Even for Warden, that was unbelievable.

"You comin' in?" He pushed at the door.

A blast of warm air hit me as I followed him in, and it felt good. Oh, and a blast of smoke. There were five of them, all Bashfordians, dressed in jeans, ripped jeans that is, with work shirts or T-shirts with Jefferson Airplane graphics on the front, and boots.

"I brought Stafford," said George, matter-of-factly. I didn't know he even knew my name.

Everyone stopped smoking, playing guitars, lighting pipes, setting up the bong, and they stared at me. I knew they knew I was on silent treatment. Hell, everybody knew. So I wasn't sure what they would do next. One by one they turned to look for guidance to a guy with a pronounced brow, almost Neanderthal, deep-set eyes, with long brown hair pulled back in a ponytail. He was taking a hit on a joint, so he stopped in mid-hit and looked me over. Then a smile broke out on his face.

"Hey, dude," he said. "Want a hit?"

"Sit there," said George.

Someone handed me the joint, and I thought for a moment about all the rules I would be breaking, the instant expulsion if caught, the shame I would bring onto the family—and took a hit. The rolling paper was an ivory color, the ember small and round, and the joint was small now—the end very close—and my fingers burned. I drew the smoke into my lungs, trying to be hip as possible in the "I do this all the time" kind of way. And of course unable to hold it. Out came a barking cough. The big guy horse-laughed.

"Go again."

"Yeah, go again," they all yelled.

So I took another hit, more gracefully this time. And as I finished the hit, the high flowed over my brain, the getting-high wave, and it flowed over me like a wave from the ocean. I laid back and exhaled all the smoke. It felt great.

"Yeah," the guy next to me said. "Give that here." Smiling, I passed the joint.

"Okay, introductions," said George. "You know me. I'm George. This is Rennes."

"Dude," said Rennes.

"His first name is David, but the last guy who called him that got kicked in the teeth, so I wouldn't. This is Jamie O'Connor—"

"I know you," I said. "From football."

"Yeah, that fucker Warden almost got you killed." Jamie was not as tall, but thin, with a wickedly handsome face, brown hair just over the ear, so not so long, but shaggy—a strong lean body and large ears.

"And this is Peter Chartson. We call him Charts." He was the least friendly, looking me over, but not unkindly. He was taller, maybe the tallest, with short, wiry hair with little curls, a broad, almost-fat face, big teeth, round eyes, and a cigarette dangling from his mouth.

"And this is Barker, or Bark for short," said George. "He's fucking nuts. I mean, we're all fucking nuts, but he's really nuts." Bark was real thin, and not very tall, with a shock of brown hair parted to one side, a jaw that stuck out a mile, birdlike eyes, a tall forehead, and a body that looked like it belonged to a ninety-pound weakling.

"Hey," he said, smiling.

"So, I gotta tell you guys what happened," said George, his eyes blazing. "I was coming down from the dorm with all this pot, so I wasn't going anywhere fucking near Founder's and I saw this jeep flying out of the woods"—he was really throwing himself into the story now—"and then I saw Stafford here running like a motherfucker and I knew they were hunting him, so I followed along. The security fuckers kept circling back, but Stafford ran into the woods and they finally gave up. Right?"

"Yeah," I said. "Kind of."

"He outran them—and they were in a jeep!"

"Cool," said Rennes, taking a hit and passing me the joint.

"Uh, yeah."

"Roll another," said Charts.

Bark took out his plastic bag filled with pot, took out his pack of rolling papers and a sheet of rolling paper, and placed the paper on his lap. He then placed his hand in the plastic bag and with two fingers selected a nice bud. Crushing it, he let it all fall into the rolling paper.

"More," said Jamie.

"I know how to roll a joint."

"Just roll."

Bark licked the gum side of the paper and sealed it into a fat joint. Charts flicked his lighter and held out the flame, and Barks, leaning into it, lit the joint, drawing the smoke deep into his lungs. Then he let it out in a trail of smoke crossing the room.

"Yeah," said Rennes. "Nice, dude." Rennes took a hit, a long one, a deep one, and then while holding it, stuck his arm out and offered it to me. Not around the circle but across the circle. To me. I took it, gripped it, and took a hit.

"Let's play," said Rennes with a husky laugh. He reached for his guitar, George reached for his, Jamie got out the bongos, and Charts got his drumsticks.

"What?" said Jamie.

"Born?" asked George.

"Born," Rennes said.

"Do you know the words?" George asked me.

"To what?"

"'Born to Be Wild.'"

"Oh, you're the guy no one talks to," said Charts in a sudden flash.

"Yeah," I admitted.

There was a long, silent pause.

"Fuck them," said Rennes. "Let's play."

George tuned his guitar, Jamie set up his bongos, Charts got his drumsticks out and practiced on the back of a chair. When Rennes hit the first riff on his guitar, everyone pounded, and I mean pounded, their guitars and bongos and drums, and out it came. Steppenwolf.

Born to be wild . . .
Born to be wild . . .

Even I got into the action, singing, "Born to be wild" at the top of my lungs, though singing is not my strong suit, but it just felt so good. After that we played Crosby, Stills, Nash & Young, "Southern Man," and it went on and on and on, and I didn't want it to stop. I sang the chorus again and again, and Rennes nodded to me when I sang, like I got it right.

Barks grabbed some little round white sugar-coated doughnuts out of his backpack, and we sucked those down and drank bug juice from the dining hall from a thermos Jamie brought.

We left the cabin at sunset, and I started back the way I came. But George stopped me. "No, this way. They'll be looking for you that way." We headed north instead of south, hopped two fences, found a bridge over the Farmington River, got onto the road into school from Windsor, and walked right down the middle of the road as if we had been in town.

"See you, dude," said Rennes, and they split. I went back to my room, where Warden was waiting.

"Where you been?" he said.

"Shut up, Warden."

"What's with you?"

"Nothing," said I. "Nothing that affects you, anyway."

I got up to go to dinner. "Hey." He looked apologetic. "Can I go with you?"

"No."

At dinner I grabbed my tray, loaded it up, walked to my empty corner, and sat. George came over a minute later.

"Fuck that," he said. "Come sit with us."

I took my tray, walked past Warden and his football players, put my tray down next to George, with Charts, Rennes, Jamie, and Bark.

"What the fuck?" Jamie scowled at Warden and his moron football players.

"Yeah, what the fuck," said George.

Yeah, what the fuck, I thought.

Chapter Seven
Are You Experienced?

"Dad, I need a stereo," I said, standing at the pay phone in the dorm, talking with my father with five guys behind me waiting for the phone—and yelling every few seconds, "Hurry the fuck up."

I could hear my father's resistance to getting me anything that could play rock 'n roll. "That's a big expenditure, son. We should talk about—" Yeah, like that was a lot of money to him. He just didn't want to buy me a stereo, because on that stereo I might play rock n' roll, for God's sake.

"Dad, everyone has a stereo, and I need one."

"Son, why don't we talk about it when you come home for Christmas?"

"Because Christmas is still a month away and I need it now."

"Son, this is something—"

"Dad, I need a fucking stereo and I need it now."

"Don't use that kind of language with—"

"Dad, if you want me to stay in this awful place, you'll go buy me a tuner, an amplifier, a turntable, and speakers, and get it to me as fast as you can."

After a long pause he said, "All right, where do I get this stuff?"

"Liberty Music on Sixty-eighth Street."

"Okay."

"And have Fritzy drive it up to me tomorrow."

"Fritzy has a job, you know, and—"

"I'll be waiting."

"Anything else?" he said in that pissy tone.

"Yeah, extra needles."

"What's all this going to cost me?" he said.

"Dad, you can handle it."

The next afternoon just before dinner our silver Rolls Royce pulled up in front of Founder's Hall, with me there to meet it. I knew the boys would make fun of the Rolls, but I said, *fuck it, who cares,* I wanted my stereo and this is how I had to get it.

"Hello, Tommy," Fritzy greeted me, jauntily stepping out of the car with his chauffeur cap on, probably for the benefit of the boys hanging from their windows and whistling at the Rolls Royce. "I have some boxes for you." The stereo system came in six boxes, and Fritz handed me the extra needles in a brown paper bag.

"You should do very well with all this, Mr. T," said Fritz.

"Thanks for bringing it up," I said. "And I forgive you for, you know, last time."

"You like this place?"

"No, but this will help." The stereo boxes were sprawled all over the drive.

"I'm going now. I'll get some dinner at Howard Johnson's and be back in the city by nine."

"Thanks, Fritz," I said. "You're a friend."

"Good luck, Mr. Tommy," he said, fast footing it to HJ's.

"Hey, you," I called to some unsuspecting freshman boy walking past. "Help me with these." He considered, then complied, so we carted the stereo to my room. Looking at his disappointed face, I gave him a five-buck tip. And perking up, he said thanks. Luckily, idiot Warden was off with his moron buddies, so I got to set up the stereo.

Warden opened the door an hour later. "Out!" I yelled.

He hesitated, then fled. It took me another hour to get it all set up: the two speakers on either side of my desk, the tuner perched atop of the amp, the turntable on top of the amp. Then it struck me. I didn't have a record. What was I going to play? I needed a record, dozens of records. I tore out of the room, straight across the Quad to Flagg and up to the second floor, where I pounded on George's door and without waiting for an answer flung myself in.

"Whoa," he said, "steady now."

"George, I just got it!"

"The stereo?"

I nodded.

"And you need to christen it?"

This was a moment George lived for, the first record on a new stereo, and it had to be just right. *Just right.* So he pondered as I stood there, waiting, waiting . . .

"I got it," he decided. Without hesitating further, he flipped through his two-foot-long album collection, whipping out an album. "Come on, let's roll."

We ran straight out across the Quad and back to my dorm, and a few moments later George stood above my stereo, eyeing it. He nodded approval as he looked over the turntable, tuner, amp, and speakers.

"Nice, dude," he said. "Nice."

"So what is it?"

"There is only one album for a christening, only one, and I have it right here." With a great circling of his arm, he brought out a brightly colored album with a giant Afro on the cover.

" 'Are You Experienced?' " said George. "That's the one. Jimi."

"Jimmy?"

"Jimi," said George. "Hendrix."

"Hendrix," I agreed because it sounded right.

He took the album out; no, he let it slide carefully out of the cover into his hand as if catching a baby and held it along the edge with a flat hand to keep from touching the vinyl. This was not just a record but was a sacred element; and we were not just playing music; it was a godly act. As if he were handling nitroglycerin, he placed it over the center bullet and let it slide down carefully onto the turntable. He nodded. I hit the switch, and the phonograph started to turn. He picked up the needle and laid it down carefully on the vinyl. It hissed as it went around, hiss . . . hiss . . . hiss . . . and Jimi started to play his electric guitar, and it might have been the most amazing thing I've ever heard.

Are you experienced?
Have you ever been experienced?
Well, I have.

George sat back and closed his eyes. The door opened.

"What's that?" said Warden, wrinkling up his face.

George yelled, "It's Jimi Hendrix, you fucking idiot. Jimi fucking Hendrix. Okay? Okay? How in fuck's sake do you not know that?"

"I'm going to dinner," said Warden. And he split. We laughed.

At dinner, word went around that Tommy had a new stereo, so after dinner we all met in my room. Rennes brought the Crosby, Stills & Nash double album with Neil Young on it, and we played "Southern Man" and yelled "Southern Man" every time it came up. Jamie brought the Allman Bros and put it on.

"Sweet Melissa."

As it played, a new world opened up to me, a world that seemed perfect to me, at least at that moment, the world of Gregg and Duane and Dickie Betts and the sweetest slow song I ever heard.

Crossroads, seem to come and go . . .
But back home he'll always run
To Sweet Melissa

When it was over, we sat silent, overcome. Until . . .

"Let's go smoke a joint by the river," suggested Rennes, and we piled out, but not before I carefully turned off my tuner and amp, putting the needle up, and closing the clear plastic top on the turntable.

We jumped the short wall and headed down the river, walking along the tree-lined edge till we got far enough away so no one would see the matches or the burning embers in among the trees. When George lit up first, we stamped our feet in the cold, passing the joint around. We skipped rocks on the river and when I got an eight-skip, everyone said, "Whoa, dude." As we were finishing the joint, a car stopped on the road above and just stayed there.

"Security," yelled Jamie. With that, we all split in different directions, making it back to the dorm just before lights out. I still don't know if it was security or not, but hell, what fun it was to run from the car, whoever it was, and whatever it was, and feel the rush of danger.

Chapter Eight
Gucci Gone

I neglected to lock my door after I got back, so Warden burst in with his moron buddies and fists flew. There were five of them, or six, I wasn't sure, 'cause to protect myself I had to put my arms over my head. Ordinarily, they didn't really do much damage—it was just the act of beating me that they liked—but tonight it was different. They unloaded on me. This time it was serious. After Warden dragged me onto the floor, they took turns kicking me in the ribs and on my cheek. And then, like lightning, they were gone, just gone, out the door—the door shut behind them. A stillness in the room. I got up. At the sink I washed off the blood and saw for the first time the black and blue under my eye. I got into bed and laid my head gently on the pillow and drifted off. I'm not sure how long it was before someone shook me awake.

"Hey, what you doing in bed?" said a voice, with light flooding in from the open door. It was George. I lifted my head to see what he had.

"Holy fuck, what happened to you?" He was horrified.

"Nothing."

As he raised my chin his eyes hardened. "I'm getting Rennes. He's got to see this."

In a moment he was back with Rennes and they just stared down at me. Rennes didn't say anything, just looked. A slow fury came over him.

"Come on," he said. He grabbed me by the shirt and lifted me out of my bed. Charts, Jamie, and Bark fell in behind us. George brought up the rear.

"Where are we going?" I asked.

Rennes didn't respond, so I shut up and let myself get dragged. We went up one flight, pushed through the door into the hallway, walked halfway down the hall, stopped at a door, and Rennes put his ear to it.

"Are they—"

"Shh," said Rennes. "Shut up."

He heard what he needed to hear inside and put his shoulder to the door. In we went. We burst through the door and found Warden and his moron buddies sitting on the bed and the chair, smoking cigs. Rennes went straight for Warden, made a fist with his shirt, lifted him off the bed, and pushed him against the wall. Bark, Geo, Charts, and Jamie each seized one of the other guys and froze them in place.

"What the—" screeched Warden.

"See what you did?" said Rennes, looking back at my face. "See it?"

"What?" said Warden. "I didn't do—"

"Let me tell you something," said Rennes. "This"—and he looked back at me—"is never going to happen ever again. Got that?"

"Get your hands off me."

" 'Cause if you and your fucking idiots here touch one hair on his head, you'll hear from us. And next time won't be so nice. Got that?"

Warden shut up, and that was sweet silence.

"Come on," said Rennes, letting go of Warden, who slumped down against the wall. He was heading out, with us following, when Warden blundered in the blunder of all blunders.

"Fuck you, Rennes, you stupid Neanderthal."

Now, truth be told, Rennes did look a bit like a Neanderthal, with his protruding brow, deep-set eyes, and massive forehead, and he was a little sensitive about it. Warden woke the volcano. In a split second, Rennes, reversing course, had Warden up against the wall again, by the neck, closing off his circulation. I thought for a moment he was going to kill him.

"Scissors," yelled Rennes.

Rennes held out his hand and Jamie placed a pair of scissors in it. Hand on Warden's neck, he raised the scissors.

"What are you doing?" screamed Warden, struggling to break free.

Rennes sliced off half his hair, the whole right side, in three major clips of the scissors.

"What are you doing, you stupid fucking idiot?" screamed Warden.

"Missed a spot," said Jamie, pointing.

"You stupid—"

"Looking good," said Charts.

"Oh, nice," said Bark. "Half a head of hair."

And there he was, my tormentor, the angry man of Bashford, the beater of my head, sprawled on the floor, gasping for air, with half a head of hair and the other half flopping all over the place. We split.

"I got this," said George as we headed back down the hallway. He dragged me to my dorm and instead of going to my room banged on Mr. Howe's door.

"Don't say anything," he ordered.

The door opened. Mr. Howe stood there in his undershirt—a little shocking to see him that way— proving once again that dorm monitors had lives too.

"Mr. Howe," said George.

"Boys, what can I do for—" He saw Tommy. "What happened to you?"

"This—is what your guy did to Tommy here," said George. "Warden. He beat him senseless every night. Every night, Mr. Howe. That's what he did."

Mr. Howe took me by the chin and turned my head this way and that, so he could get several angles of my black-and-blue face.

"Sorry, I thought Warden was a good guy," he apologized. He seemed to mean it.

"You were wrong, all right," said George, in an unapologetic way most kids never talked to teachers. "So we're taking him."

"Taking him?"

"He's moving to Flagg. And if you don't say yes, you'll have a big lawsuit on your hands."

Mr. Howe considered. "Good night, boys," he said, closing the door.

George laughed. "That was a lot fucking easier than I thought. Come on."

Rennes and the guys were back in my room. It didn't take long to box and bag all my stuff up and head out the door and back to Flagg, where a bed magically appeared (you never knew where this stuff came from), and I was set to bunk in with George.

"Cabin," Rennes gave the order.

We scattered in different directions, George and me along the river, Rennes and Jamie across the lacrosse field, Bark and Charts into town and then backtracking across the Farmington Bridge. There first, George and I started a fire. The little cabin warmed up in no time. The others arrived pretty soon after, Bark carrying a brown grocery bag. He threw it on the little makeshift table. I thought it was food, but he threw the bag at me.

"Here," said Bark, "put these on. You can't wear those clothes anymore."

I opened the bag. A light blue work shirt, ripped jeans, a red bandana, a big leather belt with a silver buckle, and Dingo boots. Charts nodded at me, and I got busy changing. I took off my Gucci shoes, my grey flannels, my white Brooks Bros shirt. I balled up the old clothes and put them in the brown bag. I heaved the bag into the garbage.

"Oh, no," said Rennes. "Give here." I pulled it from the trash and handed it to Rennes. He walked out the door with it and we all followed. In an old oil drum Jamie had a nice fire going outside. Rennes threw the bag of clothes into the fire. And as we watched it burn, I felt my life from before fading away, turning into ash, going the way of the Rolls Royce and the Gucci shoes.

Bark broke out a bottle of Jack Daniels, and we took hits off it. Jamie passed me the bottle and then looked at my head, examining it, cocking his head at it, and I realized he was looking at my short hair. He reached up and mussed it.

"Don't worry, dude. It'll grow," he said.

They played.

I'm a joker
I'm a smoker
I'm a midnight toker
I sure don't want to hurt no one

Chapter Nine
Jimi Lives!

November turned raw. The wind blew harshly off Farmington River. All this partying started to get to me, so to clear my head I started running in the morning. Jamie played football and liked to run, so every morning we headed out and ran to the edge of campus by the main road, then down by the river. I showed Jamie the place where we threw the rocks and broke the windows, and he thought about trying it but decided it was bad luck. I told him it was good luck 'cause without that day I never would have found the cabin.

"You don't get it, Tommy," he said.

"Get what?"

"You, man, you."

He shook his head and took off running. We ran in the rain, which turned to freezing rain, and at first I was cold, but then something came over me, and the wetter I got the more fun it was. We were soaked and laughing when we got back. Jamie went to take a hot shower. I wandered out onto the balcony and watched as people below in the Quad hurried to their dorms. So I couldn't help but turn my attention to this solitary figure who came out of Founder's Hall, walking slowly right down the center of the Quad, as if it were the sunniest day in the history of Bashford, slowly, deliberately. He was black, tall, and walked strong. He had a massive Afro, rising over his head like a halo, and I could see one of those black combs with the big teeth sticking out of the top of it. A maroon scarf at the top of his forehead pushed the hair off his face.

He wore purple-and-pink bellbottoms, a red peacoat open with a yellow-and-black shirt underneath, open to the wind, open to the world.

"It's Jimi," I yelled. "Get out here." And the dudes piled out to see—even Jamie in his towel.

"Holy shit," said Jamie. "It is."

"It looks just like him," said Charts.

"It's him. I know it's him. It's Hendrix," said George.

"Jimi's dead," said Bark. "Drug overdose."

"Fuck that," said George. "He's right there."

Rennes stepped up to the balcony wall and yelled, "Hey, Jimi."

"Hey, Jimi," we yelled after the walking man.

He kept walking and didn't turn around.

"Jimi lives," yelled George.

He stopped. He slowly turned around and he looked just like . . . Jimi.

"Holy fuck, it really is Jimi," said Charts.

He smiled and bowed. We hooted. He kept his head down for a long time, so as to let us admire his Afro. Then he straightened up and kept walking.

"Jimi," we yelled after him. "Jimi."

We looked for him at dinner, but no dice. We asked around, but no one seemed to know him. Until we grilled Mr. Howe in his office.

"It's Winton Monroe," he said. "He's a transfer."

"Well, we know he's a transfer," said George, "but who is he?"

"It's Jimi Hendrix," said Bark.

"He's from Suffield. He's here on a football scholarship."

"He plays football?" asked Jamie.

"Yes, he's a halfback. Now, go to class, boys, and let me get on with my work."

Winton showed up in my English class, and sat in the front, so I had to peer over his Afro. He wore another Hendrix outfit—a purple vest, yellow shirt, black pants, a maroon scarf—and had that black comb sticking out of his hair. Mr. Rock gave him the treatment, you know, but he seemed ready for anything.

"Yes, I've read Donne, and Coleridge, and Yeats and Dickens, and while the latter two are clearly high Victorian, as you constantly remind us, in their outlook,

I'm more partial to Hunter S. Thompson and Kurt Vonnegut," he said. That shut up Mr. Rock. He had no idea who Thompson and Vonnegut were. Neither did we. George and I found Winton after class.

"Who?"

"Great new writers," he said. "Read them."

"I'm not sure they are in the library," I said.

"Come by my room. I'll lend you my copy," he said.

So we trooped over to his room, downstairs in Flagg, and entered a different world. All his walls, every single inch, were covered with books. Some authors I knew, like Alexander Dumas and Tolstoy, Fitzgerald and Hemingway, but there was a whole world of writers I had never heard of. Jerzy Kosiński. Isaac Bashevis Singer. Tom Wolfe. Saul Bellow. Joyce Carol Oates. And E. L. Doctorow.

"Who are all these?" I exclaimed.

"Writers who write," said he. "Here." He handed a me a dog-eared copy of *Fear and Loathing in Las Vegas* by Hunter S. Thompson, with a magnificent ink drawing on the cover by Ralph Steadman.

"This is *now*—" said Winton. "Not some freak from the 1800s. Not Shakespeare or Milton or Dickens or Thackeray, not that I have anything against them, but Hunter S. Thompson."

"Never heard of him," said Bark.

"Can I borrow this?" I asked.

"I'm giving it to you."

"I'll return it."

"No, when you're done, give it to somebody else. That way it keeps going round."

"I hear you play football," said Jamie.

"Yeah, I play football. I have to."

"You have to?"

"I'm on scholarship. Can't afford this place otherwise."

"Oh." Most kids hid the fact that they were on scholarship, but not him.

"Do you have a record collection?" I asked.

"Do I have a record collection?" he said, with that look that said *of course I have a record collection.*

"Why do you dress like Hendrix?" Charts asked.

"I don't," he said. "Hendrix dressed like me."

We nodded. Very deep. Very *deep.*

"I have to go to football practice."

"Jimi lives," said George as we went back to the room.

"It's not Jimi," I said, "not really."

"I know," said George. "But fuck, who cares?"

He laughed that George laugh. I opened up *Fear and Loathing in Las Vegas: A Savage Journey to the Heart of the American Dream.* Why was it savage? Was there something wrong with the American dream? Just what was the American dream? I hadn't really thought about that before. I was just trying to get through my physics class.

"Let's go to dinner," said George.

"See you there," I said, reading. And I read and I read and I read. Hunter S. Thompson was a journalist, which meant I guessed a reporter, and he and his three-hundred-pound Samoan attorney went to Las Vegas and did a lot of drugs, a LOT of drugs, and the attorney threw a grapefruit in the bathtub while Thompson was taking a bath, and Thompson thought it was a radio and thought he was being electrocuted. But it was a grapefruit. And then they did more drugs and wandered through the casino. And there was a lot of talk about politics, which I didn't really understand, and then they drove out to the desert and, well, did more drugs. And somebody let them publish this? This was a real book?

At two in the morning, I found myself standing in front of Winton's door, knocking softly. When you are trying to wake somebody up, you should knock loudly, right? But it was late; the red exit light was burning in the hallway, and so I knocked softly till the door opened, and Winton stood there in the red light, bleary-eyed. He looked down at the book I was holding.

"You got Thompsonized," he said. "Happens to us all."

"Got another?" I said.

"Wait."

He went back into his room and I heard books moving around till he reappeared with another book.

"Kurt Vonnegut. *Breakfast of Champions.*"

"That's the title?" I said, astonished again.

"Yeah, here." He handed it to me. "And get some sleep. It will be there in the morning."

On my way back, I slipped my copy of *Fear and Loathing* under Bark's door and went back to my room. George was asleep. I opened the Vonnegut book and read the first line: *This is a tale of a meeting of two lonesome, skinny, fairly old white men on a planet which was dying fast.* What!!! What was I reading? Who was this guy, this Vonnegut? And who let these guys write this stuff?

We went to the football game on Saturday, on campus, against Choate. There was something about Choate being our archrival and all that, but we didn't care about that: we went to see Winton play. During the anthem he stood with Jamie in their white uniforms with maroon numbers, and then they went their own way—Jamie on defense, Winton at halfback. They didn't play Winton in the first quarter.

"He doesn't know the plays yet," said Rennes.

"You know about football?" I said.

Bashford fell behind 20–7 at the end of the first half. It bored me, just two teams, one in white, one in blue, with Ben Warden at halfback doing nothing, each team charging each other, falling down, getting up, doing it again and again. Lots of whistles and lots of guys running off the field for no reason I could figure out. "Let's go," I said at halftime.

"Stay," said Rennes. Bark nodded at me, so I sat back down.

Choate had the ball first in the second half. I put my head in my hands and almost fell asleep. It was cold, just sitting there in the bleachers. After three running plays, Choate came off the field, and Bashford fielded the punt. The offense ran onto the field.

"He's going in," said Rennes.

I looked up. Sure enough, the lean figure of Winton ran onto the field. Number 36. Bashford set up, Winton in the backfield. The quarterback took the snap and handed off to Winton. He started for the line just like Warden had for all of the first half. The Choate players circled him and moved in for the tackle. Then something amazing happened. Winton wouldn't go down; they couldn't touch him. He backed up three steps, zigged left, cut back, zigged right, cut back, sidestepped two tackles, and headed to the outside. The Choate defensive ends chased him, but Winton turned on the jets and beat them around the corner.

Now he was running, faking this way, going another, down the sideline, ten yards, fifteen, twenty, twenty-five yards. A Choate player got the angle and forced him out of bounds. The whistle blew. Tossing the ball to the official, Winton headed back to the huddle, very nonchalantly. Like whatever.

"First down," called the ref, signaling with his right arm.

Bashford's next pass fell incomplete. So they gave the ball back to Winton, and he broke free, five, ten, twenty yards—and crossed into the end zone.

"Did you see that?" said George. "That dude can fly."

The cheer went up as the scoreboard changed to 20–14.

"And he and Jamie smoked a joint before the game," said Rennes.

"Really? They did?" asked George. "Amazing."

To make it even better, Jamie intercepted a pass in the fourth quarter and ran it back for a winning touchdown, 21–20. They came off the field arm in arm, Jamie and Winton, smiling, walking past Warden, now on the bench.

"You're a loser," yelled Charts at Ben Warden.

"There's gonna be a party tonight," said Rennes.

"Yeah," said Winton, "where?"

Chapter Ten
Fire and Rain

Everyone said that Chalmers, the girls' school, was "down the road." What I didn't know was that it was actually down the road. A mile away. Bashford shared stuff with Chalmers, like playing fields and the theater and the auditorium. The girls, in their sexy plaid skirts and white blouses, floated by like sirens. You know, the sirens that enticed men to their deaths—those sirens—like in the *Odyssey*, which Mr. Rock made us read and which I kinda liked, but don't tell anybody. The girls would look at us, we looked back, and then the inevitable laws of attraction would take hold and we'd be over there chatting them up. School rules (ha!) stated clearly and unequivocally that no girls were allowed in our dorms, for the obvious reason that the school wanted no pregnancy stories to appear on the front page of the *Hartford Courant*. I mean, to me they weren't girls but women, the younger ones brusque and confident, the older ones prepping for Yale and Swarthmore and Williams and the world beyond.

But right now they were still stuck at Chalmers, and that meant those little plaid skirts that came down to the knees and the white blouses that were very hard to get off, for them and us. However, on weekends and special nights, these uniformed girls shed their uniforms and became modern women, in tight jeans, tie-dyed shirts, long hair, faces painted with little flowers, sporting some particularly seductive looks, at least to us Bashford boys.

The party was at the home of Susan Carter, a Chalmers girl I didn't even know, but her parents were away for the weekend—we always found houses with parents away for the weekend like eagles find fish—and tonight it was her turn to get her place trashed by a hundred or so kids from Bashford and Chalmers, and to try to clean it up before her parents got home. Our goal, trash the house as best we could while making sure the damage could be covered up by Sunday night. She lived in West Hartford.

"I'm going after Cindy Fox tonight," said George.

"You do that, George," I said.

We all liked Cindy. She had a car, and she was funny. And George wanted to hit on her, so we let him sit up front when she picked us up in her Ford Pinto and crammed Winton, Jamie, and me in the back. We weren't supposed to ride in any car at school, so Cindy quietly drove her Pinto down by B&G, and we piled in, shouting, "Get the fuck out of the way," and "Move over," and "Come on, let's get out of here." They could probably hear us in Hartford.

"Get down," said Cindy as we passed Founder's Hall. "Want to get me busted?" So we hit the floor till through town and onto the highway.

"You're on my leg."

"Get the fuck off."

"Oh, man, you're killing me."

"Shut up, all of you," said Cindy.

"Cindy speaks," said George. "So shut up."

"Shut up yourself, George," we said.

We hit the Interstate 91 and then went west on 41 and got off on Elm Street, headed for the Carter mansion, such as it was.

"Hey, that's Mark Twain's house," yelled Winton as we drove by the historical house. "Right there. Can we stop?"

"No," said Jamie, "we can't. We only have so much time to smoke weed and hit on the girls, so no time for literary stops."

"Shut up," said Cindy.

Taking out a joint, Winton lit it up.

"What's that?" Cindy yelled, as the aroma filled the car.

"Winton lit it," said Bark. "Not me."

"Are you out of your fucking minds?" Cindy yelled. "We'll get busted."

The clear sound of a beer can opening filled the car.

"And what's that?" said Cindy, shaking her head. "You guys are going to get me in a lot of trouble."

Bark rolled down the window and threw the beer can out.

"I think that cop saw that," said George.

"A cop? What COP?" Cindy screamed.

"Just fucking around," laughed George. "Ha!"

"George, I hate you," she said, but we all heard in her voice that she didn't hate him at all. That she liked him, and maybe, just maybe, it would be quite a night for little Georgy.

"Now, put that out," she ordered. Taking a last hit, Winton rolled down his window just a crack and gave the joint a toss. But it didn't fly out; the wind pushed it back into the car, the joint hitting the car seat. We all had to jump up, and Winton slapped at it to put it out as the joint flew across the seat and down the crack.

"Breathe it in, boys," yelled Jamie as the car filled with smoke.

"Pull over here," George directed. It was a package store. Rennes and Charts were there in an old station wagon, waiting for us. Rennes and Jamie went into the store while we waited in the car. A few minutes later they came out with two cases of beer, two bottles of rum, two bottles of whiskey, and a bottle of vodka.

"No wine?" asked Winton. "I mean, this is West Hartford, after all."

"How'd he do that?" asked Cindy.

"Fake ID," I said.

"Oh, man, I love you guys," she said, "but you are trouble with a capital T."

We drove into the West Hartford neighborhood, the big white houses racing by, one after the other, with manicured lawns and second floors with the lights on that lit up the street. All white. Not a blue one among them. White. All white houses in a row.

"That's the house. That's Suz's." Cindy pointed, maneuvering into the driveway. Parties were easily spotted, because dozens of cars parked on the street, and kids jammed the doorways.

"Nice place," said Jamie.

"Suz told me to drive around back," Cindy explained as she parked between the house and shed. We could hear the music blasting from inside the house, Airplane.

> One pill makes you larger
> And one pill makes you small,
> And the ones that mother gives you
> Don't do anything at all . . .

"Grace Slick," said George, and we all nodded in reverence. "Grace fucking Slick."

The house was packed. Maybe a hundred guys and girls. And smoky. The house was filled with smoke, both cigarette and pot. We carried the liquor in and found our way to the kitchen, where there was a veritable city of bottles, like the New York City skyline, on the island in the middle. The liquor counter at a party is a work of art, in the modern sense at least: caps, labels, empties, full bottles, plastic cups, weird napkins all balled up with scotch, empty beer cans on their sides, lemons already squeezed and lemon pits on the counter, a bottle opener, another bottle opener, a broken wine glass, beer mixed with wine mixed with whiskey all making an ocean of booze dripping onto the tile floor. Not one but two garbage cans overflowed with bottles, cups, napkins, and bags. I took a walk around.

In the living room the plush couches had flower prints, the chairs were antiques, the chandeliers glittered with diamond-shaped glass pieces, the rugs were from some *Yankee* magazine article, and the hardwoods were stained dark brown. We didn't care about any of that; we only cared how many bedrooms it had upstairs. For later. Already a few couples were making out in the living room and in the library, with the lights flickering low. Charts went straight for the turntable; taking control, he put on Jimi Hendrix.

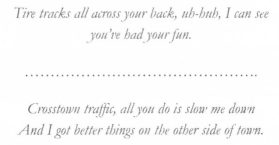

Tire tracks all across your back, uh-huh, I can see you've had your fun.

. . . .

*Crosstown traffic, all you do is slow me down
And I got better things on the other side of town.*

I wandered around checking things out, the keg on the porch, the mixing station in the kitchen, the lock on the father's liquor cabinet, the girls teasing the Bashford boys, and the boys trying to get them on the couch to make out. I ended up on the porch with Rennes, Jamie, and George, smoking a joint in the back of the house. The door to the house opened and the screen door slammed shut. A girl came running down to join us.

"Hi," she said.

"Hi."

"I'm Susan."

"Carter?" said Jamie.

"Yeah."

"This your house?" I asked.

"Yeah," she said, "can I?" She reached for the joint and took a hit.

"Cool house," George observed.

"Wait," said Susan. Out of her coat she produced a bottle of rum, took a swig, and passed the bottle around. We all took a hit off the bottle.

"Cool," said George. "Thanks."

"Look," she said, making a white puff with her breath. We all made little white puffs until the rum was gone. We went inside. The music was loud, like we liked it, but we couldn't talk. The dancing started. Susan looked at me, like *you going to ask me to dance?* And I was summoning my courage when Jamie let out a holler, grabbed her by the wrist, and pulled her onto the dance floor.

"Jamie's fast," said Rennes with a laugh. "But it won't last."

"You smell something?" Bark sniffed the air.

"Yeah, you," said Rennes.

"Something burning?"

Shrugging, Bark went to dance with Marcy Downe, a blonde who wore Patchouli oil and lots of jewelry. Rennes and I found some girls along the wall, approached them, and nodded towards the dance floor; they giggled, and we all went out and danced to the Steve Miller Band, "Fly Like an Eagle." Jumping up and down, Winton played air guitar. Bark was pawing young Marcy. Jamie was whipping Susan around the dance floor, knocking into everyone and everything, nearly upsetting the lamp on the side table by the sofa. Someone put on Hendrix again.

Have you ever been (have you ever been) to Electric Ladyland?

I was headed to the kitchen to get another beer when Susan appeared in the hall, and our eyes met briefly.

"Hi," she said.

"Hi. Nice party."

She looked around like she wasn't really thinking about that. We had to yell over the music.

"You're Tommy Stafford," she said.

"I am."

"We all, you know . . ."

"No, I don't know, what?"

"We all know who you are."

"You do? Why?" I was clearly dumbfounded, wondering why in the world Chalmers girls would possibly know who I was.

" 'Cause, you know, you're cute," she said.

"Cute?" I exclaimed, genuinely shocked. "Whoa, that's new."

"Well, you are."

"You were dancing with Jamie," I said.

"Yeah," she said. "I like Jamie, but . . ."

I didn't know what to say to that, and I didn't have to because someone came running into the room and yelled, louder than the music, "Fire!"

"Oh, my God"—from the kitchen—"Look."

"It's on fire!"

Ben Warden came into the house, yelling, "Fire, fire."

We tore off in the direction of the voices that yelled *fire*, and a bunch of us pasted our faces against the kitchen window at the same time. We looked out onto the back driveway and the shed through the reflection of orange flames in the kitchen window. Cindy's car— was on fire.

"My car," Cindy screamed.

Her little red Ford Pinto had flames lapping against the ride-side slightly open window.

"Oh, fuck," said Bark.

We ran outside, all of us, coalescing into a little crowd around the vehicle. The fire raged. The paint on the roof bubbled. It *bubbled* 'cause it was so hot. In the whole back seat flames leapt up everywhere.

"My car," screamed Cindy, walking towards it as if in a trance, and Charts grabbed her and restrained her.

"It's gonna blow," bellowed George. "Get down." We all hit the ground and watched the fire leap out the windows until, well, it didn't blow. Running into the house, George came back out with a jumbo-sized jug of apple juice.

"What are you gonna do with that?" asked Bark.

"Fuck if I know," said George. "I just grabbed it."

"Here," I said, taking the jug. With a towel that someone handed him, Bark ran for the car. Seizing the back-door handle, he yanked the door open, but as the flames leapt out and singed his down jacket, he fell back from the heat. I charged forward, squeezing the plastic bottle harder and harder, till a stream of apple juice came gushing forth and flooded the back seat.

"Good one," said George. Now in a steady stream out the back door liquids of all kinds were paraded from the house. George grabbed the next one, a gallon of milk, stopped at the back door of the flaming car, and squeezed with everything he had. Then came Bark with orange juice, Winton with lemonade, and Charts with fizzy water. The flames went down but did not extinguish. Then, magically, a keg appeared. George and I carried it to the car door and set it down.

"Pump," yelled George. So I pumped with all the arm speed I had. "Pump." After a dozen or so good pumps, I stood back and George aimed the hose, letting fly a steady stream of beer.

"More," yelled Rennes. And we flooded the back seat with beer till the flames went out, leaving lingering in the air only a thick grey smoke. Rennes moved towards the car, grabbed the seat, yanked it several times. And miraculously, it lifted out. As it lay on the driveway, George poured beer from the keg on it till the flames were all extinguished.

"Look," yelled Bark. Grabbing the hose from George, I went back into the car, under the seat, where the embers burned red and orange, and doused them with beer. Goodbye, fire.

"Holy crap," said Charts.

"My car!" yelled Cindy, looking at the smoking, beer-soaked interior and the bubbled paint on the roof. "My car."

Winton approached Cindy. "I'm sorry," he said. After a moment, she turned to look at him inquisitively.

"I think it was me."

"Holy fuck," said George, "you dropped the joint."

"Sorry," said Winton again.

"My dad's gonna kill me," wailed Cindy.

"Sorry . . . Want me to call him?" Winton asked.

She thought about it, like, *would you?* And then it must have hit her that some weird guy calling her father at midnight saying he lit her car on fire might not be the best way to approach this. She turned back to the car, still belching smoke.

"No, I'll do it."

"We're gonna need a ride home," said Rennes. We all looked over at him, to say *nice going, man, she didn't need to hear that*, and Rennes shrugged, like *right, but we still have to get home.* The party was over. Some girl who lived near campus offered a ride, so we grabbed our coats and headed out. Susan smiled at me in the weakest kind of way, and I could tell she was thinking about her house and the fire and the car burning in her driveway. Rennes threw his arm around me, laughing that husky laugh of his.

"It could have blown, you fucking idiot," he admonished.

"A car almost blew up in your face," said Jamie.

"Yeah, you were possessed, man," said Charts.

"Yeah, well," said George, in that *aw, shucks* kind of way. He threw his arm around me and we stood there, wet beer all over the drive, a smoking hulk not far off, and half the school standing and watching from the back door and windows.

"Oh, they're gonna be talking about this for a long time," said George.

One thing bothered me about what happened, and I slowly turned to see standing in the crowd Ben Warden, who looked on with a Cheshire-cat grin. For the life of me, I couldn't figure out if he was just happy we'd fucked up, or if there was more to it.

Tire tracks all across your back
I can see you've had your fun...

Chapter Eleven
Coming Out Alive

"Mr. Stafford, you are late. Again."

As I made my way to my seat, Mr. Rock stopped class and coldly stared at me.

"Sorry."

"Sorry? Sorry? Bashford men are not sorry, are they, boys?" Some boys actually nodded in agreement, those fucking brown-nosers. "We do not ask you to be sorry, Mr. Stafford. We ask that you get to class on time. That is what Bashford men do. Are you a Bashford man, Mr. Stafford?"

"You know, I hadn't actually thought about that much," I said.

"Are you or are you not?" asked Mr. Rock.

"Well, I go to school here, so I guess I'm a Bashford man."

"Incorrect, Mr. Stafford," intoned the prof. "Most incorrect. You don't become a Bashford man by just being here—"

"You become a Bashford man when your father coughs up the bucks," yelled George from the back of the room.

"Also incorrect, George. You become a Bashford man by living by the principles of the Bashford School code. Those principles include honor, dedication, adherence to the motto in Latin, *Super omnem virum*."

"Man above all," yelled the class, knowing the Latin.

"Man above this," yelled Charts, holding up his middle finger.

"That will be quite enough, Mr. Chartson." He turned to me. "Mr. Stafford, I'm going to send you to see Dean Harper and see what he has to say about your being late time after time."

Dean Harper! We also had a motto, and it was *Et irrumabo sede a Dean Harper*, which translated roughly into, *Stay the fuck away from Dean Harper*. He was famous for his cruelty, and his teeth, which had gaps between them, and the air whistled as it went through. Dean Harper, the whistling troglodyte of Bashford School.

"So go," said Mr. Rock.

"Um . . . I won't be late again?" It was formed as a question, as in, give me another chance.

"Go," he ordered. And then there was that awful silence, the kind where you know it's not going to end well—and it didn't. I got up.

"You can do it, Tommy," George urged. "Give 'em hell."

"Fight on," said Winton.

"Live strong," said Charts.

"Return," said Rennes. "Return to us."

"Shut up," I said.

"Take your book, Mr. Stafford."

"My book?" That meant I wasn't coming back, and that meant trouble.

"Yes, take your book," said Mr. Rock. The ominous words hung in the air. Charts started singing "Taps," slowly and low down, and Jamie and Rennes joined in. Rennes stood up.

"Mr. Rock, can I address the prisoner?"

"He's not a prisoner. Oh, go ahead."

"God be with you," said Rennes. "Go forth."

I shook my head. On to the dean!

It took me fifteen minutes to walk downstairs to the Dean's office, a two-minute walk on a slow day. Arriving outside his office, I stood there, weighing my options. I could just run, leave school, never come back. I was seriously considering it when I heard a voice. The Battleaxe. The Dean's secretary, almost as fearsome as Dean Harper himself. She was, well, a bit on the heavy side, short but squat, in sensible clothes, a long skirt and a white blouse, her hair pinned on her head with long pins with jewels on the end.

"Mr. Stafford," she said.

"Yes?"

"Are you coming in?"

So I went in. And the Battleaxe stared me down.

"I'm here to see Dean Harper," I announced.

"You don't have an appointment," she said with suspicion.

"Mr. Rock sent me down."

"Hmm, I see." And I'm sure she did see, me being one of those kids who required the rack. And if she had her way, I'd get it. "I'll tell him you're here."

Stepping into the adjoining office, she shut the door. A massive school crest hung on the wall like a sentence over me. I looked up at it. Maybe I wasn't a Bashford man, after all, I thought. The door opened and the Battleaxe came out, looking stern.

"The Dean will see you now."

I walked the seven steps to his office, as if I were walking the gang plank, and ushered myself into a long, rectangular room, the walls lined with books, a table covered in green felt with several stacks of files piled here and there, and a gargantuan wooden desk that the dean sat behind, adorned with lots of swirls in the woodwork.

"Sit down," he told me. A leather chair awaited. I sat. As if I weren't even there, he kept on working, not even looking up. I assumed he was signing the death warrant for some poor unsuspecting student, who by lunch would be strung up on the flagpole.

"Yes?" he said finally, putting down his pen and looking across at me. I heard that slight whistle as the air rushed through his teeth.

"Mr. Rock sent me down," I said.

"Did he?"

"He did."

"And pray tell, why did Mr. Rock send you down?" I didn't know what "pray tell" meant, but I got the idea.

"I was late to class." I said it nonchalantly, like what a trivial thing to send someone down for, don't you think?

He pushed back his chair to size me up. It's a very unnerving thing to be sized up by a known sadistic torturer, so I squirmed a bit in the chair, which did not seem to bother him in the least.

"Mr. Rock did not send you here because you were late, Mr. Stafford."

"He didn't?"

"No."

"Oh. So why did he send me down?"

"Mr. Rock sent you down because you are not performing up to par," he said.

"I'm not?"

"Mr. Stafford, we took you on here at Bashford because you came from a very prestigious school in New York—"

"And because my father paid the tuition?"

"—which matters not at all, I should say, and we had great hopes for you as a Bashford man."

He opened a folder on his desk to look it over. Not just any folder. My folder. The whistling torturer had my folder on his desk already. Not a good sign.

"You started off well," said he, "with A's and only one B at the midterm, and then your teachers report to me that you don't come to class, you don't do the assignments, and you are disruptive in class. Is this true, Mr. Stafford?"

"Well, logically, if I don't go to class, I can't be disruptive, can I?" I said. It fell flat, even if I thought it was funny.

"Hmmm," said Dean Harper. "Teachers don't lie, Mr. Stafford. Do they? Not here at Bashford."

"No, sir, they don't."

"Then what's to be done?" said Dean Harper. "This is your senior year, and you'll be applying to college soon. Where are you wanting to go?"

"Yale, sir. All my family went to Yale, so—"

"You won't be going to Yale with this kind of record, Mr. Stafford."

"No, sir —"

"Shall I call your parents?"

Everyone always threatened to call parents but never did, because parents didn't want to be bothered and they knew it.

"I can give you the number if you like," said I.

"That won't be necessary," he replied. "Another day perhaps."

We sat staring at each other, and suddenly I wasn't really scared anymore. I had a feeling of power over Dean Harper, and frankly the whistling through the teeth was starting to get to me. "All right."

He stood up. "Consider yourself warned, Mr. Stafford. You must do better. You must improve or you will not be asked back next semester. Do you understand?"

"I do." Not asked back? I never wanted to come here in the first place.

"Let's be clear. We will meet again at the beginning of next term, and if your performance does not improve, you will be expelled. Do you understand?

"You betcha, Dean Harper," I said.

"It's not a joke, young man," he said.

"No, sir."

When I opened the door to go back in class, Mr. Rock stopped. He had not expected me back. He obviously expected Dean Harper to chew me up and spit me out, and not back into his classroom.

"He made it," bellowed Bark. "God is merciful."

Thinking that saying nothing was best, I just walked to my seat and sat down. George raised his hand.

"Yes, George?" said Mr. Rock.

"Can I go to see Dean Harper?"

The room erupted in laughter, and Mr. Rock rolled his eyes, gave up and went back to teaching *Love's Labor's Lost* by Willie You Know Who. I settled back in and basked in the glow.

"Not everyone comes out alive with Dean Harper," whispered George.

"You made it, kid," said Rennes.

Chapter Twelve
Rum and Coke

For a while I missed my work job in the kitchen, too busy. Then one day at lunch Wugs came looking for me inside the dining room. Wugs didn't come into the dining room much, so it was kind of a big deal. The room quieted down as he made his way to my table. When I looked up, I knew I had fucked up, even before he said anything.

"Where you been?" he demanded. I was sitting with Jamie and Rennes and George. They all looked up at him as well.

"Sorry," I said, "been busy."

"No one's shining the silver," he said. And he winked.

George picked up a knife, looked it over and said, "Looks okay to me." Wugs ignored him. "You coming back?"

"Yeah, sure, I'll be back," I promised.

He gazed at me for the longest time, stared a hole right through me; then he did an about-face and walked straight back to the kitchen, with all the boys watching him go and jeering a bit.

"Whoa, what was that all about?" said George.

So I explained to them that it was my work job and that I had stopped going and that Wugs had been the only person on campus to talk to me when no one on campus would talk to me, and that maybe I had let him down, because there was no one to polish the silverware or work the line.

So that night at my regularly scheduled time, I reported for kitchen duty. With Rennes. With George. With Charts and Bark and Winton. All of us. Reporting for duty, sir. Wugs chuckled one single chuckle and found us all aprons and hats, turned them all backwards, and put us to work. In no time George was shining the silver; Rennes (always the leader) went on the line and made the mashed potatoes. Bark stacked the dishes. Charts folded the napkins. And I worked with Wugs, concocting the Turkey Surprise.

"Quite a crew," said Wugs as he finished up and hung up the aprons. "Got a way to go, but not bad for a start. You can come back."

"Oh, we can???" we said.

The fall term moved on. Winton led the football team to the league championship. Charts got into a fight with his math teacher. Then he clogged up the sinks with paper towels in Founder's Hall and turned on the faucets full blast, so they came in the next morning and found two inches of water on the floor, with the rooms below drenched. Charts got a week's suspension, which just gave him a chance to come back with a pound of pot and two bottles of Dewars White Label. We had quite a party.

Dean Harper's threat to throw me out didn't do much. I did not start going to class, and when I did go, I wasn't, well, cooperative. Like in science, I had to do a project. You know the kind: if the car is moving at X speed and the force minus the friction equals the fuck who cares, then what the hell are we doing here? I did my project on the topic "the heat of a marijuana joint when it reaches full-ember capacity." I wrote, "The heat of the ember in combination with inhaling of the air by mouth creates a vacuum in which temperatures of 225 Fahrenheit are achieved, and in the midst of the inhale, temperatures can rise to as much as 250, in order to meet the standard operating temperature for proper joint efficacy."

Mr. Scott, the noble science teacher, was not amused but did not turn me in. I mean, knowing about smoking weed, or writing about it in science projects, was not the same thing as actually smoking it. Was it?

"Taking orders," said George, with J. Geils Band on the stereo as he burst in.

"For what?"

"My cousin is coming down from Boston, and he'll bring whatever we want."

"He can do that?" I screeched. Meaning, was he eighteen? Could he buy?

"Yep."

Rennes thought about it. "I'll have a case of rum," he said.

"Me too," said Jamie.

"All of us," said Charts.

The rum arrived a week later, by way of a box that said Lacrosse on it, and they ran it up the stairs, past Mr. Maroni, who lived across the hall from me but smoked weed himself so didn't really care what we did. I took out a bottle and slid the box under my bed.

"Party in my room tonight," I said.

I had a small refrigerator in my room, the kind with the door that barely shuts, which leaks onto the floor, where ice crusts around the freezer. But it made ice. At nine they all piled in till we had fifteen people in there. Bark brought coke, and I made run and cokes, and the cigs came out, even though we weren't allowed to smoke. With the rum flowing, Rennes got out his guitar and rested his rum and coke on the desk, the desk that held the textbooks I never used, and played, well, you know . . . CSN&Y.

Wooden ships on the water
Very free and easy . . .

The only thing we didn't ever do in our rooms was smoke joints, 'cause we knew it would smell no matter what we did, and we'd get caught. So about eleven, we snuck out of the dorm, trudged down by the river, and in the cold glow of the moon smoked two joints, passing them around with our frigid fingers. We walked back in silence, dew on our boots, the foggy fields before us. Barks threw up walking back, too much rum. But it didn't matter. We put our arms around him, helping him back, and put him to bed.

"A nightcap?" said Jamie from the hallway.

"Fuck no," said George, heading off to bed around two o'clock, proving that there was a limit to debauchery, even for a Bashford man.

I shook my head no as well and went to my room.

"Fuck," yelled Jamie, "Isn't anybody gonna have any fun around here?"

Chapter Thirteen
Black Ice

George shook me awake at dawn. "Get up."

"What the fuck, George. What time is it?"

"Get up."

"Leave me alone." I rolled over.

"No school."

"What?" I said groggily.

"No classes. They've been cancelled."

"Why?"

"Black ice. Grab your skates, and let's go."

"What's black ice?"

George explained on the way to the river, with our skate laces over our shoulders and the skate blades bouncing off our chests. It was cold, real cold, so cold our ears froze sticking out of our hats.

"It's this Bashford thing," said George, winding up as he always did to tell a story. It rushed out of him like lava from a volcano. "So you have to have the right conditions," he said. "It's got to be warm one day, like it was yesterday, and then the temps have to plummet that night and drop well below freezing, way below. And here's the most important thing—no wind."

"No wind?"

"None. That way the river freezes flat as a pancake, and that's what we want."

"Why?"

"Cause that's when you get black ice. It only happens every ten years or so, and it happened last night."

We pulled the scrambled eggs folded in white toast from our pockets that we made in the dining hall and munched them down. In like three bites. The dudes—Winton, Rennes, Bark, Charts and Jamie—met us at the log, the place usually reserved for smoking joints or cigs. This time it was all business. Sitting on the log, we laced up our skates.

"What the fuck are those?" said Charts, staring horrified at my skates.

"My skates," I said.

"Figure skates . . . ?" protested Jamie.

"Why do you have figure skates?"

"Cause I do. That's how I learned to skate."

"Can you do all that shit?" said Rennes. "You know, the spins and the jumps?"

I walked to the edge of the river, pushed off, gained some speed, knowing everyone was watching, did two loops, skated backwards, and executed a double axel, landing it perfectly.

"You gotta be fucking kidding me," said Rennes.

"What the fuck . . . ?" said George.

"*What the fuck* is right," said Rennes. "We got ourselves an Olympian."

With several giant strides, I sped up to them and at the last second did a full stop, with ice spraying everywhere.

"Where did you learn to skate like that?" asked George.

"Wolman Rink."

"What?"

"I grew up across from Central Park and took skating lessons from two years old at the rink there."

"Was that near the Pierre Hotel?" teased Charts.

"And dancing school?" asked Bark.

"I'd shut up if I were you," said George. "Look at him."

"Upriver," said Rennes. "Let's go."

And so we set off up the river, right in the middle of that great waterway, and it was kind of eerie to skate past the houses, under bridges, in the middle of the river. We went past bonfires on the water's edge. Our faces burned red and our legs tired and our thin gloves left our hands cold. We went miles upriver, maybe five, maybe more, and after the usual hijinks, the wrestling and the falling and the attacks, we ended up on a bend in the river at a bonfire with some Chalmers girls hanging out by the fire.

"Better watch out," said George as we skated over. "That's Trixie Harper."

"Who's she?" I didn't know her, I didn't think.

"Oh, watch out," he said with a laugh. "She'll get ya."

We skated over to the bonfire and took off our gloves. At first, we pretended to be warming up, and I looked around to see which one was Trixie. When I caught her eye, I saw Trixie checking me out. The other girls giggled and huddled together, but Trixie (I could tell it was her, for some reason) stood apart, staring straight at me.

"You have chicken legs," she said, looking me over.

"What?" I replied.

"Chicken legs," she repeated. "You have them. I mean, otherwise you're cute, but I can see when you skate you have chicken legs. Come, stand by me."

"Okay."

"You're Tommy, aren't you?" she said. "All the girls know who you are."

"Really?"

"Yeah, they all talk about you, all the time, Tommy this and Tommy that, and doesn't he have cute blond hair and all that. Kind of annoying, actually."

"And you? Were you talking about me too?"

"Oh, no, I don't care about that stuff, and I had never seen you before, so I couldn't say, now, could I?"

"And now?"

"Oh, they're right. You are cute, I guess, but you have chicken legs. Take off your hat."

George cut in, "Don't take it off," he said.

"Oh, quiet, George, he has to do what I say."

I took off my hat. She looked me over. "Okay, they're right, but don't think that impresses me, you know. I don't just go out with anyone, you know."

"Who said anything about going out?" I shot back kindly. "I didn't ask you out, that I can remember."

She smiled at me. "You will," she said. "Come on." And she skated off.

I just stood there, till George nudged me. "Go, stupid. Don't keep her waiting."

Trixie skated with that determined, deliberate cadence. You know, push, push, push, glide, push, push, push, glide, all while looking straight ahead. Catching up with her, I skated around her several times, showing off my skating skills, first frontways, then backwards. I could tell she could see me but pretended not to be impressed. Like a bulldog, she just kept skating forward, head down. I could see her better now, how pretty her face was under the knit cap, how slim her body under her peacoat, how shapely her legs were with the knit stockings, how her dark hair poured out from under her cap.

"Yep," she said, finally looking up, "chicken legs."

"I do not have chicken legs," I retorted. "Whatever those are."

We had found our way another mile upriver into a small, secluded cove surrounded by oak trees with massive trunks.

"Do you kiss well?" she asked.

"Kiss well?" I sputtered. "No complaints so far."

"It's very important that you kiss well," she explained. "I mean, what's the point of being handsome if you then mess it up as a bad kisser?"

"Uh, I think I'm okay."

"Well, maybe I'll let you kiss me and we'll find out."

"I'll alert the *Hartford Courant*," I replied.

She giggled, almost against her will. "You're funny. You know that?"

"I've been told."

"A girl likes that. Later on she wants somebody who has some bucks. That's what my mother says, anyway, but now we just want handsome and funny. You may be both. Or you may be stuck up. Are you stuck up, Tommy Stafford?"

"Uhhh, I don't think so."

"Well, you come from New York City, so you are probably insufferable. Are you insufferable?"

"Uhhhh, no, I'm not. I don't think."

"Well, that's for me to decide, isn't it?"

"Is it?" I said.

She had me all tied up in knots now. I got flustered and stuttered my way forward.

"Don't worry, it happens to all the boys I go out with," she said. "They can't handle me."

"Define stuck up," I said.

"When you don't give a damn what anybody says, and you're rude because of it. That's stuck up."

"Sounds like me."

"Are you going out with anybody?"

"I don't even know any girls here . . . yet."

"A man is defined by his girlfriend, is he not?"

"Is it okay to say that I have no idea what you are talking about?"

"So underneath all that good looks you're stupid?"

"I . . . I don't think so."

"Don't argue with me. It's tedious."

"I can't argue with you?"

"Not if you want to be kissed. Do you want to be kissed, Mr. New York City? You know, no one cares that you're from New York City. I'm from West Hartford, a fine place, and so what if you came from New York?"

"I never said—"

"Say what you like, but it doesn't really matter. Where are you going to college?"

"Yale. Well, I'm supposed to go to Yale, but Dean Harper says I'll never make it the way I'm going."

"Dean Harper says that?"

"Yeah, he hates me. He wants to throw me out."

"Now kiss me and let's see how you do."

I had just met this girl, who now wanted to kiss me. Right here on the river. I edged closer, not sure if I would do it or not. She made a turn towards me. Her face glowed and she looked so pretty I just stopped and stared.

"Well?" she said.

So I kissed her. And about a second into it, I realized it was the best kiss I'd ever had. She leaned into it, so I leaned into it. And she put an arm around my neck so I put an arm around her and started to really get into it.

"Slow down there, big fella," she said, pulling back. "It's just a first kiss." She then smiled shyly and said, "It wasn't bad, you know. You have potential."

"Potential?" I protested. "Just potential?"

I blushed. It was something I couldn't control, a full-on flush of the face. I went redder than a lobster.

"I blush sometimes too, but not like that! Don't worry, I won't tell."

She took my arm, and we skated back to the bonfire to rejoin everyone. Cindy had arrived. George was huddling with her by the fire and cracking her up. Trixie made sure everyone was looking at us, and they were, and then without even a look she turned and skated away with her girlfriends down the river.

"Did you score?" asked George.

"Yeah, *did* you?" asked Rennes.

"I don't know. She kissed me. I kissed her."

"It's a mini-score," said Bark. "A mini!"

"Are you in love?" asked Charts, howling.

"Oh, fuck, not that, please," said George.

"Home for rum and cokes," said Rennes, and we were off down the river. We passed Trixie and Cindy and her friends skating together, but I kept my eye on Trixie. She wouldn't look at me, but at the last minute, just before we passed them, she looked up and caught my eye. No smile, nothing like that. But she looked up.

"And little Tommy's caught the bug," said Charts.

When we piled into our dorm room, George and I got out the ice and made the rum and cokes, and all of us drank and warmed up—and mostly laughed at me for being so stupid. I didn't mind, but I couldn't get her out of my head, either.

"She's a preppie," said Jamie. "Not one of us."

"I know," I said. "But . . ."

"She wears turtlenecks and peacoats and plaid skirts, even when she doesn't have to," said Bark, a horrifying thought.

"She's stuck up," said Charts.

"Yeah, but Tommy likes her," said George. "I can tell."

I blushed again, and they razzed me something terrible, but I didn't mind all that much. I just laughed and hung my head.

"You get anywhere with Cindy?" Rennes asked George.

"No, but I'd like to," he replied. That got a raucous laugh out of everyone. I poured, and we sat back with our rum drinks, just one ounce of which would have gotten us all thrown out of school—sipping them like the gentlemen we aspired to be.

Chapter Fourteen
Ben Fucking Warden

"Jamie, I have a lot of people counting on me, and my rum," I said. Jamie was trying to get me to go with him and I wasn't budging.

"You're coming with me," he said.

"I am not. I'm going back to my room. I have rum and cokes to make."

"You're coming with me."

"Where?" I asked.

"To the rink."

"The rink? The ice rink? What for?"

"You're trying out for the hockey team," he said.

"And why would I do that, when I could go back to my room, have a few rum and cokes, walk down to the river and smoke a joint and head to the dining hall for Turkey Surprise?"

"I've seen you skate. That's why."

"Oh, lead on," I said, resigned.

I followed him like a puppy dog to the rink and found a pile of equipment on the bench in front of my locker. It all smelled like dirty locker room.

"What are these?"

"Shin guards."

"Right." So I put them on, then the shoulder pads, then the baggy pad-filled pants, then the knit socks, then the jersey, then the elbow pads, then the helmet, and remarkably, it all pretty much fit.

"Wait, my skates," I said.

"Here, I got them from your room." Jamie produced my figure skates. "We have to get you some hockey skates, but wear these for now."

I laced the white figure skates all the way up the ankle, wrapped the laces around my ankles twice, and tied them tight.

"Here," said Jamie, handing me a stick.

"What do I do with this?" It was a joke, but truth be told, I had been to plenty of New York Rangers games, but never held a stick.

"Very funny."

"No, I'm serious. Really."

We skated counterclockwise around the rink—red line, blue line, center line, blue line, red line, again. Some guys shot disgusted looks at my skates, but I couldn't care less. I was here for an afternoon, and then it was back to the rum and cokes. The coach came out. They called him Muzzie, Coach Muzzroll, and he ordered some drills. Which I couldn't do. I mean, I'd never held a stick before. Muzzie watched me with the assistant coach; he watched me lose the puck time and again and shook his head. We did a drill where I was supposed to slip past the defenseman along the boards. The defenseman creamed me against the boards and crumpled me onto the ice. Jamie skated over to see how I was.

"You okay?"

"I think my leg is broken."

"The only thing broken is your ego," he said.

"Can I go now?"

"What the hell did you bring him here for?" asked Coach Muzzie when the team had left for the locker room and it was only me, Jamie, and the coach on the ice. "He can't play hockey," said the coach. "Why is he here?"

Jamie turned to me. "Skate," he said. I shook my head. "Skate," he ordered.

"No."

"Skate!" said Jamie.

So, to hell with it, I skated. My pride took over. I put my stick down and picked up speed, rounding the corner with arms out like the figure skaters. I flipped from back to front again and again, then executed a perfect double twisting jump and stuck the landing, moving from there into a spin, the kind with the arms up in the air that goes faster and faster and faster. And stopped, arms up, like I was going for the gold. All in my bulky hockey uniform.

"That's why he's here," said Jamie to the coach.

"Well, I'll be damned," said Coach Muzzie. "Our first game is right after Christmas break. Think you can get him ready?"

"Leave it to me."

"Leave what to you?" I said.

Coach Muzzie shook his head like he'd never seen anything like that and left the ice.

"What did you just do?" I asked.

I was a hockey player, despite it all. But yet sometimes things work out, 'cause we were walking back to my dorm, still in my hockey gear, and carrying my stick over my shoulder, like I was a pro, when Trixie came walking towards us, going the other way.

"Look," said Jamie.

"Well, hello Chicken Legs," she said.

"Well, hello," said I.

"Hey, I gotta run," said Jamie with a nod, walking ahead.

"I didn't know you played hockey," she said, touching the uniform.

"Well, yeah, I do. Sort of."

"I like a man who plays hockey," she said. "Especially the fights. Do you fight?"

"Well, sure, if I have to."

"Oh, you have to fight. Hockey is about fighting, not playing, fighting. Walk with me."

I was going the other way, and she knew it, but I turned around. It felt good walking next to her in all my gear.

"You didn't call," she said.

"Call?"

"You're supposed to call, silly, and you didn't. It's very rude. I kissed you and the least you could do was call."

"Uh, sorry. I didn't know I was supposed—"

"There's a phone on your floor."

"I know."

"You were probably afraid my father would answer."

"Uh, yeah . . ."

"Everyone's afraid of my father, but he's not so bad."

"Who's your father?" I inquired.

"You don't know? I thought everyone knew."

"No."

"Dean Harper."

"Dean Harper is your father?" I blurted out.

"Yes, yes. Now should we go on a date?" she said.

"I don't know . . . Dean Harper is your . . ." I trailed off.

"Oh, stop it—it doesn't matter."

"A date?"

"But you're not getting *that*, you know. I'm not putting out. Not yet, anyway."

"Then what's the point?" I said, a big smile on my face.

"Oh, you!" She slugged me on the arm. She hit mostly pads but got the point across.

"I have a boyfriend, you know. That's why I can't, you know . . ."

"You do?"

"Yeah, a senior like you."

"Who is it?"

"Wouldn't you like to know?"

"Tell me," I said, a little more serious than I should have been.

"I'll tell you if you promise not to tell him that I kissed you," she said.

"My lips are sealed."

"Ben Warden," she said. "Do you know him?"

"Ben Warden? You're going out with Warden?"

"Yeah, for like two years," she said wearily. "He's in love with me, poor boy."

"Ben Fucking Warden?" I repeated. "Really?"

"Yes, really. Why do you keep saying that?"

"I gotta go," I said, walking away.

"Where are you going?" she said. "Tommy. *Tommy.*" I just kept going.

So I played hockey. Jamie got me up early each morning, and we hit the rink and skated, stickhandled, learned hockey turns.

"I can't stand it anymore," he said, handing me a pair of hockey skates. "Take those off."

Christmas break was coming, and I was to go to New York to see my parents, which I didn't really want to do. I thought I'd be bored. Then I ran into Trixie on the last day before break.

"I can come down to the city over break," she said. "If you want."

"What about Warden?" I asked.

"Oh, him," she replied. "We broke up. He keeps saying, *I love you*, but I don't love him. Oh, I like him and all that. I just don't love him, and it's boring he keeps saying that. So I'll come to the city."

"What about your father?" I wanted to know.

"Oh, Cindy has an aunt in the city. I'll say I'm with her."

"Your father won't let you come to the city if he thinks it's to see me."

"So I won't tell him."

"Okay."

"And bring George. I think Cindy likes him."

Chapter Fifteen
Christmas in the City

Christmas break arrived and we packed up for the holiday. I took the shuttle to the train station in Hartford. Jamie and Rennes were going home to Virginia. George was headed to Pittsburgh, Charts to Boston, and Winton to Bridgeport, so he was on my train. Winton didn't have the money for the train, so I bought his ticket. Jamie and Rennes ran for their train, waving goodbye. Charts tried to buy a beer at the station canteen and got turned down, and George and I shook hands.

"See ya, dude," he said.

"Come to New York," I said. "Cindy will be there."

Winton and I ate peanuts while we waited. Two girls walked by, and one said, "He looks like Jimi Hendrix," giggled and walked on by. Winton watched them go.

"You know why I dress like Hendrix?" he said.

"Why?"

"Cause Jimi was somebody." He paused. "Somebody."

"You're somebody."

"On the football field, maybe. But otherwise, I'm Jimi."

"Okay, be Jimi. See if I care," I said. He smiled and shelled a peanut. The girls giggled again, not far away, looking at Winton.

"See?" he said.

The 11:20 to New York boarded at 11 o'clock. Jumping on first, we got four seats facing each other, near the back.

"You know," I said, "I might not be able to come back."

"What?"

"Dean Harper said I might get expelled."

"Did you fuck up?" he asked.

I shrugged. "I don't know. I don't go to class, don't do my homework, and I give teachers a hard time," I said.

He thought about this for a moment, considering. Then he said, "So go to class, do your homework, and don't give teachers a hard time."

"Yeah," I said, after thinking a while, "maybe I will."

"You gotta come back, dude," he said. "You gotta."

As we got closer to Bridgeport, Winton got more uptight. The houses out the window were smaller. Stray dogs ran along the tracks; the clotheslines were filled with sheets. I could tell something was wrong but said nothing, looking out the window. At Bridgeport he shook my hand and got off the train, waving to me through the window. A black man in an Army coat who must have been his father met him, and they headed off. I wanted to go out and tell him it was all right, but that was impossible, like a lot of things in those days, so I just watched.

The train let me off at Grand Central Station about two-thirty, and immediately the old world came back. I walked home, giving myself time to adjust. So many people, going fuck knows where, going past me like I didn't exist. I had my backpack on, and no one else had a backpack, and that made me feel kind of good, you know, different. I wore my jeans, my work shirt, my leather belt with the silver buckle, the Dingo boots, the bandana. The doorman looked at me suspiciously, then recognized me and flung open the door.

"Tommy," he said, "welcome home. You look good!"

My mother heard the elevator and rushed to greet me. She threw her arms around me, and I hugged her. Stepping back, she looked me over, with that mother eye.

"My," she said, looking me over, "you've changed."

"I haven't changed," I replied.

"Wait till your father sees," she said. "At cocktails."

I went to the guest room and unpacked. Dinner was at seven. We had cocktails first in the library. My mother had a vodka. My dad bourbon, and I had a beer.

"You're a hippie now," said my mother with some degree of horror.

"Oh," said my father. "Is that right?"

Agnes the maid came in, to collect the glasses.

"Hello, Agnes, how have you been?" I asked.

"Very good, Tommy. Thank you for asking." I smiled at her, and she didn't dare smile back at me, but our secret about her man friend was safe and she knew it.

"Dinner is served," said Agnes.

Dinner was lamb with mint sauce, not jelly, asparagus with hollandaise, scalloped potatoes, a Waldorf salad, and mousse au chocolat, served with a noble 1955 Listrac Hosten wine from, where else, southern France.

"You like the wine?" asked my father, pleased as punch.

"Very much."

"French wines are the best, followed by Italian, and then none. California wines are so bourgeois, and all the others—Australians, Chile, New Zealand—those aren't even worth mentioning at all, let alone drinking."

"I like it."

"Listrac Hosten is a small vineyard in southern France and I buy a case or two every year. How is it?" asked my father, refilling my glass.

"I like it," I said again.

He burst with pride. Coffee was served in the library, and my mother poured.

"Sugar?" she asked.

"Yes, please," I said. When she put in two lumps, I motioned for more.

"More?" she asked, as if sugar were somehow worse than the ferocious amounts of alcohol they consumed. Those little cubes were a joke but asking for more seemed like I was mainlining cocaine, so I let it go. With coffees safely in hand, my mother turned to speak.

"Honey, we have a surprise for you. Don't we, dear?"

"Yes, we do," said my father.

"I'm all ears," said I, sipping delicately from the good china, my longer hair almost falling in the cup. I had to brush it aside.

"Your father and I have been talking—" said my mother.

"We have," he agreed.

"And we've decided that you don't have to go back to *that* school."

I coughed, and my coffee sprayed the table. "Really?" I sputtered.

"Yes, we see now that sending you off to that school was a mistake, and you don't have to go back," said my mother.

Warning, warning, enemy ship approaching.

"I've spoken to Mr. Lacklan, and he said you could come back to your old school, starting next term. Isn't that marvelous?"

"Yes, that's, uh . . . marvelous," I managed.

"You can go back to school here in New York, move back into your room, and even go back to dancing school, and go to Yale next year."

It was then, in that *you don't know what you got till it's gone* kind of moment— thank you, Joni Mitchell—that I realized the last thing I wanted to do was come back to ballroom dance at the Pierre, not that I had anything against the Pierre. But I realized in that split second I actually liked my new school. Liked hanging out with George and Rennes and Bark and Charts and Winton. And well, I didn't want to leave.

It hit me like a truck going a hundred miles an hour, looking around at my Fifth Avenue apartment—with the doorman and the Rolls waiting outside, the good china for the coffee, the interior-decorated living room, the antiques, the *money*—that it all seemed so . . . irrelevant. *Think, you bastard, think. Do something!*

"Good, it's settled, then," said my father.

"Well, that's a very lovely offer," I said (and I did actually say "lovely"). "But there is one thing."

"Yes?" said my mother, raising an eyebrow.

"Well, I'm there now, so . . ."

"Oh, that doesn't matter," said my father.

"Yes, but I'm doing very well in my French class, and I'm not sure we should interrupt it." Lame, I know, but I was playing for time. *Think, you bastard, think.*

"Oh, nonsense. You can get French here, can't you?" grumbled my father.

"And colleges may not look so well on me moving in the middle of the year," I tried.

"Well, I'll just have to give Yale another wing on their library," said my father, huffing with laughter.

"Then that's that," said my mother. "I'll call the Bashford in the morning and withdraw you."

Warning, warning, Will Robinson. I knew that I had about ten seconds to save myself, to come up with something that might do the trick. And for the life of me my mind went blank. For a second I thought I was totally fucked. Hello, Pierre Hotel. Hello, Fred Astaire dancing. Then came a flash.

"I'm on the hockey team," I blurted out.

My mother swung her gaze back to me. My father stared as well. Now, here's the deal. In our family there were only three things that mattered. One was, you know, the family; the second was the investment-portfolio return from Ernst & Young, and the third was the New York Rangers. Yes, the hockey team. We had season tickets in the yellow seats, almost among the regular people, about halfway up, close to center ice, with four seats across. My mother went to every game—I mean every game—and my father went as much as he could, which was quite a lot. I went whenever I could before going off to school.

We cheered the line of Jean Ratelle, Rod Gilbert, and Vic Hadfield, the GAG line, or goal-a-game, as well as Brad Park on defense, Jim Neilson the enforcer, and Eddie Giacomin in goal, who wore no mask, with their blazing blue jerseys with the Rangers lettering running diagonally from shoulder to hip. Wednesdays and Sundays were hockey nights, 7:35 p.m. at Madison Square Garden, during which my polite and respectful mother would holler like a dock worker and swear at the opposing team and shout, "Kill him. Kill the bastard," when we played the Boston Bruins. She hated the Bruins. She loved the Rangers. And she loved hockey.

"You're on the hockey team?" asked my mother with something bordering on reverence. I knew right away I had hit upon something, something big perhaps.

"Yes, I went out."

"You're playing hockey?" said my father, with real respect in his voice.

"Uh, yes, I'm on the team. Well, actually, I am not on the team till the first game, but I'm working out and think I'll make it."

"But you don't play hockey?" she said.

"Well, no, I didn't. But when they saw me skate—"

"You skated for them?"

"Yes, figure skated—on the river."

"You skated on a river?"

"Yes, I did. It's a long story."

"And they saw you?"

"I got recruited and I made the team. I think."

"Well," said my mother, "that certainly makes a difference."

"Yes," said my father, nodding in agreement. "But we thought you hated it there, son?"

I moved in for the kill. "Yes, father, I know, but don't you always say, never give up, never give up, never never never." I might have overplayed the emphasis on *never*, but it worked.

"I do. I do say that. You listened?"

"Well, like father, like son, I'd say," I said. "I'm not a quitter."

"Quite right," said my father.

"But look at you," implored my mother, looking over my jeans, long hair, boots, work shirt, and bandana. "You're *different*."

"Yes, we're worried about you, son."

"We still wear jackets and ties to dinner on Monday nights, Dad, so you have nothing to worry about."

"Oh," said my father, "well, that's something."

And that was that. I was back in. It had been a close call, but I was back in. In the end I just had to reassure them that their precious boy was not going to become some post-Woodstock, pot-smoking, degenerate hippie type, driving around in a VW bus with my face painted with flowers and girls who didn't shave their armpits. Which actually sounded pretty good to me. Because, in fact, that's exactly the way I was going, but didn't want them to know. So I played up the hockey. And in the end the hockey did it, 'cause more than anything, my parents just wanted to see their son, the dancing school boy with the white gloves on, knock someone wickedly on his ass in a hockey game, with them in the stands yelling, "Kill him. Kill him." Good boy that I was.

Chapter Sixteen
Roger the Wrestler

"*L iving on reds, vitamin C, and cocaine . . . ,*" played the Dead, over and over again on the stereo, as I had only a few records at home and this was one.

"Tommy, phone for you," yelled my mother over the cocaine lyric.

I had worn down the record groove, home in New York now for four days. I was bored out of my mind.

"Don't you want to call Joanna Danforth?" my mother asked on more than one occasion. "She's home from Kent, and her father owns NBC."

"No," said I. "I don't want to call Joanna Danforth."

"Why not? She's a perfectly respectable girl and quite pretty."

"Because I don't want to go out with Joanna Danforth. That's why."

"All right, you don't have to be like that," she snapped. "What about your other friends? Don't you want to see them?"

I didn't want to talk to any of my old friends. I knew it would turn into the usual discussion about Gucci and who's a debutante this season and who's got a new house in the Hamptons. So I stayed in my room.

"Tommy, phone," yelled my mother again.

"Who is it?"

"I don't know. Tracy or Trixie or something like that."

"Oh, man." I ran for the phone, which was located in the little phone closet off the hall.

"Hello."

"Do you still have chicken legs?" said the voice. It was her.

"Hello, Trix."

"Are you bored without me?"

"Horribly," said I. "But I've been pretty busy, you know. It's New York."

"I'm coming to the city, and if you aren't too busy . . ."

"What about Warden?" I blurted.

"Oh, we broke up," she said with finality. "He's so annoying sometimes. I hate him, actually. All he wants to do is have sex. Isn't that so boring?"

"Uhhhh . . ."

"Anyway," she rattled on, "he went home to New Jersey, or Philadelphia, or wherever he lives and I'm coming to the city."

"What about your father?"

"I told him I'd be at Cindy's and he said okay."

"So what do you have in mind?"

"Don't be silly," she replied. "I'm the best-looking girl at school. You're the best-looking boy. We have to be seen together."

"You *are* the best-looking girl at school," I agreed, "but I'm *not* the best-looking guy."

"Oh," she exclaimed in mock exasperation, and if I had been there, she would have smacked me in the shoulder. "My train gets in at three-forty. Be on the platform."

Just as I hung up, the phone rang again. I answered instantly. It was George.

"I just heard," he said. "I'll be there tonight."

So it was settled. Cindy and George, me and Trixie, out on the town, and hopefully, if her parents weren't home, at Cindy's place afterwards. My mother was standing there in the hall when I came out of the phone room.

"Can I have some money?" I said.

The train from New Haven came to a screeching stop on Track 14 on time at 4:35, and the passengers untrained (that's what you do in NY; you "untrain"). With the platform filling up with people, I stood there as if in a movie as the passengers went by. I saw Trixie get off five cars back, with a weekend bag over her shoulder and heading towards me. She saw me two cars back and gave me a little smile and a little wave. Then she ran the last few steps and planted a little kiss on the cheek.

"You're a doll to meet me."

"Did I have a choice?"

"Not really." She smiled that Trixie smile.

I took a good look at what she was wearing. She wore jeans, but they were new. Very blue. No fading. New. She wore a white blouse under a green sweater, and very brown penny loafers. And around her neck a scarf. Not a bandana like I wore, but a scarf like her mother wore. Only, she wore it stylishly, if only to show that she wasn't her mother. Yet. She took me by the arm, like in the movies, and we walked off the platform into the station.

"Buy me a drink," she said.

We entered, somewhat gingerly, the Oyster Bar. It was between meals and the waiters waved us to a table without much thought. A waiter came over.

"I'll have a rum and coke and she would like . . ."

"A gin and tonic," she said.

"ID," said the waiter, gruffly.

I took out my fake ID, a driver's license from Maryland, and handed it over. He flipped it over nonchalantly and handed it back.

"I don't have one," said Trixie.

"Sorry," said the waiter.

"I'll have a coke," she said calmly.

"Then I'll have one too," I said.

The waiter shrugged and went off. He came back a few moments later with two tall, thin glasses filled with those wonderful round ice cubes, and the coke looked so very inviting. I drank mine down before the waiter even left and said, "Another." He brought another coke as we sat watching the commuters head for the trains back to Connecticut.

"Oh, isn't this marvelous," she purred.

"It is."

"Okay, about tonight."

"Yes?"

"Cindy needs a date."

"I have one."

"Who?"

"George. He'll meet us for dinner."

"He'll do, I suppose."

"Cindy likes him."

"As if that matters," she said. "Where are we going?"

"Steak 'n Brew," I said. "They won't card us there."

"Then?"

"Mallory's." I knew that would make her happy because everyone would be at the bar and we'd be seen by, uh, everyone. Which I knew she wanted.

"What time is dinner reservation?"

"Seven."

"Okay, put me in a cab."

I put her in a cab on Lexington and walked home. I didn't want to go home, but I had nowhere else to go. When I got home, there was a message for me.

"You're getting a lot of calls," said my mother.

It was from Trixie, at Cindy's house. I called her right back.

"You know," she said when she came to the phone, "you may get lucky tonight. Not that lucky but lucky, if you play your cards right."

I didn't answer immediately.

"Does that meet with your approval?" she wanted to know.

"It does."

"I thought so." And she hung up.

George got a cab from Penn Station, arriving at my house about five, and immediately made an impression on my mother—dressed in the usual stuff, jeans, jean shirt, bandanas, Dingo boots. But George had brought a sport coat to show some respect and charmed Mother right off with his best Eddie Haskell imitation. "Oh, Mrs. Stafford, you are looking particularly beautiful in that dress tonight," he said. My mother fell for it.

"Are you all staying for dinner?" she asked.

"No, we have plans," I said. That sounded awfully grown up. *Dinner plans.* She nodded. If there was one thing my mother understood, it was dinner plans. We cut out about six just to get out of the house and walked through Central Park, finding a quiet tree under which to smoke a joint and then head over to Sixth Avenue. We arrived at Steak 'n Brew right at seven, feeling like there was no other place in the world we'd rather be. Two beautiful girls waited for us at the table, dressed to look, well, like their mothers actually. But sexier.

"Hello, men," said Trixie. Which sounded quite good. "Let me introduce. George, you know Cindy," she said, pairing them off.

"Uh, yeah," said George, and he and Cindy giggled right off.

"Okay, give each other a peck on the cheek—now," said Trixie. "Go ahead, do it. No tongues, mind you. Just a nice little peck. Like this." She pecked me on the cheek, and I looked at her, like *is that all?* George pecked. Cindy giggled.

"Good, now we can sit down. Drinks everyone?"

Just as I said, they didn't card us. Trixie got her gin and tonic and Cindy a fancy drink. George ordered two pitchers of beer, and that was fine with me. As I was pouring, I felt Trixie's leg under the table push against mine, which made me spill some beer on the table.

"Silly boy," she said, with a mischievous smile. "Here, let me"—wiping it up with her napkin. "Now, George, you talk to Cindy, and I'm going to talk to

Tommy here." It was an order, laid down by the sheriff, so we squared off.

"How do I look?" asked Trixie.

"What?" I said.

"How do I look? I mean, do I look good?"

"You always look good."

"Tommy, you're driving me *crazy*. How do I look?"

"You look great."

She let out a long breath. "Well, thank God for that. I spent hours to look this good. Beauty like this takes time, Tommy."

"Well, it shows," I said.

"And I wanted to look good, you know, for later . . ."

"But later, you won't be wearing any clothes at all," I replied.

She slugged me in the arm. "What I want to know is, do I look like you'd want to . . .?"

"What?"

"Oh, Tommy."

"Of course I want to," I replied.

She took a sip of her gin and tonic. "Beer is so boring," she said, "but I wouldn't mind having one."

"Here," I said, grabbing an empty water glass and filling it. She drank it down.

"Oh, that's divine."

We had steaks medium rare and baked potatoes and salad from the salad bar, with gigantic croutons, and blue cheese dressing with huge hunks of blue cheese.

"Another pitcher," yelled George to the waiter, who returned with the suds moments later. The girls both got up to go to the ladies' room.

"Could be a good night," George summed up.

About ten, we piled out of Steak 'n Brew, and the girls bundled up against the howling winds whipping up Sixth Avenue.

"Fix my scarf," said Trixie. I adjusted it as she looked into my eyes.

"There," I said, patting it.

"What's next?" Cindy wanted to know.

"Mallory's," I said. And off we trooped, jumping into a hansom cab.

The cab let us off on Seventy-ninth Street, and we walked the block to Mallory's Bar, a seedy rundown place packed to the rafters with drinkers, mostly underaged, because they never carded. People always said they paid off the police to stay open. We fought our way in, to the bar, where I ordered drinks and handed them over the crowd to George and Cindy and to Trixie next to me. Everyone from school, and I mean everyone, was there. It was like Bashford on the Hudson, with dozens of Bashford kids and Chalmers girls there too. Winton came through the door with a black girl named Chloe, who bunched up the skin around her nose when she smiled. I liked her right off.

"When'd you get here?" I asked.

"About an hour ago," he said. "I called your house from a pay phone and talked to your mother. Nice lady."

"I told her I'm on the hockey team."

"Come, look at this," said Winton. He took me over to where the pinball machines were lined up against the wall. One had only a flat screen, like a TV screen. It was very odd. It had a whole bunch of red, blue, pink, and yellow men—chompers with tiny eyes and a marauding mouth that ate up the dots on the screen.

"What is this?" I asked.

"Pac-Man."

"What's Pac-Man."

"Take a look," said Winton. "It's a video game."

"A what?" So I played it and it was kind of fun but lost interest after a while and went to find Trixie, who was surrounded by clingy Chalmers girls. When she saw me, she threw her arms around me and hugged me like saying to everyone, *this is my boyfriend and don't any of you forget it.* Like they could.

We bounded out of Mallory's about one o'clock in the morning, just as a bunch of what looked like fourteen-year-olds went in.

"We could go to my house," said Cindy. "My parents are in the Bahamas." That's what we wanted to hear.

"Sounds good," said Winton, with his arm around Chloe.

"My brother is there, having a party," she added.

We grabbed a cab, paying extra to take six of us. Piled four in the back and two in the front, we went over Seventy-ninth Street and then down Park to Fifty-seventh and then across Fifty-seventh Street, all the way to the East River. George paid the driver, and we all huddled together on York Avenue, watching our breath in the still December air. It was two days before Christmas. The Fifty-ninth Street bridge hung in the air over the river, the silver girders all lit up.

"It's around the corner," said Cindy.

Riverview Terrace, a little exclusive side street facing the East River, had its own park below it, and six brownstones with stairs coming down to a cobblestone street. We walked to the fifth house. *"Love the one you're with,"* blasted out the window. Two dudes and a girl stood on the stoop, smoking a joint.

"Share the wealth," bellowed Winton, and they passed him the joint. He took a hit. Wanting no part of that, Trixie waltzed inside. We all followed, barely able to see through the smoke at first. When it cleared, we saw dozens of kids in jeans standing around an apartment that looked like it came from the *New York Times* style section. It was a pretty typical New York City holiday party, everyone holding a drink, girls dressed up but not wanting to show it, a few guys in blazers over their jeans to show that they knew where they were, guys heading out the back to smoke a joint, girls wearing just a little of their mother's perfume, guys parting their hair in the middle and chugging beer. Glasses lined every shelf and tabletop, as the maids and housekeepers had been sent home. Ashtrays were overflowing. And someone put on The Who, *"See me, Hear me, Feel me, Touch me."* Trixie turned up her nose, looking peeved.

"I'll get you a drink," I said.

I went to the bar. A tall boy was fixing drinks, in a blazer with jeans.

"And who the fuck are you, may I ask?" he said.

"Tommy Stafford," I yelled over the din, taking no offense.

"Your name is not what I seek," he yelled back. "This is my party, so I get to ask, why the fuck are you here?" He was drunk, not falling down but weaving, so what the fuck.

"I'm here with Cindy."

"Oh, my sister." He nodded his head, a little too much.

"Yeah."

"Where is she?" he said, looking around. He was really checking to see if I was a crasher.

"Uh, she's back there."

"Okay, there's one thing you should know."

"What?"

"I go to Kent, and I'm the wrestling champ for Western Connecticut."

"Very impressive," I yelled over the music.

"What?"

"I said, very impressive."

"So if I were you, I wouldn't fuck with me."

"I won't."

He laughed. "Just kidding, kidding, my fine friend. I'm Roger. Cindy's brother. What would you like?"

Winton came walking up, getting drinks for him and Chloe.

"I'd like you to meet Winton. He plays football," I said.

"Football, huh," said Roger. "I'm the wrestling champion for Western Connecticut."

I left them talking wrestling and went back to Trixie with her gin and my rum and handed her the drink, but I could tell she wanted nothing of this scene.

"Come on," I said, leading her out the front door into the little garden that looked over at the river below and the Queensboro bridge with a string of lights dancing in the cold air.

"That's better." She sighed, taking my arm. "Oh, Tommy," she said, in her best imitation of Zelda Fitzgerald. *"Oh, Tommy."*

I wanted to say, "What?" but that seemed such a pedestrian thing to say, so I just looked out at the river, thinking silence was better than saying something un-Fitzgerald-like.

"I'm so unhappy," she said.

"Why?" I blurted. "You're a senior, going to Harvard next year. Everybody wants to go out with you. You boss everybody around, and you're gorgeous. Why the hell would you be unhappy?"

She gave me a look, like *that's not how you play this game.* "I hurt," she said, with her suffering face.

"You hurt?"

"I know this should be the best time of my life, that it'll never get better, that I'll never look this good, or be this wonderful—"

"You're wonderful?" I asked.

She smacked me on the arm, but not that hard. She said, "It will all fade, this year. You'll go off to Yale, and I'll go to Harvard, and we'll write for a while and see each other once or twice. Then you'll start dating some insufferable Yale girl, and I'll be pushed off into oblivion."

I wanted to remind her that we had only kissed once. No, twice if you count the peck on the cheek, and while I liked her . . .

"Promise me you'll let me down easy," she said dramatically.

"I promise," said I. She hugged my arm tightly as we looked up at the bridge and the twinkling lights. I mean, I think they were twinkling.

"I supposed I should kiss you now," she said.

"I won't complain."

She turned and we kissed, and I must say I'd never kissed anyone like that, with such force, like she actually liked it and couldn't control herself because of . . . me. I couldn't help but admire what a good kisser she was, and I wanted to tell her that, but I didn't want to seem like I was grading her or keeping score, and it's awfully stupid to say, "Great kiss" after you kiss a girl, so I just shut up and kept kissing her.

"Hey, get a room," yelled Winton from the steps above. He whistled. And I heard Chloe say, "Stop that. Leave them alone."

"Don't mind him," said Trixie and turned and held my arm. "You're a good kisser."

We went inside, and I saw George leading Cindy up the stairs. He didn't see me. Someone opened two bottles of champagne, probably from her father's wine cellar, and we drank out of small paper cups like we were slumming it. Trixie brightened completely with four quick shots of the bubbly in her.

"What do you do at Bashford?" asked Roger the Wrestler. He obviously didn't recognize me from before.

I knew what he wanted to hear. "I play hockey."

"Ah, hockey," he replied. "I'm a wrestler."

"A wrestler? Really? I didn't know."

Winton showed up from nowhere, Chloe now nowhere to be seen. "I'm a wrestler too," said Winton. I wandered off with my drink. "Really?" I heard Roger say as I drifted off.

George came running downstairs, with his shirt open, grabbed a half-drunk bottle of champagne, and ran back upstairs. "Just passed second, racing for third," he said. Trixie laughed, and she had a nice laugh.

"Ladies and gentlemen," announced Roger from the living room. "Can I have your attention, please? We are now going to have a wrestling match, right here in this room, between me and Winton . . . what did you say your name was? Oh, never mind. So, if you would all move back. And move that furniture back."

Somehow Roger the Wrestler had challenged Winton the halfback to a wrestling match. I didn't think this was going to go well. We grabbed the wingback chairs and the coffee table, pushing it all against the wall, so there was a big open space on the carpet. Roger took off his blazer, struggling a bit more than he should under the weight of gin, and Winton took off his shirt, so he was bare-chested. Roger then took off his shirt, so he was bare-chested too, and he was ripped.

"Wait, wait," said Roger, "we need an announcer." For some reason, he handed me a candlestick, to be used as a microphone. So I walked to the center of the room and held the mike.

"In this corner," I said in that mock-announcer voice, "from Bridgeport, Connecticut, weighing in at 174 pounds, from Bashford School, the Connecticut

Colossus, Winton the Wunderkind." The crowd now went wild. "And in this corner, from New York City, weighing in at 162 pounds, from Kent School, Mr. Kent Courageous, Roger the Rapacious." I was making it all up, but people liked it.

Roger waited a dignified second, then assumed the wrestler's crouch. We all stepped back for the fight. The crowd got right into it. Trix took my arm. Instantly, Roger lunged, catching Winton by surprise, and got him around the waist, pulling him down, almost ending the match. But Winton wrestled free and retreated to behind the sofa to pull himself together. Roger, full of confidence now, approached slowly like *where's my kill?* He lunged again, but Winton just sidestepped. Roger looked around; his face said, *this isn't going to be as easy as I thought.* The two boys met in the middle of the room and like two bulls pushed against each other, and Roger got him crossarm and threw him across the room. Winton smashed into the coffee table.

"Oh, fuck," said Cindy, eyeing the remains of the coffee table.

In desperation Roger lunged, and at that moment he figured out Winton was the star running back on the Bashford football team. Winton dropped down low, hit him at the knees, knocked him back, tackled him, then fell on top of him. Roger squirmed and grunted but couldn't get away. Winton now moved in for the kill, pinning his shoulders to the light green rug.

"One, two, three," I yelled. I slapped the carpet hard.

The match was over. Winton had won. He threw his arms in the air in triumph and paraded around the room.

"I lost," said Roger miserably, picking himself up off the carpet. "I fucking lost."

His girlfriend, or what passed for a girlfriend, ran to him and he pushed her away. He got up and walked away. "Win-ton, Win-ton, Win-ton," chanted the crowd.

"Shut up, all you fuckers," yelled Roger. "Or you can get out of my house."

"Come on," said Trixie, "it's over." She led me by the hand upstairs. The first room was locked; the second was taken, so we went up another flight of stairs, found an empty bedroom, and went in. She locked the door behind us. That's a good sign, the locked door.

We fell on the bed together, ripping at our clothes much like you rip open a big box from Bloomingdale's. Soon our shirts were off. I reached back for the clasp of her bra, and a moment of panic came over me. What if I couldn't get it off? A man was not a man if he couldn't get a bra off. When I pulled the two straps together, the clasp released. Thank God, I thought. Ever so slowly the bra came off slowly and our bodies met; it was the warmest, most wonderful feeling ever. We kissed for a while, and as I said, she was a fantastic kisser, and now she wrapped her legs around mine and pressed her jeans to mine. Boy, did she press. My hand reached for the button on her jeans. This was the moment of truth. This is the moment when her hand could come down and take mine, which meant *no, not that.* But it didn't. The button flipped open.

"Do you have protection?" she asked.

Now, this was always a tricky question. If you have a rubber in your pocket, waiting to bring it out, you get slapped, figuratively at least, because you had the audacity to think she was going to put out—*and what kind of a girl do you think I am?* And if you don't have it, you're a loser who isn't confident enough to bring protection.

"Uh, no."

"Okay, you'll have to pull out," she said. "Okay?"

"Okay," I said. Hell yes, okay. And the next few minutes went by in a blur, with jeans coming off and panties flung across the room and hitting the floor, and bodies meeting as one in that great cataclysm of ecstasy. Of course, I was about to come too soon, so I tried thinking of my physics homework. It worked. And then suddenly she grabbed me and held me tight and called out a name as she came. It just wasn't my name.

"Oh, Ben, Ben, oh yes! Benjiiiiiiiii."

Benji? Benji? Ben Warden? Was she calling out *his* name during sex? Shouldn't I be offended? And

Warden, of all people! The girl I was having sex with was calling out someone else's name. But I was too far in to turn back now. And she didn't even seem to notice—maybe because she was drunk, I don't know— that she called me by the wrong name. So if she didn't care, I didn't care. Right?

After it was over, we lay there in someone else's bed, in someone else's brownstone, under someone else's sheets, holding each other. It might have occurred to her at some point that I was not Ben, but she purred quietly and I held her. When she fell asleep, I got up and walked down the hall, naked, to get some air from the balcony, when something caught my eye. There, on the balcony, overlooking the East River, was Roger the Wrestler, totally naked, on the other side of the railing, clutching a can of beer, while holding the railing with only one arm, maybe even a few fingers. Five stories up, with a death drop below him, he looked at me in the most pathetic way. Only his fingers, just the tips of his fingers, kept him from falling.

"What are you doing, Roger?" I said slowly, in that *don't excite the beast* kind of way.

"I lost," he said, his words slurring. "I fucking lost. I'm not the wrestling champion anymore."

"Who the fuck cares?" I said.

"I care." He took a swig of beer, which did not seem to me to the best idea for someone hanging fifty feet in the air over certain death.

"Roger, you're hanging off the wrong side of the railing," I said. "Why don't you come back over?"

"He beat me—the little fucker beat me. I am the wrestling champion of Western Connecticut. I am!"

"Roger, come on back."

"Maybe I should just jump. Maybe that's best," he said, swigging his beer. He rolled around on the other side of the railing, and I thought he was going to fall. "Roger!" I yelled.

"It's over," he said. "It's fucking over."

"So what if you lost?" I said again, trying to calm him.

"He's not even a wrestler."

"He plays football," I said, hoping that might cushion the blow. "He's pretty good too."

"He doesn't wrestle," he yelled back. "And he beat me."

"So fucking what?"

"I just don't know," he moaned. "The only thing I care about, the *one* thing, is wrestling champ. And now your friend took me out."

"Yeah, you've made that pretty clear."

He was starting to annoy me. I wanted to help him and uh, save his life, but I also wanted to get back to bed with Trixie.

"Is there any point in going on?" He moaned.

"Probably," I said. "You used to be wrestling champion of Western Connecticut, and you are still the wrestling champion of Western Connecticut."

"That's true," he said, as if it hadn't occurred to him.

"So here's the deal. You can wallow in self-pity, give up, have everyone give you shit for the rest of your life, and wander off in obscurity . . ."

"Or?" He was catching on.

"Or you could go back to school, get back in the ring, win some matches, and be the champion of Western C.T. all over again."

"Yeah, maybe I could . . ." It was getting through to him, through the haze of a gallon of gin.

"Worth a try," I tossed out almost nonchalantly.

He climbed back over the rail. "I need another drink," he said. And he walked inside, out of the pouring rain, right past me.

"I'd put some clothes on," I said, my voice trailing him.

When I got back to the room, Trix was up and changing. "Where's Cindy?" she asked, stress now in her voice. The moment had passed. No second round tonight.

"Somewhere with George."

"We have to go."

"Okay."

We pulled George and Cindy out of a room, then found Winton talking to Chloe in the living room, smoking cigarettes. Roger came in, hugged Winton, and said it was okay.

"It's okay, man. I love you," slurred Roger.

Winton hugged him back, and they did a shot of tequila together.

"To us," yelled Roger. "To the warriors!"

"To us," yelled Winton, draining the shot.

It was after two o'clock. We put Cindy and Trixie in a cab on York Avenue.

"Hope my doorman lets us in," said I, walking home.

"Did you score?" asked George.

"Long story," said I.

"Did you nail Dean Harper's daughter?" he asked. "That's all I want to know."

I took Trixie to the train station next day, and we stood on the platform for the 11:40 to New Haven, steam pouring out of the engine.

"I'm going to tell Ben I don't love him anymore," she said

"I thought you already told him."

"You know what I mean."

"Right."

"See you back at school," she said. "Got to run." She hurried toward the train, stopped, came back, kissed me, and ran again. Just before getting into her car, she turned and waved, then was gone. She didn't see me wave back.

Chapter Seventeen
Dear Dean Harper

I t was the day before Christmas, and I sat down and
wrote this letter:

Dear Dean Harper,

*I know you are reviewing my record and thinking about
expelling me from school. I realize that you might have
reason for that. I haven't been a very good student, I see
that now. I just wanted you to know that I've made a
change and turned the corner, as they say. I am
committed to being a better student, a better athlete, and
a better person. In short, I think I am becoming a
Bashford man, and I'd like to have the chance to show
you in the next semester.*

Sincerely,

Thomas Stafford
Senior, Class of 1973
On the hockey team

Oh, come on, be real, I didn't mean a word of it, of course, but maybe it would get me into my second semester of my senior year, and maybe I could ride it out and graduate. I added "on the hockey team" because if there was one thing they liked at Bashford, it was someone who could help them win. When I went to drop it in the outgoing mail for my building, as it would happen, in our mail was a letter from Bashford addressed to my parents that looked like my grades, so I folded it up and stuck it in my pocket and took it back to my room. Sure enough, it had my grades.

English D
French C-
Math D
Science D
History B

The last one caught my eye. B in history? *I'll take that*, I thought. I mean, not quite sure how I did it, but hell, if they thought I was a B student in history, I was a B student in history. The rest of them? Well, let's just say I'm glad I intercepted the letter.

Christmas was a blast. I took great pleasure in watching my parents warm up to my long-haired friend. They especially liked George's infectious laugh. Somehow, without me knowing it, he had snuck out to Bloomie's and got my mother a scarf, actually wrapped in a Bloomingdale's box, with an actual ribbon around it. A fucking ribbon!

"Why, Mrs. Stafford, it's most beautiful on you," said George as my mother put it on Christmas morning, and she really seemed to like it, I think.

"Would you like some more coffee, George?" she asked, holding out the china coffee pot.

"Why, yes, I would, Mrs. Stafford," he replied, with great self-satisfaction that generally annoyed me.

George even did some magic tricks for my parents with two silver loops he bought from a head shop on Second Avenue. My father laughed heartily when the loops went together, then came apart.

"Marvelous," he roared.

On Christmas morning we all sat around in our pajamas, with baseball caps over our long hair. My mother had bought presents for George too, and when we opened them, George tried on his argyle sweater and refused to take it off.

The phone rang after presents—Jamie calling from Virginia. I took the call in the phone room and then came back and announced, "I have to go back to school tomorrow."

"So soon?" asked my mother.

"Hockey practice," I said, and that ended that.

"Well, we're sorry to see you boys leave," she said, "but we don't want to stand in the way. Are you a hockey player as well, George?"

"No, I mostly just drink beer," George quipped, which my parents thought was oh, so funny, and they laughed and laughed. Jeez, George.

We all gathered in the foyer next morning to say goodbye. George, I noticed, got the biggest hug.

"Fritzy's downstairs to take you to the station," said my mother.

"In the Rolls?" said George. "Right on." Then we were off to the station in the Rolls Royce. George kept rolling down the window, yelling to other cars, "Excuse me, do you have any Grey Poupon?"

We caught the 2:40 to New Haven, then the 5:10 to Hartford. And who should be there to get us at the station, but Jamie and Rennes.

"What are you doing here?" I asked.

"Come on," said Rennes.

He had brought an old station wagon from home in Virginia and drove us back to school. Because having a car was illegal, we hid his car in the woods by Building and Grounds, then carried our suitcases through the empty school.

"Is the rest of the team here?" I wanted to know.

"No," said Jamie. "Not back till next week."

"Then why are we here?" I demanded, suddenly annoyed.

"I got one more week to make you into a hockey player," he said. "And it ain't going to be easy. And now you've told everyone in New York you're on the hockey team, you better make the team."

He woke me at six o'clock the next morning.

"We have all day," I complained, as he dragged me out of bed. "Why so early?"

"Two a day," he said.

"Okay, but how about at ten and two?"

He laughed. The rink was empty and cold—the ice hard. I did a few turns.

"You skate like a pussy," he said. "Skate like you mean it."

"And how am I supposed to do that?"

So, I skated. We did the line drill, red line, blue line, back to red line, back to center line, back to red line, back to blue line, and on and on. At first Jamie kicked my butt, but after a few days I could keep up. And then on one cold day in a cold rink I skated my heart out and beat him by a yard.

"You skate like a pussy," I said.

He appeared satisfied. He had me skate backwards at full speed while stickhandling, then around the cones for an hour, then wrist shots, then slapshots, then more skating drills. By the time the team was back on campus, I wasn't half bad. Jamie never said a word to me, never asked for thanks, never paid me a compliment. Until in the first game of the season, when he had the puck behind the net and I was on point, and he came around and could have taken a shot. But he passed it to me coming in. I took a slapshot and scored over the shoulder of the goalie.

"McConnell, I don't know how you did it, but you made this kid into a hockey player," said Coach Muzzie. "I may have to keep you two on the same line."

While walking back from the game, I came face to face with Dean Harper and his whistling teeth, that, strangely, I was kind of getting used to.

"Mr. Stafford, I've been meaning to speak to you," he said. "I received your letter. I've decided that you may remain in school, at least for the time being."

"That's great, Dean Harper."

"What did you parents say about your grades, I wonder?"

"Well, they were disappointed, but I told them I'd do better this term."

"Will you?"

"Yes, sir, I will."

"Because you'll never get into Yale if you don't."

"Yes, sir."

"All right, then, let's leave it at that, Mr. Stafford. We'll give you another chance, and you'll put the nose to the grindstone."

"Yes, sir."

He moved off, but he wasn't done.

"Oh, Trixie says hello," he said. "She likes you, for some reason."

I nodded lamely, feeling strangely guilty, not sure what he knew. George came walking up as the Dean walked away.

"What did Whistler want?"

"He said I could stay."

"Do you think he knows you nailed his daughter?"

"Leave it alone, Georgy—would you please?"

Chapter Eighteen
Hot-bagging It

Winton showed back up at school the next day, sporting a new Jimi Hendrix purple coat, a mauve scarf over his forehead, red and black bell bottoms, and a green shirt, with a pack of cigarettes rolled up in his sleeve. Bark showed up that afternoon and Charts the same day. We met for dinner over Salisbury Steak and milk from those massive stainless-steel dispensers. With no homework, it felt like a holiday, even though I didn't do homework anyway. We worked in the back with Wugs for an hour or two, just to get the rhythm back, until Rennes put up his apron.

"Come on," said he, "Freak's back."

Freak. The legend. Freak's real name was Frank Wells, but everyone, including the teachers, called him Freak. He was a senior, like me, but we rarely saw him. It was said he was a genius and wrote math papers for the University of Connecticut—also that he performed physics experiments his teachers couldn't even understand.

There was one place at school completely safe from teachers, Dean Harper, even security. And that's where Freak lived, in rooms over the gym—five dorm rooms in a line that had been converted from storerooms. Freak had one, and nobody could go there without an invitation from His Greatness. As a genius on his way to M.I.T., Freak could do whatever he wanted. And what he wanted to do, when he wasn't being an astrophysicist, was smoke dope, drop acid, and smoke hash. *That's* another reason why they called him Freak.

Freak was pencil thin, with the longest hair of anyone at school, down to his waist, parted in the middle, straight as a ruler, shiny black. He wore a Sergeant Pepper jacket, wire-rimmed spectacles, ripped jeans, and snakeskin boots. He rarely let anyone into his room, so we felt like we were entering the inner sanctum being invited to *Freak's lair*.

We bundled up against the cold in our olive coats with the orange linings and the fake fur on the hood, walked across campus to the gym, and took the back stairs. The hallway walls sported graffiti and weird art from Japan and a New York City subway map. Rennes led the way as we took the stairs two at a time. He waited outside Freak's door until all of us gathered; then he knocked. Freak yelled come in. Music was on . . . Hendrix.

So uh, are you experienced?
Have you ever been experienced?
Well, I have . . .

Electric Ladyland. He had tapestries from India on the walls hanging in great arcs, a mattress on the floor, a stack of books higher than my head, a small running fountain with smooth round rocks, posters on the wall of Jimi Hendrix, Janis Joplin, and Jim Morrison of the Doors, and five beanbag chairs in a circle.

"Well, hello dudes," he said. "You like Janis Joplin? I was just putting some on."

"Sure," we said.

"Good, sit down, why don't you?" We sat without a word. Well, there being no chance for a word, 'cause Janis was playing pretty loud.

Oh, Lord, won't you buy me a Mercedes Benz
My friends all got Porsches, I must make amends
Worked hard all my lifetime, no help from my friends
Oh, Lord, won't you buy me a Mercedes Benz?

"I know all about you guys," he said. "You guys don't take any shit."

"No," agreed Rennes. "I guess we don't."

Freak looked right at me. "You're Tommy Stafford, right? Dean Harper hates your fucking guts."

"I guess," I said. It wasn't a very articulate response, but I couldn't think of anything else.

"He's a fuckhead," said Freak. "He represents the old. We need a new paradigm."

That was a cool word, *paradigm*, but I had no idea what it meant. He went on. "High school as a fundamental concept just doesn't work anymore, does it? We go, but the modality is outdated, don't you think?"

I just nodded. What the hell was he talking about?

"Look, we all live on this planet, right?" he continued. We nodded. "And this outdated system of education has lost its way. We should be working on an organic farm, harvesting wheat."

"Wheat?" I asked, genuinely confused.

"Yes, wheat. Or barley. Or rye. Or whatever. It doesn't matter. That's true education. What we have here is *faux*."

"Faux?" I repeated.

"Fake," said George.

"Right."

Freak tore on. "Look, we study stuff here that makes no sense. Calculus. French. Physics. Math. We should learn what we need to know on a farm, or a school in Harlem."

"But you're a math genius," I blurted. "And you're going to MIT."

He ignored me. "Or at Woodstock," he went on.

Woodstock. *Woodstock.* If there was one thing that stopped a conversation in its tracks, just saying

"Woodstock" would do it. The actual concert happened a few years back, and only a few hours away from this very spot. Not actually in Woodstock, but in Bethel, New York, and everyone was there—Jimi, CSN&Y, Airplane, the Dead, Santana, Arlo Guthrie, Richie Havens, Johnny Winter, Joe Cocker, I mean everybody.

Nobody went to church anymore, because there was Woodstock out on a field with tents for people who had bad acid trips. In a thunderstorm that almost electrocuted Crosby, Stills, Nash & Young, and where free love was best practiced in a parked car to keep out of the mud. We revered it. We *worshiped* it. And if anyone even mentioned the name, it was our job to genuflect.

"Right, Woodstock." Rennes nodded sagely.

"That's real education," said Freak. "Not French class."

Without thinking, Jamie blurted, "Aren't you fluent in French?"

"The point is, we need to think differently," said Freak. "New things are coming. Called computers. They're coming and it's going to change everything."

"Oh," I said, not quite sure what to say, "that's cool."

"Want to get high?" Freak quickly shifted.

"Yeah," we all yelled because that at least was something we could understand.

Now, normally there was a procedure to getting high. Someone rolled a joint in EZ paper, licked it closed, placed the joint fully in the mouth tip first, pulled it out to wet it, removed it again, showed it off, took out a lighter, flicked it, and lit the joint. Whoever rolled the joint took the first hit. After that, he passed it, usually to his left. With four or five people, you could usually get two hits off it before it was played; then someone pinched it and put it with all the other roaches for when you got desperate later on.

But that's not what Freak did. He took out his pipe and blew through it to clean it. Then pulling out a pipe cleaner, he threaded it into the stem. He then pulled an ounce bag from his drawer, filling the bowl with pot. So, it looked like we were going to pass a pipe around.

"Cool, dude." Rennes gestured approval.

"No, wait," intervened Freak. "Wait till you see this."

He lit the bowl, took a small hit, and drew it into his lungs.

"I have something you'll like. It's a new invention I've discovered," he said, letting out the smoke in a blast across the room. Freak then pulled a box out from under his bed and opened it. Inside was a giant plastic bag, with a white hose sticking out at the bottom of the bag. We all recognized it right away as the bags used to hold milk in the giant milk dispensers at the dining hall. He took a pair of scissors and cut the bag at the opposite end of the white tube, all the way across. Then in the sink he rinsed it out till there was no milk left in it.

He carefully wrapped the plastic bag completely around his head, then a scarf around his neck to keep the air in, and when he couldn't breathe, he grabbed the white hose where the milk came out and sucked air through it. He motioned with his arm, but we couldn't read him. With his head completely covered in plastic, his words came out muffled.

"Oh," said Rennes, catching on. He took the pipe from Jamie, attached it to the hose, put his mouth over the pipe, and blew backwards into the pipe so the smoke went backwards into the bag and it filled with smoke. First the white smoke shrouded Freak's face; then the smoke hid his eyes and mouth; then the smoke filled the bag and we couldn't see his head at all.

"Holy fuck," said Jamie.

"You can say that again," said George.

Rennes took the pipe out of the hose and let a little air in, but now we could hear Freak's breathing as he sucked in the smoke.

"I want to try that," said Charts. "I got to try that."

Soon the smoke started to dissipate. And we could see the outline of his head again. When it was totally gone, Freak ripped the bag off his head, sucked in a huge deep breath, and yelled, "It's the only way to get stoned! Not one molecule was wasted this way. Try it, dude. It's so radical."

Charts slipped it over his head and repeated the whole thing. He started to cough but got himself under control, sucking it all in, and came out with a gigantic stupid smile on his face when we pulled off the bag.

"It's called hot-bagging it," said Freak. "It's my invention."

"You ain't going to MIT for nothing," said George.

It was George's turn. His head disappeared in white smoke, and he stuck his thumb up to say he was okay, as if this were some kind of NASA exercise. Freak turned to me.

"Hey, aren't you going out with Trixie Harper?"

"Uh, yeah, kind of."

"She's a bitch."

"Uh, well, I don't know about—"

"She's a bitch. What happened to Warden?"

"She dumped him."

"Well, that's good. But she's still a bitch. You go."

My turn. I slipped the bag over my head, wrapping the towel around my neck to keep even the smallest smoke from escaping. For a moment I panicked, when I couldn't breathe, so I grabbed for the white hose and sucked in air; then Rennes took the hose and blew the smoke into the bag. The room got hazy, then far away, then foggy, then obliterated; then there was just the whitest white you've ever seen. I took my first breath and started to cough. But I got that under control. I took my second breath, then third, then fourth—what happened after that, I don't remember. When the smoke cleared, I tore off the bag, glad to get it off, but with the best high I've ever had, really stoned—like best ever—but the room was sharp, clear, focused for me like a laser. Everything made sense: the school, this room, my dorm, Mr. Rock, Dean Harper, George, Rennes, Jamie, Winton, Bark, and Charts. And Trixie Harper, who appeared like an apparition, beckoning me towards her. It was like a dream. And then Trixie became a demon and her eyes glowed red and snakes came out of her eyes, and then Susan Carter floated above me with a smile. I got up.

"Where you going, dude?" said Charts.

I fell into one of Freak's beanbag chairs, not able to get up, and dreamed of rivers and fields of golden wheat, mountain gorges and purple mountain's majesty. I don't remember saying goodbye to Freak or going back to the dining hall, but I got there and went right into the kitchen to see Wugs. Hugging him, I told him he had saved me. He could see it in my eyes. Taking pity on me, he put me on the silverware line, where I shined the knives and spoons and forks till they gleamed, saying aloud again and again, "Look at that spoon. Is that not the most incredible shine you've ever seen? I mean, look at it. *Look at it. It's so . . . fucking shiny.*"

"Okay, let's get him out of here."

"Wait, just look at this fork," I said, turning it over in my hand. "Can you see it? It's the most incredible fork ever. Ever! Duuuuuuuuude, just look."

They just shook their heads.

"No more weed for him," said Rennes.

Chapter Nineteen
Of Human Bondage

The new term started the next day. After class I walked to Chalmers and looked around in the usual places for Trixie but couldn't find her: not at the bus, not at the caf, not at the Quad. And she hadn't sent me a note or anything. I found Cindy in the Snug.

"Seen Trixie?" I asked.

"Not today."

"Here." I handed her the note I'd written in Science. "Give this to her."

"Okay, but . . ."

"But what?" I asked.

"Nothing."

When she took the note, I felt better, thinking Trixie would call me that night, but the call never came. I fell asleep that night, thinking about her—about how she hit me on the arm, how she made me do little things for her, how she asked me if she was pretty, and, oh yeah, that one magical night in New York.

"Oh, fuck, you're far gone," said George.

I even called her house. And her mother answered, thank God, not Dean Harper. I heard some muffled back and forth, before her mother came back on and said, "Trixie's not here right now. Can I take a message?"

I wrote another note *("Trixie, I need to talk to you")* and slipped it in her school mailbox. And waited. But nothing. I went to Chalmers and walked the hallways, hoping to run into her, even looked through the windows into classrooms, hoping to see her. A teacher came out and said, "Can I help you?" I went back to Bashford. Chalmers girls were always coming onto campus, so I checked all of them—every face, every possible girl—and never was it her. The next afternoon I caught up with Cindy.

"What's going on?" I demanded.

"Tommy, look," she said. "It's Trixie, okay? It's Trixie."

"I know it's Trixie, but why doesn't she want to see me?" Shaking her head, Cindy just walked off.

And then I saw her. I was walking back from hockey practice, and she was en route to her faculty house. I saw her first. Then she saw me. She looked quickly for a way out, but we were on a passageway between buildings, so there was nowhere to go.

"Hi," I said, as we approached each other.

"Hi," she said, kind of coldly. I waited. "Look, I'm sorry," she said. "I really am."

"For what?"

"I wanted to tell you, but—"

"Tell me what?"

"Oh, I'm just gonna say it. I'm back with Ben."

"With Warden?" I shouted. "With Ben Fucking Warden?"

"Quiet down," she admonished, looking around. "Yes, we came back to school, and he apologized and I realized that I loved him."

"He's a fucking idiot," I yelled.

"Tommy."

"But in New York, we—"

"New York was fun, but—"

"Fun? It was fun?"

"Tommy, look, I like you, I really do."

"Oh, that's nice."

"But what I mean is, we have to stop seeing each other."

"I don't want to stop seeing each other."

"That's somewhat obvious," she said as we stood there, on the walkway, she in her stupid plaid skirt and me in my clumsy hockey uniform—knowing I had to hold onto this moment, now and forever, 'cause if I didn't, I was totally fucked.

"When I got back, Ben was there and we had a fight, a really big fight. He told me he loved me, and I said I might love him and—"

"You said you didn't even like him."

"I never said that. I just said—"

"But what about us?"

She paused, as if she had something to tell me that she wasn't sure she should say. But she said it.

"You're not a serious person, Tommy, if you must know."

It stung. "Not . . . serious? What does that even mean?"

"Ben is serious. He's going to go to Harvard. He wants to be a lawyer."

"And me?"

"You just want to get stoned all the time."

"Not all the time," I protested.

"Well, I didn't mean all the time, I meant—"

"Yes, what did you mean?"

"I meant that all you want to do is have fun," she said.

"Instead of what—doing physics and French?"

"Well, yes. Those things are important."

"Give me a fucking break."

"See what I mean. You aren't serious."

"Trixie, what happened in New York, it was . . . you know . . ."

"Yes, I'm sorry about that," she said.

"You're a slut." I blurted it out. I knew right away it was a mistake. But I was red hot.

Whatever was left between us, and there wasn't much, disintegrated in that instant. I knew. Her face told me, and there was not much to say. She got that pouty look, and tears welled up. Her lips trembled as she turned her back on me and walked off without another word. *Say sorry*, I screamed inside my head. *Say sorry!* But I didn't. When she turned the corner, that was fucking that.

I walked back to my dorm. And what came over me was a completely new feeling. Nothing mattered anymore, not school, not George, not Rennes, not Charts or Jamie, not classes (well, they never mattered), not my mother or father, not smoking pot or hanging by the river, not Dean Harper coming after me, not nothing, not nothing at all. Just the overwhelming feeling of being crushed, right down to the bone. I slammed the door. George came in a moment later.

"What's the matter?"

"Nothing."

"Doesn't look like nothing to me."

"I said nothing, okay? Okay?" I yelled.

"Ohhhhhhh," he said, "you saw Trixie." He sat down. "How did it go?"

"I got dumped."

"She dumped you, huh?"

Tears filled my eyes and I sat back in my chair. "Yeah."

"Is that so bad?"

"Just leave me fucking alone."

After that, a blur: George got up, receded; the door opened; it closed behind him, and it was quiet again. For three weeks I didn't leave the room, not for class, not to eat. When I was hungry, which wasn't very often, I ate cheese from my little square fridge. Well, I did do one thing. I went to hockey practice. Because that was the one thing I could do without talking to anyone, and I could cream people into the boards and walk away without caring.

"What the hell got into Stafford?" asked Coach Muzzie. "He's an animal."

"He got dumped," said Jamie.

"Well, maybe all of you should get dumped."

But other than that I stayed in my room. I lost five pounds, then ten. Then fifteen. Instead of going to classes I would wander over to the Chalmers campus and pretend I was walking around for some reason, or go to the Chalmers library for a book, just hoping to see Trixie. I knew she wouldn't talk to me, but maybe I could just see her face, her smile. Be near her, on the same walkway as her. Anything! Just be around her, be with her in some way. Then I'd go back to my room. I didn't sleep, at least not much. I didn't open a book. George would bring food, like a tray from the dining hall, and leave it there for me to look at. And he'd say, "She's not worth it."

One day I waited on the hill opposite her faculty house to see her come out. I couldn't stop dreaming that she'd come up the hill, sit next to me, and say, *"Tommy, I tried to stay away. I tried. But now I realize I can't be without you, and so kiss me and hold me and tell me you love me."* When she did come out, it was with Cindy. And instead, Cindy came up the hill, stopped, and looked down at me, a pitiable sight.

"Tommy, what are you doing?" she said in that pissy tone.

"Nothing."

"You've got to stop. It's creepy."

I looked at her, and she looked back with a mixture of pity and loathing. Then I looked at Trixie at the bottom of the hill, and the most abominable pain coursed through me.

"Tommy, be real," said Cindy. "This isn't working. It's Trixie. She likes you being this way—she's a sadist-and she's not going to talk to you, because you called her a slut."

I slunk away. I knew I had blown it. She was back with Warden anyway. That was the last day I went there, never again. I lost five more pounds. I wasn't sure I had much more to lose. I didn't care.

Back in my room, I played "Tied to the Whipping Post" over and over until Jamie yelled through the door, "Enough! That's fucking enough!"

Oh, Lord, I feel like I'm dying...

George made one last try. He forced his way into the room, and sat down, and turned off The Allman Bros.

"Okay," he said, "I talked to Freak and he told me this. There's the ego, the superego, and the id. You got 'em all. We all do. So, the id is the monster, the guy on your shoulder who says, *do it, do it, kill him, or whatever.* He rampages all over the place. He fucks with everything. That's the id."

"The id?"

"Yeah, then there's the ego, and you got yours fucked up."

"Is this scientific?" I asked. " 'Cause it sounds like bullshit."

"And then there's the superego, and it referees between the id and ego. It can't do its job right now."

"The superego?"

"Look, Trixie just triggered your ego; it's been raising fucking hell ever since."

"Tell me something I don't know, George." So he gave up and left me alone.

Hard to believe I lost another five pounds, and Coach yelled at me, "Eat a burger, would you, Stafford?" But I got faster on the ice, so he liked that.

I'm not sure how I did it without food or sleep, but I did. It had been a month since Trixie dumped me.

Rennes finally stepped in. On a Saturday just after lunch, as I was wearing out the groove on my Allman Bros record, he and Jamie and George and Charts and Winton and Bark showed up in my room.

"Okay, get him up." The boys moved in, grabbed me, threw on my coat, and carried me down the two flights of stairs. Once outside, jumping the guardrail, we made our way across the field to the river.

"Where we going?"

"Shut up," said Rennes.

After trudging through the back woods, we ended up at the cabin. Jamie lit a fire and I sat sullenly in a chair, refusing to talk at all. George lit a joint and passed it around, and they made me take a hit. Charts had brought some Schlitz malt liquor cans, which they cracked open. I turned the beer that made Milwaukee famous down. Rennes tuned up his guitar and I thought he was going to play, but instead of playing he put it aside.

"Tommy, you got dumped," he said. "We've all been dumped."

"Not me," said Charts. "I've never had a girlfriend."

"Except for Charts. Believe me, it hurts. But you know what? You know what?"

"What?!"

"You've been fucking MIA for a month."

Everyone looked at me. Waited for me.

"I can't stop thinking about her," I pleaded. "I can't."

Rennes leaned in. "She's not the one. Give it up. Just give it up."

Funny thing, in that instant the cloud lifted. She had taken me in and wrung me out, consumed everything I had, sucked my world away, reduced me to ashes, and I thought I would be forever lost, I just wanted to die. All that—went away, just then. The weight lifted from my chest. It still hurt, but not in the same way at all. It was like recovering from a terrible illness, one you thought would kill you, but then you realized you were going to live after all. There was suddenly color in the world— the green fields, the white fluffy clouds, the purples in Winton's Jimi Hendrix wardrobe. And I knew something that I didn't know before. Trixie could hurt me, but she couldn't take me down.

"And one more thing."

"What?"

"I promise you that before the end of the year, whatever happens, we will get revenge on Ben Fucking Warden."

"Yeah," I said. "Can we do that?"

"Here's to Tommy," George saluted.

They held up their Schlitz malt liquors, yelling "To Tommy!"

And I drank, and it was good. "*Au revoir*, Dean Harper's daughter." See, I did learn something in my French class.

Chapter Twenty
Sweet Goodbye

"Harper," yelled George, bursting into the room, arms flailing. "Code red, code red."

Code red meant a bust. Dean Harper was coming.

We scrambled out of the room, out of the dorm, and into the Quad, just in time to see Harper enter the side door. It was a Saturday, normally a quiet day around the Quad.

"He's going for Bark," said George. "Fuck."

Bark sold pot from his room on the second floor. Bark was a pure dealer, which meant he bought a pound, cut it into sixteen ounces, put each ounce in a plastic lunch baggie, rolled it up, and sold the bag for fifteen bucks. If there were too many stalks, he sold it for less, but he had a good relationship with his dealer so there weren't usually many stalks. Everyone knew he sold from his room; he'd done it all year.

"It's Bark," yelled Jamie. "Come on." We charged up the two flights of stairs and out into the hallway. But Dean Harper was already there, in front of Bark's room.

"Mr. Barker, open this door," he ordered, pounding on it.

No answer.

"Barker," said the dean, "open up."

No answer.

"I don't think he's in there," said Jamie. The dean scrutinized Jamie, saying with his eyes, *he's in there all right, he's there, and we're gonna get him*—then continued to knock. Bark wouldn't open.

"The master key," said the Dean smugly. A teacher with him delivered the master key, and Dean Harper put it into the lock and turned it. The door would not open.

The dean pushed harder, and it opened a crack. The dresser on the other side was blocking it—a common trick we all knew.

"Barker, open this door," yelled the dean.

"I won't. This is my room and I refuse entry," yelled Bark. "I have my rights."

"You have no rights, Mr. Barker, none. *Now, open this door.*"

The idea of rights was something we threw around a lot, and the idea that Bark didn't have the right to sell pot from his dorm room three nights a week seemed, well, ridiculous to us.

"You can't come in." Bark resisted.

"Help me push," said Harper to his henchmen, and push they did. Little by little the door gave way. A moment later the dresser was pushed aside, and Dean Harper burst into the room, with us following.

"We have reason to believe you are selling illegal drugs out of this room," said the dean.

"I'm shocked, shocked you would say such a thing," said Bark. "It's calumny!" *Calumny* was a word we had just learned in English from Willie S., so I knew it right away. It meant no fucking way.

"It's not true," said Bark. He snuck a quick look at Jamie and nodded his head in the direction of the window. He kept motioning his head towards the window, and finally the light went off. Jamie tore out of the room. George grabbed me and we hustled after. We ran down the stairs in giant strides, out the side door, to the courtyard below, and sure enough, there were a half dozen packages on the ground under Bark's window.

"Oh, fuck," said Jamie. "Come on."

We were on our way to grab the packages and take off when security arrived and cut us off, surrounding the packages.

"What is it?" said Rennes, showing up.

"They got Bark."

Dean Harper marched Bark out of the dorm across to Founder's Hall, where he disappeared for several hours, despite our repeated attempts to get into the

Dean's office. Finally, he came out, and we gathered around him outside the Dean's office.

"I'm gone," he said.

"They're throwing you out?" I said in shock.

"Yeah, they called my parents." Calling parents could only mean one thing; he was gone. "My dad's coming to pick me up. Tonight."

"River," ordered Rennes, and we ran for the river, once last time for Bark.

"Sorry," he said, when we got there. "I let you down."

"No, you didn't. No, you fucking didn't," said George.

It was a strange thing to see a parent that night at nine o'clock in the dorm. Bark's father shook all our hands, not seeming to blame us in any way. With his arm thrown around his son, they walked to the car. Bark turned back at the car, and we all just looked at each other for a while. Then he nodded—it was over—and got into the car, which slowly drove away. Bark was gone. Gone.

Next day after smoking we were coming back from the river when I saw Trixie Harper walking towards us. Rennes saw her first, then George, and they all closed ranks around me, until I was surrounded. I wasn't sure why. That's when I saw her. It hit me hard when I saw her, a jolt, but then I was fine. And we walked by her without a word. Yes, oh yes, she turned to look back at me. Or at least that's what George told me, because I didn't look back. 'Cause Trixie Harper was history now and forever.

Chapter Twenty-One
Night of Nights

The game was against Exeter, and my parents showed up. I had made the team, and even during the worst of times worked hard, learning how to stickhandle and pass and play defense. And of course, I could skate better than anybody, so what I lost in play I made up in skate, if you know what I mean. Anyway, I was on the third line—not even sure I would get much playing time, and that would have been embarrassing to my parents—but somehow word got out, and Muzzie moved my line up to second. It felt good to hit the ice, skating to warm up. I looked for my mother and father and saw them up in the stands at center ice, twenty rows up: Mom in her mink coat and Dad in his camel hair.

"Hope we get some playing time," I said to Jamie as he skated by.

"We will."

The game got going. In the first few minutes there were lots of crashes—it was that kind of game.

"Second line," yelled Muzzie, and over the boards we went. I skated out to center ice, keeping one eye on my parents to make sure they knew I was on the ice. My mother pointed, so I knew. I felt good on my skates, full of energy, maybe because Jamie had me up every morning at six to skate for an hour, maybe it was my parents, maybe just the game. I don't know. But something came over me just then. The puck dropped and off I went. First, an Exeter wing tried to get around me with the puck, and I took my angle and creamed him into the boards. He crumpled onto the ice. It was such a good hit I thought I might get called for it, but the ref saw it for what it was, a good hit. *Bloodlust.* I snuck a look up into the stands and saw my mother standing, fist outstretched, yelling like a banshee. The bench erupted in yells, and the adrenaline jolted me as I skated down ice. Jamie got the puck behind the net and saw me charging. He sent a perfect pass just left of the circle, and I wound up and took a slapshot, which went between the goalie's pads, and the red light came on. The place went nuts.

"What the hell happened to you?" said Jamie, hugging me.

"Fuck if I know."

Jamie looked up into the stands and saw my mother screaming. "Man alive," he said, as we skated back to the bench.

Two Exeter guys skating past looked over at me, as if to say, *nice game you got*. Me. They were looking at me. "Man alive."

I scored one more goal on that night of nights. It was a junk goal, swatting at it in front of the crease, but it went in. Then I got an assist, and it was a work of art, coming straight out of the confidence you get from being on a roll. *If you think you can do it*, sometimes you can. Now we all knew about my figure skating days, but I always seemed to lose the puck. So when I picked up the puck in my own end this time, I said, "Oh, fuck, I'm gonna lose it," but I didn't. I deeked one guy out and took off with the puck.

The guys yelled at me from the bench to "Go, go." So I went. I skated right, then left, moving in the flow of players. When an Exeter guy moved in to take me out, I faked a pass and went around him. When I came in on the goalie, he had my angle blocked, so I increased my speed, went in front, pulled back, the goalie flopped in front of me, and I sent a lovely pass over to Jamie, who flipped it over the flopped goalie for an easy goal.

"That one's for my mother," I said to myself, mobbed by my teammates.

When I looked up, I saw my parents clapping, not yelling, very respectfully. So I did something funny without thinking. I bowed my head to them. Just a head nod really. They nodded back. The final score—we won 5–4. We beat Exeter. *Exeter.*

"Can we take you boys out to dinner?" said my father after we showered and showed up outside the rink. "I'll take as many as you like. We'll go to the Griswold Inn."

"Sounds good to me," said George. "I've never been there."

"I'll round up the guys," I said. I found Rennes and Winton and George and Charts, and we piled into my father's car.

At dinner my father found something to talk about with each of us. To Rennes he talked Virginia, as my father, when spending some time in Washington DC, traveled to the horse country for weekends. To George he talked sailing, which George knew from growing up in Maine. To Charts they talked about hot dogs, 'cause Chart's father once entered the Coney Island hot-dog eating contest. My father loved hot dogs. To me and Jamie, he talked hockey. My mother only wanted to talk hockey, to which Jamie said okay, and they talked about it all night. Things were different when we left the restaurant, because my mother and father were now more than Mother and Father. They had become people who actually could talk about other things than my grades and dancing school.

"Oh," said my mother, drawing me aside, "we're thinking about spending Spring Break at Lyford Cay. Think any of your friends would like to go to the Bahamas with us?"

To the Bahamas! Like yeah! "Hey, guys, who wants to go to the Bahamas?"

Chapter Twenty-Two
Last Chance

Spring break was still six weeks away, however. Each dreary February night was succeeded by a still more dreary February morning. We played hockey. I never had another game like that, but I blended in and played okay. We smoked joints by the river. We smoked cigarettes in our room with air filters we bought in Hartford. We had rum-and-coke parties on weekends. I shined silver in the dining hall. I went to classes a bit more, but still not much, and Dean Harper finally called me in.

"The reports I'm getting from your teachers are not good," he said. "I took a chance on you, Mr. Stafford. Don't let me down."

"I won't, sir," I said.

I left his office and went straight to the river to smoke a joint. I thought about this study thing. Somehow Winton always got A's. Jamie and Rennes, who never seemed to study, got A's and B's. But of course I slept till eleven and met them by the river at ten at night, so it was possible, indeed probable, that they sneaked in a bit of homework while I was out smoking. Hearing that I was on shaky ground, Winton came by and gave me a schedule. Homework seven to ten o'clock every night. Then I could have a drink and go for a smoke. But that was so fucked up, so I bagged it. I went to class and discussed the book, even though I hadn't read it.

"Have you actually read the book?" said Mr. Rock.

"Sir, I have," I replied.

"Well, then you must be extremely stupid."

"Yes, that is a distinct possibility." It was harder to fake physics, so I didn't really try. I'd pick up the odd thing here and there in class, which helped on tests, and usually I got a C-or D+, so I got by.

At our next meeting, "I'm not seeing much improvement," said Dean Harper. "I must see improvement."

I applied to Yale and a few other places. Not that I thought I'd get in with my senior-year grades. But my father expected me to apply to Yale, so I did. The Yale hockey scout came to one of our games, but it was not a good game for me, and he didn't wait for me outside the locker room.

"Mr. Stafford," said Mr. Rock, after class one day.

"Yes?"

"You will report to me every day five minutes before class, and I will determine if you are approved to come to class," he said.

"Approved?"

"If you are prepared, you may stay. If not, you will not waste our time."

I wanted to say, "Mr. Rock, you report to me every day, and I'll tell you what an asshole you are," but I didn't.

So the next day when I came to class five minutes early, he grilled me: "What did you think of the assignment?" Not having read the assignment, let alone know what to think about it, I wasn't sure what to say; frankly, I did not know what it even was.

"It was enlightening," I started.

"In what way?" asked Mr. Rock.

"Made you think."

"In what way did it make you think?"

"In a most fundamental way," I responded.

"Mr. Stafford, did you read the assignment?"

"Of course."

"Well, then, kindly tell me what it was."

When he found out I had not read it, he said, "Go to Dean Harper. He may recommend disciplinary action."

"I'll read it," I begged.

"Oh, it's much too late for that," said Mr. Rock.

"One more chance?"

"You can only get one more chance once, Mr. Stafford, and you've had about ten."

"What are we going to do with you, Mr. Stafford?" said Dean Harper, seated now across from me in his office, with a face that said, *I don't know what to do with you.*

"Valedictorian," I quipped, thinking that was better than being serious.

"Oh, you're a long way from that, I'm afraid. It will be a miracle if you make it to graduation."

"Oh, I'll make it," I said, "if Mr. Rock will get off my back."

"He's just the messenger. I'll admit he does not like your presence in class—"

"He's a rat."

"He's not a rat, Tommy. He's just reporting to me."

"He's a rat."

"Mr. Stafford, I will give you one last chance if you are interested, or you may pack your bags today."

"One last chance?"

"Yes. But there are conditions."

"What?"

"You will attend every class," he said, the wind whistling through his teeth. "You will raise your grades above C. You will report to my office every morning and show me your homework. You will be confined to your room after dinner on every night but weekends."

"In short," I said, "you want me to be a Bashford man?"

"Precisely."

I walked down to the library after dinner that night to think it over. I got a book on dinosaurs from Mrs. S and headed to the back stacks to read through it and think about my life. I had just reached the Brontosaurus era when I looked up, and who would be standing there, but Trixie Harper.

"Hi," she said.

"Hi," I said coldly. I had nothing else to say to her.

"Listen, I know you hate me and you have a right to," she said. "But, Tommy, they're going to throw you out of school."

"Maybe."

"Not maybe. My father said—"

"It's none of your business," I said, going back in my book to a lovely Stegosaurus.

I could tell from her expression she thought about walking away at this point, but she took a deep breath and forged on. "I'm just saying, Tommy Stafford, I know you can do it. So just try. Just try."

"Why do you care?" I blurted.

"Oh, Tommy, come on," she said.

So I decided to try. I mean, come on, give me a break, I had to try, didn't I? Otherwise, it was the end of the road, back to the city and dancing school at the Pierre and debutante balls and drinks in the Hamptons.

And I'd lose everything I had worked so hard for: the nights smoking dope by the river, the cases of rum under the bed, hot-bagging it in Freak's room, the parties in West Hartford—all would be lost. *All that!*

So I would become a Bashford man, after all.

I stopped drinking, well sort of, I kept a case of rum under my bed for Saturday nights. Stopped smoking pot. Until after lights out, anyway. Stayed in my room after dinner, actually opening a book. Of course, I could barely say, *"Bonjour"* and *"À bientôt"* in my French class and in geometry had no idea what parallel lines were. But funny thing, if you actually looked at the books, they started to make sense. Then I got the idea to outdo Mr. Rock: write the best essay ever written by a senior at Bashford School. First, I read the book, *The Odyssey*, with a lot of Greeks and sailing and weird sea monsters. At first, not to my liking. I say at first, because George came over, looked down at my table. and said, "Fucking great book." I looked at him. "You've read it?" "Sure, everyone's read it." So, they were all holding out on me. They all actually did homework. Who knew? Who fucking knew? *Those Bastards.*

Chapter Twenty-Three
Tabitha

My grades rose. I actually started to like some of my classes—the history of the Revolutionary War, conjugating the verb *être*, and how fast a car was going when it amassed twenty pounds of pressure per square foot, or whatever torture the physics teacher could come up with. Funny thing, my teachers showed great pride in my recovery, as if they had had anything to do with it. I let them bask in the glory. I just didn't want to get kicked out. I just didn't want to leave Rennes and George and Charts and Jamie and Winton. I didn't want to end up like Bark, with my father showing up at nine at night in the car to collect me and my things.

"Mr. Stafford, my reports tell me you are doing much better in class," said Dean Harper. "And you are on the hockey team, and doing your work study job. In short—"

"I am now a Bashford man," I said.

"Precisely."

"And because of that, I am allowing you to go on spring break."

My heart skipped a beat. What, you're telling me that was on the table? 'Cause there was no way I was going to miss spring break in the Bahamas. Dodged a bullet there, I thought. So there was a reason I did all that work. I just didn't know what it was.

"It was never in doubt," I said confidently.

"Well, have a good time," he said cordially. "Where are you going?"

We took the train from Hartford to the city, arriving at dusk at Grand Central, then squeezing into a cab to my apartment. Me, George, Charts, and Winton. Rennes and Jamie had to go home to Virginia to do some farm chores, or walk horses around, or whatever they did in rural horse country of VA. Their parents said no, they couldn't go to the tropics. George had said yes right away, even before asking his parents. Charts and Winton negotiated for a week before coming into my room and shouting, "In." So it was the four of us.

It was now middle of March and I hadn't had a haircut since August, so it was growing out nicely, and the other dudes had hair even longer. I could snicker at the thought of the elderly guests at Lyford Cay, at the eastern end of the island of Nassau, as we paraded into the dining room, four men straight out of *Easy Rider*.

"Fuck ya," said George.

Together with my mother and father, we caught the 9:40 Pan Am flight from JFK, nonstop to Nassau, my parents firmly seated in first class and the four of us in tourist. Two hours and forty minutes later, we stepped out at beautiful Nassau International. For those who haven't experienced the rush of warm, tropical air after a winter in Connecticut, it's awesome. Getting off the plane, you are transported. One minute you were in the cold, damp, bone-chilling misery of a New England winter. And the next— with that wonderful, warm wind in your hair as you walk down the stairs to the tarmac— you are in tropical paradise. My parents had this bemused look, as if they were transporting some new species to this land.

"Wow, listen to that accent," said George after a smart-looking customs inspector asked for our passports.

"Do I need one?" said Charts.

"Don't joke."

"Just give it to the officer," said I. Charts handed it over.

The officer looked at us, and the smallest of smiles appeared on his face. Then he looked at my parents with that *oh, man, what are you in for?* look, and handed us all back our passports.

"Welcome to Nassau," he said in his lilting accent.

"Welcome to Nassau," said George as we walked away, mimicking the accent. "Welcome to Nassau."

"I have arrived," said Winton as he blessed the crowd.

"Maybe I can get a girlfriend here," said Charts.

"Doubt it," said George.

We drove the forty-five minutes east across the island to the Lyford Cay gate. A nattily dressed uniformed man met our cars. My parents were in the lead car, so the guard passed us through.

"We're going to party!" yelled Charts to the officer. The officer, who had seen it all before, smiled politely and said, "Yes, have a good time, but be careful."

Our house sat atop the fifth hole of the golf course. Not on the water. That was too rich even for us. It was a nice two-story job, with lots of verandahs and storm windows for when the hurricanes came through. March was not hurricane season, so we didn't have to worry about the weather, but we knew that if a hurricane was to come, it would be us making it.

"Mrs. Stafford, you are looking particularly lovely tonight," said George, on our way to dinner at the club the first night.

"Thank you, George."

"Eddie Haskell," I said.

"Enough of that, Thomas," she rebuked me. "I think George is being very polite."

"He's a kiss-ass," said Winton, adding "Sorry."

"Oh, it's okay, Winton," she said. "Heard it all before."

"Use the bar tab while you are here," my father informed us, giving permission. "Our number is 5757. I think you are old enough now."

Had I heard right? My father had just declared open bar for all of us, for the whole vacation.

"Rum punch, here I come," said Charts.

"Just be careful," said my mother.

"Oh, we won't let anything happen to your precious son here," said George.

The clubhouse was full of palms. You know, the big leafy things in the corner and in front of the stairs. This was the Lyford Cay Club, with the waiters in bowties and white jackets, and the maître d in tails. You entered into a massive lobby, a super shiny floor, and paintings on the walls of, well, beaches. Just in case you didn't want to walk outside and see an actual beach. A wide staircase went up to the rooms on the second and third floor. On the main floor was the bar, a festive place filled with drinkers, a game room with backgammon boards set up here and there, and a dining room.

At dinner the main dining room filled to over-flowing, and afterwards the band played calypso music. A Limbo Man came out in a flowered shirt and did the limbo and got lower and lower until the bar was only a few inches off the ground. Even then, he got under it.

"Wow," said Charts, "unbelievable."

After dinner, my parents said goodnight and took the car back to the house, leaving us to make our way back with the club shuttle, any time before midnight. My dad, all ginned up, almost hit a parked car, backing out of the parking lot.

"Don't worry about us," I called after them, but they couldn't hear.

"Talent at two o'clock," said George, coming up behind me in the dining room. I scanned the room and saw a table of girls sitting with their parents. Three girls—one a bit younger, two about the same age, like maybe late high school, well, like us.

"I saw them first," said George. "I get first pick."

"Second," said Winton.

"I'm going in," said George.

"Right behind you."

The girls wore tropical dresses, not stupid tourist things like sarongs, but tasteful spaghetti-strap numbers in white and yellow. Their faces were both red and brown, so they had been there sunning for a few days at least.

"Second from the left," said Winton.

"First on the right," said George.

"What about me?" I asked.

"What about Charts?" said George.

"He gets the mother," I said.

Charts was over surveying the band and measuring the height of the Limbo bar off the ground.

"Well, let's roll." Maneuvering right over to the table, George sat down. I next to him.

"I didn't see you on the Limbo floor," he said, natural as can be, to the girls.

"I didn't see you out there either," said the older girl, clearly the leader.

"I'm going to sing the 'Girl from Ipanema' later, so I'm holding back," said George.

"Oh, really?" She smiled, a wicked smile.

"You won't want to miss it."

"I'm George, and this is Tommy," he said.

"He's cute," remarked one of the girls.

"He might be good looking, but I am a much better kisser," said George.

"Is that right?" said the lead girl. "I am Cecilia Roberts," she said. "And this is my sister Tabitha, and my friend Cara Sanders. Cara and I go to Rosemary Hall."

"Oh, I hear a lot of bad things about girls from Rosemary Hall," teased George.

"And?" said Cecilia coquettishly.

"And I like it," said George, matching her smile.

Cecilia was hot, Cara not quite so hot but still pretty. And Tabitha looked, well, youngish, maybe fourteen. As it happened, George paired off with Cecilia, Winton with Cara, which left me with Tabitha. Not that I didn't like Tabitha—she was cute and bubbly and fun—but she seemed, well, young. I smiled at her to make her feel better.

"Let's get some Planter's Punches," said Cecilia, indicating her preference for the strong red-orange cocktail.

"Now we're talking." George happily ordered from a nice waiter, and a few moments later we all had the concoctions in front of us, filled with Myers's Rum, and they went straight down. Except for Tabitha, who had a Shirley Temple.

"City girls grow up early?" I said, pointing to her Shirley Temple.

She giggled. I liked her giggle. Her being young didn't mean I couldn't hang out with her. Her sister Cecilia rose and the other girl rose too. "Let's go," she said.

"Where you going?" said Winton.

"It's Casino Night."

"Casino Night!!!"

"It's not for real money—just chips," explained Cara. "And whoever gets the most chips wins."

"Wins what?" asked George.

"Wouldn't you like to find out?" said Cecilia, crinkling up her nose.

We made our way to the large rectangular room game room, painted in calypso colors, with beach furniture and white tablecloths.

"Planter's Punch." George spotted a waiter and ordered.

"Yes, same," we all said, and the waiter went off.

It was so natural. The girls had left seats open at the gambling table so we could sit boy-girl. George moved right in on Cecilia, Winton with Cara, and I sat with Tabitha. She smiled at me as if to say, sorry you got me. Maybe it was the tropics, but when we sat with Cecilia, Tabitha, and Cara, it was as if we'd known each other all our lives.

"Let's play," I said enthusiastically.

"Blackjack," said the dealer.

"Deal," said Winton. The dealer was slightly older, maybe a college guy, with long hair, longish sideburns, wearing a blue blazer with gold buttons. I hadn't noticed him before. Right off I didn't like him. There was something about him. He dealt the cards. I got a six and a nine, for fifteen. I should have stuck, but I hit—*why not? I was in the Bahamas*—and got a face card. The dealer swept my cards away.

"What's your name?" I said to him, not without some hostility.

"Chas Dotter, your croupier, at your service," he replied. "I'm a guest here, but I volunteered to help out with the cards."

"Tommy Stafford," I said. He looked at me, then looked away without a word.

He dealt. I lost five in a row before I saw something going on at the other end of the table. Cecilia was winning, winning big. She got nineteen, twenty-one, blackjack, seventeen, and twenty. She won every time.

But something wasn't right. The rest of us were losing big. Then I caught it. The dealer was slipping cards to Cecilia under the table. If she got a face card, he'd slip her an ace for twenty-one. If she got a low number, like a five or six to start, he'd give her another low number, so that when she got two cards, she had ten, and then she'd hit and get another face card for twenty. I knew it was true because when she lost once, she looked at him with mock anger, so I knew she was in on it. Cheating—and winning. I looked over at Tabitha. I think she saw it too, but she kept her head down. Good little sister that she was.

"Wow, you're cleaning up," said George.

"Thanks," said Cecilia.

After ninety minutes a bell rang. Games over. The prizes were handed out. Cecilia held up all her chips when they called her name. She snuck a look to her partner in crime, Chas, who sat back with complete smugness and watched her retrieve her prize. She won a beach bag woven with the green leaves from the coconut tree.

"It's green now, but it will turn brown as the leaves die," said Chas, as if he knew, as if he knew anything.

We all applauded, especially George, who thought the real winner of Casino Night was going to be him.

"Fire on the beach," said the Chas-ster.

"Right on," said Charts, reappearing from the Limbo room with a young hottie on his arm. "Fire on the beach." She was kind of pretty and had a far-off, vacuous look in her eyes, perfect for Charts.

Another cute girl, who looked to be about seventeen or eighteen, walked up to Chas—fresh and pretty. Chas said, "Tommy, this is Melissa Morgan. I was wondering if you'd like to walk out to the beach with her."

"Uh, I'd like that very much. But I already have a date." I looked over at Tabitha, who could not restrain herself from breaking out into the most massive blush imaginable.

It was close to midnight. We trooped out to the beach, where a bonfire was being prepared by the hotel. I walked alongside Tabitha, who dangled her sandals in her hand as we walked.

"I'm fourteen," she said.

"Is that right?"

"I'll be at Rosemary Hall next year," she said. "As a freshman."

"Really?"

"And you? Are you a senior?"

"I am."

"Yes, you look like a senior, older and . . . Where do you go?"

"Bashford."

"Oh."

"At least until they throw me out."

"Why would they throw you out?" she said, with a hint of excitement.

"Right," I said, "why would anyone want to throw me out?"

"You're funny."

"Hardly."

"They call you Tommy?"

"They do."

"Cecilia always likes the guys she can boss around, but you're not like that, so she won't go for you."

"I'm offended," I said with a mock smile.

"Oh, you don't want Cecilia. Believe me." She looked at George, crowding Cecilia by the fire. "You might want to tell your friend."

"He's a big boy."

I realized at that moment that little Tabitha, cute little Tabitha, cute little fourteen-year-old Tabitha, wasn't so dumb after all.

The hotel brought rocks from the sand dunes and made a circle that we loaded up with firewood from the club, dousing it with lighter fluid, then lighting the damn thing. The embers floated up in the night sky, landing harmlessly in the ocean. The water lapped the beach just a few yards away, and the night air drifted over us lovely and warm. Charts and his hottie, whose name I never got, showed up with a tray of rum punch. We all grabbed a drink. Then someone showed up with a case of Heinekens, which we cracked open too.

"But no drugs, no smoking pot," ordered Chas. "Under no circumstances. We're in a foreign country, and if we get caught, we'll be arrested." He waited for dramatic effect, then took out a joint and lit it up.

"I'll take that," said Charts.

"Let's go for a swim," said Cecilia. She got up from the fire circle, ran to the water's edge, where the light from the fire illuminated her back. Pulling her dress over her head, she plunged into the black water.

"I'm going," said George.

"Be careful," I said. Me, saying be careful, but for a moment I was worried about Geo.

But he wasn't listening.

Pulling off his clothes as he ran, George raced to the water. He plunged in. We could see two heads bobbing, growing closer, about twenty yards out. I looked at Tabitha. She smiled.

"Come on," I said.

We ran to the water, stripping down, plunged in and swam out about fifty yards to get away from George and Cecilia, who were doing their thing. Even though Tabitha was a good swimmer, I kept my eye on her.

"My sister brought some pot," she informed me as we swam.

"Really?"

"She wrapped it in a shirt and asked my mother if she had room in her suitcase. My mother said yes and just brought it through."

"Wow," I said. "She could have landed her mother in a Bahamian jail."

"That's Cecilia. You don't know her like I do."

"No," I admitted, "that's true."

We could see all the others strip down and jump into the ocean, so there were a dozen heads bobbing in the moonlight.

"I'm cold," said Tabitha suddenly.

"Come on."

We swam back to the beach, where someone had grabbed a bunch of beach towels from the swimming pool. I wrapped Tabitha in a giant white towel so only her face showed through. Dried off, we went back to the fire.

"You're nice," she said, looking at my upper body as I dried by the fire. "Cecilia is a fool."

As George came running back from the water towards the fire, the rum punches were talking; he tripped and fell, hitting his forehead on a rock by the fire, and when he stood up the rock was sticking out of his forehead.

"George, you have a rock sticking out of your head," I said.

"Fuck me," he said, pulling it out. "Who cares?"

The blood flowed down his forehead, down his nose, and over his lips.

"George, you're bleeding," said Winton.

George grabbed a rum punch and poured it onto his forehead. "The alcohol will disinfect it." He laughed.

I could tell it wasn't that bad, mostly a scratch, so we let him laugh and then polish off the rest of the rum punch.

"You're crazy," said Cecilia.

Tabitha whispered to me, "She's the crazy one."

George told some stories while holding a bloody shirt on his forehead, then passed out. Chas moved over next to Cecilia, and Tabitha rolled her eyes. "Wait, just watch," she told me, and a moment later Chas and she got up and walked down the beach, their figures fading as they drifted from the fire.

"Poor George," said Tabitha.

"He's asleep," I said. "We won't tell him."

"Let's hit the pool," Charts suggested, getting up. We crossed a huge lawn with lounge chairs put up for the night, then came upon the swimming pool, surrounded by cabanas. Winton threw himself on the first lounge chair. Charts brought in a half a case of beer. Even Tabitha grabbed one.

"I can drink," she insisted. "I can."

"I didn't say you couldn't."

Winton held out a pack of Dunhill cigarettes from the gift store and we all lit one up.

"Bonzaiiiiiii," yelled Charts, launching himself in a cannonball into the swimming pool at the Club. What the hell? So we all went in. The guys went naked. Tabitha kept her bra and panties on.

"Okay, I got a game," said Winton, holding up a martini glass he had found in the bushes. He filled it with pool water. "You've got to go down this slide with the martini glass and not let any of the water spill out of the glass."

"I want to try that," said Charts. He came down the slide into the pool, and all of the water poured out of the glass. There were only a few security lights, so the pool water was dark.

I tried it, but water from the glass spilled all over.

"Let me," said Winton. He came down the slide and hit the water, cutting it like a knife, with no splash, and the water in the martini glass sloshed but did not spill. He held it up as he went under.

"He's a genius. With a martini, anyway."

As Winton slipped off with Cara towards the beach, George showed up, walking unsteadily, still holding his forehead.

"Where's Cecilia?" he asked.

"She went to bed," said Tabitha quickly before I could say anything.

"I've got an idea," said Charts. He walked over to one of the large leafy green plants. He lifted it an inch. "Not so heavy," he said.

George looked over at me, unconvinced. "She didn't really go to bed, did she?" I shook my head.

George went over with Charts, and together they lifted the potted plant and carried it to the side of the pool.

"Don't do it, George," I said, laughing. "Don't fucking do it."

With that, they pushed it over the edge. It made a sucking sound in the water; then there was a clunk as it came to rest on the bottom of the pool, with the leafy green top of the plant hovering just on top of the water.

"Oh, hell," I said, grabbing another plant. Charts and I brought it to the edge of the pool and dropped it in at the other end. It sank to the bottom slowly, landing perfectly upright, and the top of the plant just cut the surface of the water.

"Another," said Charts. Winton and he grabbed one and dropped it in.

"Come on," said Tabitha. So she and I got up, grabbed a plant, carried it over to the pool, and dropped it into the deep end. It hovered almost majestically on top. Now there was a jungle of plants on the surface of the water.

"What's going on?" demanded Cecilia, arriving from the beach with Chas, the disheveled look of lovers.

"You missed it," said Tabitha breathlessly. "You missed the whole thing."

It was almost two o'clock. We split up, leaving behind a trail of rum punch, cigarettes, bottles of beer, and a half-dozen plants in the swimming pool. We had missed the last shuttle by two hours. I thought it best not to call the club car, so we walked home, pushing forward in the Bahamian breezes. Charts drifted off with his hottie, whose name I never got. "What a night," he said as he left. "What a night."

Chapter Twenty-Four
Young and Dumb

Not caring that Cecilia went off in the dunes with Chas, George wanted her anyway. So as the sun-packed days lined up one after the other, and Bashford drifted further and further away from our thoughts, Geo went after Cecilia with a vengeance. Cecilia played along, and they'd take walks on the beach, where she'd order him to fetch a rum punch and he'd fetch a rum punch gladly.

"It's not good to be a puppy dog," said Tabitha as we sat under an umbrella. "Not with Cecilia."

We went for walks in the afternoon, Tabitha and I, before the partying started. We'd go walk on the golf course or on the beach, then go for a swim. When she stripped down for a swim, I could see she was going to be quite something as she got older. She even tried to flirt with me, taking off her shirt slowly and pretending she had hurt her shoulder so I'd rub it.

"I have a boyfriend, you know," she said as we walked the beach.

"Really?"

"Yes, Arnold Foxton."

"That's quite a name," I said.

"How would you know, Tommy Stafford?" I smiled at her. "Oh, I hate you," she said.

"And how long have you been going out with Arnie?"

"Oh, shut up," she said. "My sister is a fool, and I'm glad."

She looked out to sea, so I looked out to sea, and there was an understanding between us that whatever it was, that was okay with both of us and that it was good.

"Would you like to go on a date?" I asked suddenly.

"A what?"

"A date. You know, I pick you up, we go out to dinner, we hang out, I take you home."

"I've never been on a date, not a real date. Where will we go?" she said, a thrill in her voice.

"There's only one place to go, unfortunately," I said, "to the club."

"Everyone will see us," she said. "Everyone." She seemed thrilled by the prospect. "They'll all be watching. Even Cecilia."

"Then it's settled," I replied. "I'll pick you up at seven."

"Tonight?"

"Tonight."

Back at the house, I decided to take a quick nap before dinner—falling asleep in a chair outside, watching the golfers go by. I was awakened by several arms grabbing and dragging me to the jeep.

"Where are you taking me?" I demanded.

"A date with destiny," said Winton.

They threw me in, and we had a wild ride through Lyford Cay to the harbor. The jeep halted with a screech at the yacht club, where arms again grabbed me, lifting me up and depositing me into the stern of a forty-foot catamaran.

"I can't," I pleaded, "I can't go. I have a date."

"It's a sunset ride," said George. "I chartered it."

"I have a date," I repeated.

"A date?" said Charts.

"Yes, with Tabitha. I have to be back by seven."

"Okay, you'll be back by seven."

The boat pulled out of the harbor, and in a few moments we were making ten knots below gigantic white sails with blue trim. I relaxed and put my legs over the side, letting the waves wash up onto my trunks. The front of the catamaran had a netting we could sit on and watch the ocean go by below. The captain, a handsome man named Joseph, came about and headed out to sea.

"I've got to be back by seven," I insisted.

"You'll be back," said the captain.

The Heinekens came out, and the captain let us smoke a joint that George got from Chas. It didn't go far, but it was something. When we stopped to swim off the stern, Joseph set up a swinging rope. We swung out and let go, plunging into the sea.

"Charts got a girlfriend," said George. "Finally."

At five minutes of seven, the catamaran pulled up at the beach by the club; the captain came about, dropped the sail, and yelled, "Swim," so I made a perfect swan dive into the Bahamian tides and swam for shore. I knocked on Tabitha's door at exactly seven o'clock. Cecilia answered.

"I hear you're taking my sister out," she said, a little annoyance in her voice.

"Yeah," I said, sandy-haired, dripping wet, still in my bathing suit. But there. On time.

She looked me over, in trunks and a tank top. "I'm not sure they will let you in that way."

"I didn't want to be late," I said.

"Hm," said Cecilia. "I'm not sure I can let my sister go out with someone who can't dress for dinner." Tabitha came around her sister and looked me over, wet, sandy, hair uncombed, but there! "Oh, I don't care," she said.

"Oh, hold on," said Cecilia, with exasperation in her voice. She came back with a white shirt, slacks, and a blue blazer. "From my dad."

I changed in the bathroom, and when I came out Tabitha's mother was standing there.

"Do you need a chaperone?" she asked.

"Oh, Mom," said Tabitha.

"Just kidding. I trust you," she said, with a look to me that said she really didn't.

"It's Cecilia you should worry about," said Tabitha.

"Shut up," said Cecilia.

We made our escape from the hotel room to the dining room, where Marcus the maître d' gave us the look over, but then took us to a pretty good table. I held out the chair for Tabitha.

"I know what Cecilia would do now," she said.

"What?"

"Light a cigarette."

"Would you like one?" I took out my pack.

"I don't smoke, silly. Thanks for asking, though."

We ordered. A Planter's Punch (for me), and she had a rum punch without the rum.

"How do we pay for this?" she suddenly wanted to know.

"Don't worry. I put it on my father's tab."

"Oh, good." She seemed relieved by that.

My mother and father came by on their way to their table.

"So, who is this beautiful young lady?" asked my father, who knew very well who this young lady was.

"Miss Tabitha Roberts of New York City," I said.

"Hello, dear," said my mother warmly. "Make sure he behaves himself."

My father winked at me, which was wholly unnecessary, so I rolled my eyes at him to get him to go. They smiled at Tabitha and moved away. A moment later on the way to her table Cecilia came by.

"You look nice," she said to me. Then to her sister, reluctantly, "You too."

"Who you going out with tonight, George or Chas?" Tabitha asked.

"Shut up, you stupid girl," said Cecilia harshly.

After Cecilia walked away, Tabitha smiled at me, like *wasn't that fun?* I watched Cecilia walk away, in her flower print dress and white sandals, her brown hair up, her gold necklace on her tanned skin, and I had to admit she looked pretty good.

"Yes, she's pretty," said Tabitha. "George is in for it tonight."

We ordered shrimp cocktails, and she had the halibut. For me, the prime rib. And before long she was telling me all about New York City, her friends, their crushes, and her crushes and dancing school and next year.

"I can get away next year, you know, for weekends," she said, sounding a bit like her sister, "and I can come see you wherever you go. Where are you going, by the way?"

"Maybe Yale. Everyone in my family went to Yale, so I guess I'm going there."

"Tommy Stafford, give me a break," she said, sounding suddenly much older. "No one goes to Yale 'cause they *guess* they'll go."

"Okay, I'm going," I said with finality. "I haven't really done much to get there, sorry to say."

"So you'll go to Yale and make something of yourself," she said.

"Maybe."

"And I'll come visit you at Yale. We'll go to Yale Bowl for the Harvard game, and I'll wear blue and white for you," she said.

"Now I have a reason to go to Yale," I said with a little laugh.

Her voice got very low, almost confidential. "It's my first date, you know."

"Well, glad to be the first," I said.

"Of course you did arrive in a bathing suit, so . . ."

We went to the beach club after dinner and danced to The Doors, Jim Morrison . . .

She's a twentieth century fox
She's a twentieth century fox

"Come on," she said, leading me down to the beach, along the water's edge, on a perfect night, with the flames from the torches along the beach walk lighting our way. She stopped. I kept walking. After a few steps I turned around to see her standing there.

"Are you going to kiss me?"

"I wasn't going to. It's not that kind of date."

"Everyone kisses Cecilia," she said.

"I can if you want, but that's all." She smiled. I walked up to her, and instead of kissing me, she sank her head into my chest.

Putting my arms around her, I said, "You're not her."

We headed back to the clubhouse, her arm through mine.

"You leaving tomorrow?" she asked.

"Yeah," I said.

"Me too. It's been . . . good."

"It's been just great."

Charts and George and Winton met us at the clubhouse.

"Your father ordered four bottles of wine at dinner," Charts, who had eaten dinner with my parents, announced.

"He had someone to drink with," I said.

Tabitha's curfew was eleven that night, so I escorted her back to her room. On the way we saw George and Cecilia having drinks on the patio. Chas came in the front door, looking around.

"You seen Cecilia?" he asked.

"No," I said, even though I could see her right then through the door.

"Oh." He wandered off, still looking.

George came in for more drinks and he carried them back outside to Cecilia—and came back in a moment later, carrying the drinks.

"Where did she go?" he was perplexed.

I didn't have the heart to tell him about Chas.

"What the fuck?" George said, going to look for her.

I took Tabitha back to her room and we stood at the door, where she gave me a peck on the cheek and that was that. Her mother opened the door, and Tabitha gave me that look, like *what did you expect?* and went in. Nodding to her mother, I left.

Back at the bar Charts came in with his hottie, whose name I still did not know. After a quick hello, they disappeared into the dunes. Winton and Cara came by and went out to the beach. So it was just me and George.

"How did it go with Tabitha?" he asked.

"Good."

We went into the billiards room and played pool for an hour or two, and George seemed fine to me. Except he was drinking more than usual. "Another," he yelled. He yelled that several times, and each time the waiter brought him another vodka.

"Let's split," I said.

"Sure."

We walked along the golf course—he wobbly, me okay—with the beach on one side and the fairway on the other. It was almost midnight. The ocean breeze felt great, even late at night like this. I wanted to get George home. And then—a woman's voice, a moan, came from the darkness of the golf course.

"What was that?" George heard it too.

I knew exactly what it was but didn't want to say.

"It sounded like Cecilia," he said.

"It might have been."

"It was. It *was* her."

"Well, maybe it was—"

"No, it was. She might be hurt."

I wanted to stop him. But too late. He ran out onto the golf course. I lost sight of him a few yards in.

"Cecilia, Cecilia," George called out. "Are you there?"

"George," I called after him, "I think she's all right."

"Cecilia. Cecilia!"

A laugh cut the night in two. A female voice, a wicked laugh.

"Cecilia?" he called out.

Then a longer, even more heartless laugh, from Cecilia, erupted out of the night, meant to drive him away. It was two lovers on the golf course, and George wasn't invited.

"Let's get out of here," he said harshly, coming back out of the darkness.

We walked silently on the golf course back towards the road. It was dark. As we came over a rise, we stepped off a ledge and fell a half-dozen feet into a sand trap. More scared than hurt, I got up, but George stayed down in the sand, on his back. So, I sat down next to him.

"Fuck her," I said.

"Yeah, that's exactly what I was trying to do," he said, laughing.

We sat in the sand.

"I'm an idiot."

"Come on." I led us both out of the trap, back to the road.

"You know, Tommy," he said, "you don't get it."

"Get what?"

"It's this side of paradise," said George. "F. Scott."

I threw my arm around him to support his wobbly walk.

"You're Tommy"—he pointed out the obvious— the vodka speaking now, the pain of betrayal underneath.

"Yes, I know, I'm Tommy."

"There's nobody like you. You know that? Nobody."

"Right, George, there's no one like me," I repeated.

We got home. I put him to bed like a child. He started singing . . .

> 'Cilia, you're breaking my heart
> You're shaking my confidence daily
> Oh, Cecilia, I'm down on my knees
> I'm begging you please to come home
> Oh-oh-oh-oh

"Get it?" he said as he drifted off. "It's Cecilia, like the song, right? Right?"

"Right, Georgy," I agreed with him. "It's like the song."

In the morning George woke me up early, wide awake, as if nothing had happened, shaking me awake as well.

"Come on, it's our last day, so let's go for a swim and watch the sun come up," he said. He seemed fine. He was George. We went for a swim. Somehow Charts and Winton found their way to the beach early too, and the four of us swam out a few hundred yards.

"Could be sharks out here," said Charts.

"I already got bit," said George. No one laughed. "It's okay—go ahead and fucking laugh," he said, and we laughed.

Our plane back to the States left about noon from the airport in Nassau. Spring break was over, so just about everybody was headed to New York that day. My father liked to dress for the plane, so just this once we all donned jackets and ties. But we also wore leather bracelets and pucca-shell necklaces to remind us where we'd been. As with our long hair and other wardrobe surprises, my father didn't seem to mind. We took a photo—my mother, father, George, Winton, Charts, and me—standing in front of the Nassau sign, sunburned, relaxed, happy, and still alive. Charts and Winton went off to buy some magazines. George was chatting up my mother. My dad went to the bar for one last martini, and when I turned around, there was Tabitha.

"Hi," she said, standing in front of me.

"Hi."

"I'm not on your plane," she advised me matter-of-factly. "I thought I was, but I'm not."

"Too bad," I said with a slight frown.

She nodded and bit her lower lip.

"You're going to be fine," I reassured her. "Next year you'll come visit me."

"At Yale?"

"Yes, at Yale."

"Tommy?" she purred.

"Yes?"

"Thank you." And in an instant she had taken three steps, was up on her tiptoes, and gave me a kiss—not a peck but a kiss—on the lips, a real kiss, that was quick, powerful, and fast.

"Goodbye, Tommy Stafford." I saw in her eyes that she had let me go in that instant. Then she was gone, into the crowd, to the boarding gate, on the plane back to New York, and I knew if I ever saw her again, it wouldn't be the same.

And it came to me, as I watched her disappear, that even if I was forever young and dumb, that even if I had fucked up everything I'd touched for the last seventeen years, even if I never lived up to anyone's expectations, not even mine, that this time, this time right here and now, just maybe, I had done something right. *Just maybe.*

Chapter Twenty-Five
Fear and Loathing at Bashford

Back on campus next day, we parted ways, Winton, Charts heading off to their rooms, George and me for ours, the Bahamas boys no more. No one spoke of the Bahamas, like it hadn't happened. But it did and we knew it. George and I sat up, made rum and cokes, and talked about how the ice was gone from the river, a chem test coming up, and fuck knows what else. We didn't talk about Cecilia or Tabitha or the turquoise waters of the Bahamas, or day of days. We just got on.

Next day as I was sitting at lunch in the dining hall, minding my own business with Jamie and Rennes, eating this rice pudding that had way too much starch, George came running in with a book in his hands. "Tommy," he said, "you got to read this."

"Okay," I said, twirling my spoon in the pudding.

"It's *Fear and Loathing in Las Vegas*. It's fucking incredible."

"I know," I said. "I've read it."

And in spite of my comment, as if not hearing, George opened the book, seemingly about to read a passage, but immediately a good half ounce of pot slid down the crease and right into my lap. Looking down, I saw giant buds of marijuana all over my legs, fresh, super green, bursting with THC, with that fine powder of pot all over my jeans. I couldn't believe my eyes. Right there in the dining hall, yards away from teachers, my lap overfloweth with weed.

"George!" I said. "What the—?"

I looked up—but George was gone. Just gone. How he got out of there so fast, I'll never know. He was just gone. I had to act quickly or get thrown out of school. I doubled over. A hundred or so people were eating lunch all around me, so I just froze there, hunched over. Rennes and Jamie, who saw the whole thing, moved into action. They surrounded me, hiding me, pretending to get a book out of my book bag.

"What the fuck do we do now?" asked a panicked Jamie.

Rennes threw an arm around me. "You've got a bad leg," he said.

"What?" I was slow on the draw.

"You've got a bad leg," he repeated.

And with that, he lifted me up, while I was still bent over, and he and Jamie carried me out of the dining hall onto the back porch facing the river, and into a stiff breeze. Jamie opened his backpack and swept as much of the pot as he could off my lap into his bag.

"Stand up," ordered Rennes. The wind took the remaining pot and lifted it off me into the swirl of the wind, drifting off onto the fields below.

"Damn waste of some good weed," said Rennes.

"Where the hell is George?" said Jamie. And we all shook our heads, laughing.

"Fucking George," said Rennes.

Jamie led the way back inside, kicking a little stray pot under the table. I noticed Susan Carter at a table not far away, and she smiled at me. I smiled back, and then we got back to the table, and there was George, eating lunch, casually oblivious. We all just stared at him.

"I wanted to get your adrenaline going." And he laughed.

"Well, it worked," I said. "It fucking worked."

Finally, finally, spring arrived. A surprise of the senses. And the weight lifted, as it does in April in New England. The dreary, overcast days gave way to spring light, a mild welcoming light. It wasn't warm yet—that would come in May—but it was time to put away the winter coats and bring out the jackets. Winton liked it because he could parade down the center of the Quad in Jimi Hendrix outfits without a coat. Not going to the cabin much anymore, we spent more time smoking joints down by the river. I did some homework, enough to get by. And I went to my work job in the dining hall, polishing the silverware every third night until it gleamed. When people used their silver in the dining hall, no one even seemed to notice it, but it didn't matter, 'cause I knew and Wugs knew too.

One night after dinner, Wugs approached me as we were heading out. He was wearing his usual institutional white shirt with snaps, grey pants, and black shoes, with a dirty apron thrown on top.

"Can I talk to you for a moment?" he asked. Jamie, Rennes, Winton, and George said they would wait for me outside.

"Sure." I went into the kitchen with him.

"It's my sister," he said, a little out of breath.

"What about your sister?" I asked, wrinkling my brow.

"She's in Hartford, and she lives alone."

"All right," I said.

"She needs to go to the hospital."

"Then she should go."

"An ambulance costs too much. She wants me to take her."

"And you want to go get her and take her to the hospital?" I asked.

"Yeah, but I got this place and breakfast to get ready," he said.

"Wait here." I walked calmly out to the dining hall and found the guys. A moment later, we walked back into the kitchen.

"Go to your sister," I said. "We got this."

"Really?"

"Yes, now go."

He hung up his apron and beat it out the back, while the rest of us looked around at the dishes coming in on the conveyor belt and said, *fuck it, let's go to work.* It took a while to figure it all out—where the pots went, where the dishes went into the dishwashers, where the silver went, and where it all got dried. We sang "Southern Man" as we worked.

> *Southern man, better keep your head.*
> *Don't forget what your good book said.*
> *Southern changes gonna come at last.*
> *Now your crosses are burning fast.*
> *Southern man.*

And we all shouted, "Southern man," each time it came up in the chorus. It took us till eight o'clock that night to get the kitchen cleaned up and the breakfast prepared. As we left, we looked back at the gleaming kitchen, well, not gleaming but pretty nice, and all the dishes put away. Then we helped the other mini-Wugs get the dining room ready for breakfast, putting out the silver, putting the milk in the dispensers, checking the juice, mixing the pancake batter.

"Nice job, boys," said Rennes as we finished up. "Nice job."

Next day Wugs came back to work.

"How's your sister?" I asked.

"She's good, thank you." And from that moment on if there was a special dessert, German chocolate cake or rice pudding, he saved it for us, and we didn't have to fight the mob to get it.

It was spring now and in spring things happen, right? A few days later, Mr. Barnes came up to me in the Quad. Mr. Barnes was the drama teacher and he had a hot wife, Consuelo, from Spain or Mexico or some place in Latin America. When she walked in the Quad, all the guys lined up on the balconies. A few even whistled—not me, mind you—but she didn't seem to mind.

"I'm directing a play for spring, term and I want you to be my assistant director," said Mr. Barnes.

"What?"

"I want you to be my assistant director," he repeated.

"You want me to be a director?"

"No, I want you to be my *assistant* director," he said.

"I don't know anything about that," I hesitated, thinking it was probably a bad idea.

"That's why you'd be assistant," he explained matter-of-factly.

"What would I do?"

"You show up," he said. "I'll take it from there."

"I don't know," I still hesitated. "I'll have to think about it."

"Well, don't think too long. We start today at three, in the theater. Be there."

I looked him over. He was tall, thin, with a great head of black hair, which fell over his ears, pretty racy for a teacher in those days. He was awkward, but funny in a quirky kind of way.

So that afternoon, I reported to the theater, sitting and observing halfway back in the rows of seats. Mr. Barnes handed me a clipboard.

"What do I do with this?"

"Auditions," he instructed. "Put down everyone's name as they audition, and I'll give you notes."

"Okay."

I wrote NAME on the top of the page. Then I wrote NOTES. Then I had no idea what to do next. A Chalmers girl came in and waited.

"Give her the sides," he said.

"The what?"

"The sides. There"—he pointed. I saw some script pages. I handed them to the girl.

"Go ahead," said Mr. Barnes. The girl read pretty well, I thought. She left. Mr. Barnes turned to me and ran his finger across his neck.

"No?"

"No," he said.

I wrote it down. NO. If this was being an assistant director, I could do it. A Bashford kid came in. He read and returned the script to Mr. Barnes. He left. Mr. Barnes shook his head.

"What should I put down?" I asked.

"Forget it."

Then Susan Carter came in, and I gave her a script. We smiled at each other. She read. He asked her to read again *with feeling*. She read it again. Handing me the pages back, she smiled. She left.

"She was good," I said hopefully. I wanted her to get a part.

"The ingénue. Write that down."

"What's an ingénue?"

"You'll find out," he said with a sigh.

Rennes came in. I didn't know he was going to try out but handed him the pages. He read badly, but he had something no one else had, which was size. So when he left, Mr. Barnes said, "The criminal. He can play the criminal."

"The criminal?"

"Yeah, write it down."

We read another forty kids, and I wrote down what Mr. Barnes said each time. Afterwards, sitting in the row in front of me, he took out a pen and started casting. It was my job to write down each part, the character name, and the name of the actor he cast. I finished with a list of seventeen names.

"Post it," he ordered.

"What?"

"Type it up and post it on the bulletin board," he said.

"Post the list I just wrote?" I asked pretty dumbly.

"Yes, the cast list," he said with a hint of exasperation.

"Oh, okay. I can do that."

"And write at the bottom—*tomorrow first rehearsal at 3:30 here in the theater.* Can you do all that?"

"Yes."

"Okay, because I have to go see my wife."

I found that a bit strange, that he told me that he had to see his wife. I mean, didn't all married people see their wives or husbands all the time? It didn't matter, though, I had a job to do. I went to the library and found a typewriter, on which I hunted and pecked for an hour until I had the cast list finished. I posted it, and that made me feel kind of important. Several actors waiting for the post at the bulletin board looked over my shoulder at the sheet. Some squealed with delight. Some crept away, silent.

The next day, I arrived at the theater on time. Mr. Barnes did not. He was twenty minutes late, which I found strange for a man who gave orders and was in charge. He got everyone, even me, up on stage to do some acting exercises. *Improv*, he said, whatever that was.

"Float in the wind," he said, instructing us to all wander around the stage, floating in the wind. So we floated.

"See yourself on a beach," he said. Instantly, we all got down on the stage floor and played in the sand.

"Walk in the forest," he said, and we all walked through the pine needles. I kind of liked this.

Next, we did the falling-back game. One person falls backwards and four people catch them. "It's all about trust," said Mr. Barnes. One actor fell back and they didn't catch him on time, and he hit his head on the floor. Mr. B went ballistic: "Trust, trust. How can we have trust if you let him hit his head?" he yelled.

When I took my turn, it was quite a rush to fall back and get caught. I didn't hit my head, and Susan Carter was one of the people who caught me. She smiled at me, lifting me back up. Grabbing my clipboard, I went and sat in the fourth row, trying to look very official.

"Blocking," said Mr. Barnes.

"What's that?"

"It's the movement of the actors. I will tell them where to go. You write it down in the big book so we remember it."

"Got it."

"Act I, Scene I," I wrote in the book. He directed the actors where to enter, where to walk. Green tape on the stage floor marked where the furniture would be—the couch, the chair, the other chair, the side table, the doorways. Everything. He then blocked each actor's movements and led them through their positions.

"Write this down in the book," he yelled to me.

"Right," I said.

We got through half of the first scene by rehearsal's end, and everyone scattered.

"You did well," he praised me, remarkably. "Good job."

"I did? How do you know?"

When Mr. Barnes didn't show up the next day for rehearsal, the rumor went around that his wife had left him—that he was just sitting in his faculty apartment with a bottle of scotch. Not knowing what to do, I just waited, paralyzed. I was oddly aware that I should step up, but having no idea what to do, I sat scribbling in my binder, as if I were very busy with official stage business. The actors waited in silence. Finally, Rennes got up and came over to me.

"Dude," he said.

"What?"

"You're up."

"I'm up?"

"Barnes is not coming. You're the director now."

"I don't know how to direct."

"Just tell us what to do," he said.

He returned to the stage and looked at me; they all did. Taking a deep breath, I closed my binder. I rose. I walked forward to the edge of the stage. Their eyes followed me. I stopped.

"Okay, you're leaves on a tree, so sway," I said.

Right on cue, they all got up, wandering around the stage, their eyes closed, swaying like leaves on a tree. So this was theater, I thought, *and I'm a director.*

After they were done being leaves, then grains of sand, then wind, I turned to blocking. Having learned it the day before, I told them where to go. And they listened and did what I said. I gave them entrances and exits and told them to come around the couch on this line and go up the stairs (that weren't there yet) on this line. And they did it. It was the first time in my life I told someone to do something, and they did it. Of course, it went horribly at times—lots of people running into each other, then swearing at each other, then demanding to know from me who got to stand where. But I got through it and finished the first day.

Modern Theater, a book I found in the library, had a section on directing, which I read five times. That allowed me to put my foot down the next day when they read lines, "No, like this." If I said, *faster,* they did the line faster. If I said *slower,* they slowed down. If I said, *yell,* they yelled. If I said, *don't yell so much,* they spoke softly.

About two weeks into rehearsals a crew of guys showed up. With tools.

"We're the light crew," they explained. "What do you want us to do?"

"I don't know. Put up some lights," I said. "Light the stage so the audience can see the actors."

"Do you want mood?"

"No, I don't want mood. I want light—light so you can see them. Got that?"

They nodded and climbed ladders, then put up theater lights called lekos and fresnels, and the stage came to life with light. Did I want an amber hue? Why the fuck not? Did I want the light slanted or flat? Okay, flat. Some furniture arrived—a couch here, a chair there—me not quite sure where it was all coming from, but I didn't care. A couch was set down on stage, and a chair and a side table—just like the script called for. The magic of theater.

With about a week before opening night, after rehearsal one day, I had a few things to do on stage, adding more green tape to mark where the window would be for the next day's scene. When I went back to gather my binder, Susan Carter was there waiting for me.

"Hi," she said.

"Hi." I was her director, so I tried to act like her director.

"You're doing really well," she said.

"Really?"

"Really."

An awkward silence followed, so I turned the pages of my binder.

"I haven't seen you since the party," she said. And it all came rushing back, the party at her house, the car fire in her backyard, the hell afterwards.

"Yeah, sorry about the fire," I said.

"It was okay. My parents never found out."

"And Cindy?"

"She told her parents that the engine caught on fire, and they bought her a new car."

"Oh, okay." I was relieved.

"You never called me," she said.

"What?"

"You never called me after, you know, after the party."

"Sorry. I didn't think you wanted me to."

"Well, think again." And with the kind of drama that only an ingenue could muster, she threw her bag over her shoulder, letting her hair fly up, and walked up the aisle in very tight jeans that I had failed to notice during rehearsal. Whew! And yet now I was a director and didn't have time to think about those things. Did she like me because I was a director? Did people like you because of what you did, not who you were? I wondered.

Mr. Howe showed up to rehearsal next day.

"You know Mr. Barnes is not able to work," he said.

"I guessed."

"His wife left him and he's gone to pieces. Poor slob."

"Yes, I know."

"So are you okay here, doing this by yourself?"

"Yes, I am."

"Okay, then we'll let you go on," he said. "You're the director." I wanted to say, *I've been the director for three weeks*, but didn't.

"Oh, and one thing"—he looked back, about to leave—"don't neglect your other studies, or we'll have to take you off."

Oh, holy mother of . . . I hadn't lifted a book for three weeks. Everything had been about the play. I ran back to my dorm, opened my math book and worked until midnight, then read my English assignments, all of them in one night, and watched the sun come up while doing my physics assignments and conjugating French verbs: *Je travaille. Tu travailles. Il travaille. Nous travaillons.* At breakfast I wasn't even tired. I went to all my classes that day, sitting in the front row and raising my hand way too much, so Jamie yelled from the back of the room, "Put your fucking hand down, Stafford. What the fuck's got into you?"

On Saturday night—yes, on Saturday night—when I was doing homework, George burst in.

"Okay," he said, "this has got to stop. You're coming with me."

"All right," I said, "I guess I can"— closing my books.

"Bonfire on the river," he announced.

Between the soccer field and the river, just far enough away from the trees so the whole place didn't catch on fire, was the scene he dragged me to. Mr. Maroni was there, so we knew it was okay. We found Rennes and Jamie and Winton cracking wood over their knees, tossing it up onto the bonfire. Hundreds of Bashford guys and Chalmers girls milled about. Rennes gave me a funny look, and my eyes darted past him. There was Trixie, who was looking at me. Ben Warden was with her, and I thought she appeared, well, miserable.

"Don't gloat," said George.

Sitting alone on a log, just past Trixie and Warden, was Susan Carter. I walked right past Trixie to Susan by the fire. She moved over slightly for me to sit down, smiling.

"You're so serious," she pretend-scolded. "All you do is study."

"All he does is homework now," yelled George, swatting me on the head. "He went from biggest party-er to biggest bore."

That was a laugh. After just a few weeks I was a nerd, already. I'm not sure I liked that.

"I know you're the director, but here I get to tell you what to do," said Susan Carter.

"And what do you want me to do?" I played along.

She just smiled, cracking a branch, and threw it up onto the bonfire—moving easily in her down jacket, tight to her body, her red knit cap, a white scarf and white gloves. She kept bumping into me as we reached for firewood. She pulled my hat over my head.

"Hey," I said.

Jamie thought a little theater of another kind might be good, and he grabbed Ben Warden's hat and threw it to Rennes, who threw it to Winton, and when Warden ran at him, Winton spun it like a frisbee up onto the bonfire. Where it caught fire.

"You fucker," said Warden.

"Go tell your girlfriend's father that we threw your hat on the fire," said Jamie.

"Shut up," said Trixie. "He wouldn't care, anyway."

"Fuck you. Fuck you all," said Warden.

And then something came to me. "You started the fire," I blurted. And everyone went quiet. I don't know why I said it, and I wasn't even sure it was true, but something deep down made me think it was true, so I just said it.

"What?" said Winton, who thought he had started the fire.

"What are you talking about?" said Warden.

"That night at Susan's party, you started that fire in her car and let everyone think Winton did it."

Swivel. That's what everyone did. The heads swiveled around to look directly at Warden, and at that moment I knew why I'd said it—because he was so mad at that moment that he just might admit it.

"So what if I did?" he said.

Winton's eyes narrowed. "You let me think I was at fault for that fire, when you did it?" he demanded.

"I was walking by and there was smoke, so I helped it along, you know."

"With the newspaper," I said. "There was newspaper in the back of the car when we put it out."

"Yeah, I helped it along."

"Warden, I swear," said Winton. "Get the fuck out of here."

Warden got up. Without moving, Trixie watched him with her eyes. Warden looked at Trixie to see if she would come with him. After a moment's hesitation she rose reluctantly, looked at me, like *hell, it wasn't supposed to turn out this way*, and walked off with him.

"So, it wasn't you," said Rennes, laughing huskily. "Not you."

"Yeah, guess not." Winton smiled the broadest smile.

The guys, now warmed, wandered off into the looming forest just yards from us, away from the bonfire. Susan stood and threw a branch on the fire, her face glowing red from the flames.

"You went out with her, didn't you?"

"Who?"

"Her. Trixie?"

"Yes."

The silence stretched on as she played with a long stick, then tossed it on the fire.

"Are you over her?" she asked.

"Oh, yeah." I was quite convincing.

"Are you?"

"I don't even think about her anymore," I said truthfully.

"Did you? I mean, when you broke up?"

I was about to lie, when I couldn't. I felt comfortable enough with Susan to tell her the truth. "I was fucked up for a while," I confessed. "For a long while. I couldn't eat, or sleep, or anything. I could barely talk. I was a mess."

"The bitch."

She smiled and threw a big branch up onto the fire. The fire burned giant in the sky, and the sparks flew a long way up. Susan sat with me by the fire, opening her jacket when it got hot. Rennes came back shortly, then Winton and George, so it was just us, and Susan was just one of us. Mr. Maroni got cold and went back to the dorm, so Charts got out a pack of Marlboros, which he passed around, and everyone lit up.

"Come on," Susan Carter whispered to me, leading me away from the fire and to the trees by the river. She swung her back to a tree facing the river and away from the bonfire, and I walked up to her slowly, because for some reason she gave me confidence. She pulled me to her, and I kissed her. And she kissed me. It was too cold for anything else, but she lip-locked me, one leg wrapped around me, and we kissed till we couldn't kiss anymore, our lips were so cold. The whole thing felt like a play, with me an actor in it. I thought, *Am I in a play, or is this real?*

"We open next weekend," she said as we walked back to the fire. "Are you ready?"

"Am I ready? Are *you* ready?"

"Sure," she smiled. "I have a good director."

A station wagon idled on the road, and squeezing my arm, she ran for it, stopping just before getting in to give me a little wave. I waved back, and the car drove off smoothly, with the faint figure of a parent behind the wheel.

Chapter Twenty-Six
Opening Night

"Look at you—you're a fucking Bashford man," said George as I walked, books in hand, from my physics class to my French class.

I still smoked cigarettes, drank rum and cokes, smoked a joint by the river, snuck out after lights out and all the usual things, but I also did my homework, went to class, actually raised my hand, tried to speak intelligently, which was hard for me, and still had time for rehearsals.

"Work expands to meet work required," said George.

"What the fuck does that mean?" asked Charts.

"It means what it says," retorted George. "Tommy knows."

Everywhere I went in school, I had a new identity—director. "Good luck," people said. "Break a leg." For once, they looked at me as more than someone who just rolled a good joint.

Dress rehearsal was Thursday night, and I sat in the back of the theater, with the not-so-fun realization that my job was done, it was their turn to have all the fun. Directing, it seemed, ended at dress rehearsal, because you could no longer stop everything with that wonderful wave of your arms and yell, "No, no, not like that."

Mr. Howe attended the dress rehearsal, watched without changing his expression, then came up to me, said, "Good," and walked out. That was about as much praise as you would ever get from Mr. Howe, and it was enough.

We opened the next night. From my seat in the back, behind the audience, I watched the curtain go up and the actors come out. The lines started, and then I heard something in the audience that made me jump, until I realized what it was—laughter. The audience actually laughed. My first reaction was like, *what the fuck was that?* By the second scene it was like a drug, laughter. A few more lines, a few more laughs. I was thinking this was pretty damn good.

Then it came time for Rennes to make his entrance stage left through the door. The door got stuck, locking him off stage. I could hear the door scraping and Rennes kicking it. Then the whole flat, the muslin fake wall, fell down on the stage. Now everyone in the audience could see backstage. Two stagehands rushed to the rescue, picked the flat up, and held it up so that

Rennes could actually step through it onto the stage. Applause broke out—but for the wrong reasons.

"What the hell—?" I said.

Susan Carter, as the ingenue, had a gag where she pulled a fish out of a bucket. It usually got a great laugh—you know, like a fish on stage, that kind of thing. But when Susan pulled the fish out of the bucket, all that came out was a skeleton and some fish guts, and when she looked down into the bucket, all she could see was swirling fish guts. The fucking fish had disintegrated. It seemed that after the dress rehearsal someone had the great idea of freezing the fish to keep it from smelling, and when it thawed, it just fell apart in the bucket.

"What's in the bucket?" one of the actors ad-libbed.

"Well, it used to be a fish," she said, and the audience perked up, wondering what was going on. Susan did her best to get through it, and just moved on. No fish gag and lots of fish guts on the stage. We missed the laugh.

I ran backstage and found Susan in tears. "It was awful," she said.

"I thought it was funny," said a stagehand.

"That's why you're a stagehand," I said.

Just at that moment I heard a great thud on stage, a thud that shouldn't have been heard, and Susan and I looked out from the wings to see Rennes comatose on the stage floor, not moving at all. Next to him was a broken chair. It was the scene where after breaking a window into the house—he's the criminal, after all—he climbs through and stands on a chair, and the chair broke. Just fell apart. I thought about going out on stage and was just about to, and stop the show, when Rennes sat up, looked around, and ad-libbed, "Now that's an entrance," and the audience roared—but again for the wrong reason.

"My show," I moaned. "What's happening to my show?"

"It's all right. Look," said Susan, pointing to the audience, roaring in laughter, in waves of laughter.

But all was not over. From the rafters, high above the stage, from where you hang the flats that go up and down, maybe forty feet up, where the stagehands worked, there came a scream, a falling scream, the kind you get in the movies, that "ahhhhhhhhhhh," scream, and a body fell to the stage floor. It landed in a heap in the middle of the stage, and the body rolled over. The audience gasped, an actual gasp. A dead body on the stage. A horrendous accident. Rennes went to center stage, looked down at the body, turned it over, and held it up. It was a mannequin, straight out of the costume shop, with some wardrobe on it to make it look real. Rennes held it up, the naked mannequin, and after the audience saw that it wasn't real, they clapped, tepidly at first, then harder out of a sense of relief. I could see someone move up there in the rafters. I made out a face, knowing with certainty that the man who dropped the mannequin was none other than Ben Fucking Warden.

Picking up the body, Rennes said, "It looks like crime doesn't pay," and the audience roared once again. He threw the body offstage and said, actually said, "So, where was I?" The play went on. Thank God for Rennes.

The lights suddenly went dark on one side of the stage, only one side, and I couldn't believe my eyes. I ran up to the lighting booth and there found Jamie and Charts, who were running lights, smoking a joint with two Chalmers girls on their laps.

"What the hell are you doing?" I yelled.

"What?" said Jamie, oblivious.

"The lights—are off!" I yelled.

A pained look crossed his face as he looked out. "Oh," he squawked. Pushing the girl off his lap, he studied the light board.

"Do something," I pleaded.

"Not sure what happened here."

"What happened is that you're smoking a joint when you should be running the lights."

"Right, sorry." He pulled some levers, and the lights went out completely on stage.

"Jamie," I yelled. "Jamie!!!"

"Sorry."

He pulled some more levers; in a snap the lights came back on, revealing some very confused actors still in their places.

"There," said Jamie, as if everything was now all right.

"Jesus," I said, running out.

"Sorry, we were just having a bit of fun," he called after me.

When it was over, I watched the audience leave the theater, then sat down on the curb outside and hung my head. I didn't cry. It was too painful for tears. I just hung my head, wondering what I did to deserve this. Winton walked by. "Great fucking play, dude," he said as he wandered off. Susan Carter, still in makeup but now in jeans, came out of the theater and sat down on the curb next to me. She put her arm around me.

"It's okay," she said.

"It was a disaster."

"Tommy," she said.

"I thought I did something, you know, good," I said.

"Tommy, you're going to be on Broadway by the time you're twenty-one," she said. She gave me a little kiss on the cheek, got up, and announced, "Come on. We have a cast party."

Everyone left, but I stayed for a while to help the crew strike the set. Rennes waited too. Then we got his car out of the bushes at B&G and drove to West

Hartford for the party. We spotted the house by the cars parked out front. We parked on the street and went in. Stacey Durr, who did costumes, was waiting for Rennes.

"I'm gonna go upstairs with Stacey," said Rennes. "Want to come direct us?"

Everyone was laughing good naturedly about all the stuff that happened on stage, and after a while I cracked a smile. Everyone razzed me, so I shook my head and said, what the hell. We were in the living room, having a beer, when Ben Warden came stumbling in through the front door with Trixie behind him.

"Nice fucking move," said Charts.

"It was a stupid fucking play," he responded. "I just made it better."

"You're a jerk," said Susan.

"You theater people are so obnoxious," he slurred, tumbling forward onto the coffee table.

Trixie had had enough, rolling her eyes. She started to walk out, when Warden reached out and grabbed her wrist. She tried to pull away.

"Let go, Benjamin," she said.

"I don't have to fucking let go," he said to her.

"Fuck you, Ben," she cursed him.

And he hit her. It happened so quickly no one had time to do a thing. It was a backhand shot, that ripped across her face, knocking her down. Without a thought, in an instant, I lunged across the threshold and punched him as hard as I could in the jaw. Except I missed the jaw and hit him in the neck. But the force of my punch shot him over the coffee table, and we both fell, me falling on top of him, the table crashing—just like the movies--the lamp crashing onto my head, the lightbulb shattering everywhere. Everyone came running in.

Warden, holding the blood from his lip, shouted, "You're all a bunch of assholes."

"Nice lip," said Jamie.

"Fuck you."

"Don't touch her again," I said. "Got that?"

"I know what happened in New York," he said.

"Nothing happened in New York," I lied.

"Yeah, I know, I know."

At that Winton, Jamie, Rennes, and Charts, who had come running, lifted Warden up and threw him out the front door, where he landed in the hard snow.

"Fuck you," he said, sitting up.

We shut the door.

"Sorry about the lamp," I apologized.

I turned to Trixie. "You okay?" The side of her face was already turning red.

"Yeah, I'm fine. I hate him." She ran upstairs, and Cindy followed.

Susan helped me to a bedroom upstairs to clean up the blood on my temple. She dabbed it with a towel.

"What you did . . . ," she began.

"Yeah?"

"What you did for Trixie . . . I hate her, but . . ."

"Oh, I hardly knew what I was doing."

"Do you still like her?"

"No," I said. She dabbed me. "Ow."

"Sorry."

She finished cleaning up the blood. "And no matter what, I think you did a great job with the play."

"It was a mess."

"It was funny. Everyone sees it, everyone—that is, everyone but you."

She leaned over till her face was a few inches from mine. It was the most natural thing in the world, kissing her. A moment later we were on the bed, tugging at our clothes.

"Wait," she said, "hold on." Not that, I thought, not the *wait*. She got up. "I'll be right back." She went into the bathroom and stayed there for several minutes. I waited for her to come back, trying to keep from losing the, well, the passion. The door opened and she came out, with only a towel around her. The light from the bathroom illuminated her, and she looked almost otherworldly. She let the towel fall. And what a fall it was. A new world opened up at that moment, for she was beautiful and naked. She crawled onto the bed, and we kissed and fell together, the warmth of her body about the best thing ever. Then she broke off the kiss and pulled back. *The pullback.*

"Tommy," she said.

"Yes?" I said, breathing hard.

"We can, you know," she purred.

"We can what?" But I knew what.

"You know, go all the way. We can."

"Okay," I said in full agreement. "Then, let's—" I wrapped my body around her.

"But it would be better if we didn't."

Ahhhhhhhhhhhhhh.

"It would?" I said, trying to be matter-of-fact.

"Yes."

"And why's that?"

"Because." She kissed me again, a deep reassuring kiss, but not a let's go all the way kiss.

"Because why?" I asked after such a kiss.

"Because . . . it's a big thing."

"Well, it is right now," I said, looking down.

"Not that." She smacked me on the arm. "You know, going all the way."

"Well, there's nothing wrong with—"

"You're not like Ben Warden," she interrupted.

"I'm not? Well, I hope not."

"He's always wanting Trixie to have sex—"

"He is?"

"Even when she doesn't want to."

"She doesn't?"

"And so if you want to have sex, we can have sex—"

"We can?"

"But if you're okay with it," she said, with the softest face, "we can wait."

"Wait?" I said. I wanted to say, *wait for what?*

"Because . . ."

"Because . . .?"

"I'm a virgin."

Now if you say, "You are???" it's like saying, *I thought you were a slut.* And if you say, "I knew it!" it's like saying *I thought you were a prude.* So, I said nothing and she curled her lovely, undressed body around mine.

"I can see you want to," she said, looking down.

"Oh, it's okay," I said.

"Thank you, Tommy," she purred. "We can still make out."

The party broke up after one o'clock, and George and I got a ride back to school with Freak, who had showed up long enough to get everyone high and tell everyone he had gotten into M.I.T.

"Did you finish your application to Yale?" George asked me on the way home.

"Yeah, I did," I said.

We were smoking a joint when a cop car approached from the other way, and Freak yelled, "Roll down the windows." We did as fast as we could. The cop car had its windows up and kept going, without stopping. "Damn, I threw out the joint," said Freak. "Oh, Freak," we all wailed. He hid the car near B&G, and we ran up the dirt road to the school and into our dorms, well past lights out. Mr. Maroni saw us piling into my room, knowing what was going on, but he kept silent. It was late. We went to bed. I thought of Susan Carter and the big night that didn't happen and drifting off dreamt about geysers and waves crashing and the Washington Monument. *Another night of nights.*

Chapter Twenty-Seven
Bad Company Till the Day I Die

I found that, if I tried, I could do my homework in just a few hours each night, and since hockey was over and the play was done, I had free time on my hands. I wandered over to the Snug, where Rennes. Jamie, and the others had band practice. They were playing Bad Company when I came in, a song as long as the Bible, so I fell onto the couch against the wall and let it roll over me. I was the only one there when it ended, so I clapped. Rennes did not look up; he went over to his guitar case, pulled something out, and threw it at me. It was a small, rectangular case.

"Open it," he said.

I opened it. A shiny piece of silver looked up at me. A harmonica.

"Learn to play it," he said.

"Learn what?"

"How to play," he said.

"I can't learn how to play harmonica," I protested.

"We need some good harp on that song."

"So get somebody who can play," I said.

He just stared at me, and when Rennes stared at you, you knew what it meant.

"What's the song?"

"'Bad Company,' " he said. "Bad company 'til the day I die."

"Sounds about right," I quipped.

He turned to the band. "Play."

Bad company
'til the day I die . . .

I left in the middle and ran back to my dorm. Taking out the harp, I blew in it; the sound scared even me. It made the weirdest sound, like a wounded animal. But I liked playing it.

"You got the *Bad Company* album?" I asked George.

"Yeah," he said, "got it right here."

"Give it to me," I said, grabbing it and throwing it on the turntable.

I listened over and over. I played the harmonica to it. George left. If there were rats in the rafters, they scurried away to someone else's room. There came the sound of a deep, forlorn, howling animals, something out of a horror film, deep and psychologically determinative. That's what Mr. Rock would say. I tried again. Just as bad. The good news is, even I knew how bad it was. So I had an ear, I thought; that's something. I played for about half an hour, until not one but several people started banging on the walls, flooring, and ceiling, yelling at me to stop. I did stop, but only long enough to play "Bad Company" on my stereo. The harp solo comes in the middle, so I had to wait for it. Then it came, low and building, soulful and awesome. I played it over and over until I had the notes locked in my head. Then I turned off the stereo and played it by myself; it almost sounded like I got the right notes. The door opened. George came in, grabbed his guitar.

"Bad company till the day I die," he said.

He played it. I tried to play along.

"Stop," he said. "It's a three-four beat."

"Oh," I said, "What's a three-four beat?"

He played it on the guitar, perfectly, and I took my turn again, hitting the beat almost right, getting the notes almost right as well. It still sounded like a cow in heat, but the basics were now in front of me. George played the part five, six times, and I belted out the harp when my turn came. More banging on the floor, ceiling, and walls.

"Shut up," they yelled.

"You shut up," I yelled back.

"Come on," said George. We headed out of the dorm and down by the river, standing in the cluster of trees normally reserved for smoking pot. George threw his guitar strap over his shoulder and played the same riffs, with me coming in at the harmonica. The trees shuddered.

"Not bad," George encouraged. "Keep at it."

"I'm going to stay and practice a bit more."

"Suit yourself. But Rome wasn't built in a fucking day."

I played the riff over and over and over till my jaw ached. The wood between the holes on the harmonica started to expand and cut my sore lips. I literally couldn't play anymore and went in search of an aspirin from the infirmary.

"What seems to be the matter?" asked Mrs. Tauride, who we called Toad-ride.

"I have bleeding lips," I said.

"From too much kissing?" she teased.

"I wish."

She put some stuff on my lips, then gave me two aspirin, after which I went right to the woodworking shop to file down the wood between the spaces on my harmonica. The act of filing it made me feel like it was really mine.

"Be careful with that," said the woodworking teacher, Mr. Hastings.

"Why?"

"If you file it right side up, the shavings go down into the harmonica. So, file it upside down."

"Oh. Right."

I filed it upside down, making sure to let the wood shavings fall onto my hands and not into the instrument.

"That's right," said Mr. Hastings, walking away. To prevent it from ever cutting me again, I filed the wood with both the rough side and then the smooth side of the file. When all the wood was flat against the metal, I rose, thanked Mr. Hastings, and walked out into the late afternoon air. I went to the Snug and found Rennes and his band practicing.

"Play it," I said.

"Play what?"

" 'Bad Company,' " I said.

"It's only been two days," he objected.

"Play it," I said.

He played it and I tried to play along, but I couldn't yet, so I got up without a word and walked back to my dorm, continuing to play the riff as I walked along. Suddenly I felt a hand on my arm. It was Trixie.

"Hi," she said.

"Hi."

"What's that?" she said, looking to see what was in my hands.

"Nothing," I said, putting it in my pocket.

"You beat up my boyfriend," she said playfully.

"He's an idiot."

"I know, but did you have to beat him up?"

"He hit you."

Her face darkening, her soft touch went away. We walked along.

"We might be breaking up," she said.

"Might?"

"It's not working out."

"I'd say. Look, I gotta go, so—"

"Tommy."

"Yeah?"

"I'm sorry. Really I am."

"So am I," I said and walked on. I didn't look back, but I knew she stood there in the Quad, alone and still, watching me. But I wasn't gonna turn around.

I figured out how to practice my harmonica really low so I wouldn't bother anybody and could practice till midnight, then till one and two. George slept through it. After class, I grabbed a sandwich and headed back to the dorm to practice.

"Let's play," said George, grabbing his guitar.

"How's Cindy?" I asked.

"Hot."

"Right."

I would have gone on practicing my whole life, and never playing with the band, except Rennes came by my room about eleven one night and said, "We got a gig."

"What?"

"We're playing in the gym Friday night."

"This Friday night?"

"Yeah, so can you play it yet?"

"I'm not sure."

"Let's see," he said. Grabbing my harmonica, I followed him across the Quad to the Snug. George was there, setting up. Jamie on drums. Then there were two other guys I knew but not well. Everyone nodded to me, like I was just another band member. They were tuning up. George got me a high, three-legged stool, and I sat on it with one leg on the ground, one on the rail.

"Till the day I die," said Rennes to the band. And the band began to play. It was extraordinarily hard to just stand there, doing nothing, just standing, waiting for the harmonica riff to come up. It seemed like it took forever. Then came the chords intro'ing the riff. I cupped the harmonica and brought it to my lips. For a moment I panicked that I wouldn't know where to come in; then came the chord George had played again and again for me in our room, and I blew the first note into the harp. Easily, it all came out, the low, growling notes, the high blissful notes, all the notes, not perfectly but with that bold blues sound as close as I possibly could play to the original. No one stopped playing and laughed at me, which I took to be a good sign. When my part ended, I got back onto my stool. Rennes finished with strong rhythm chords and his husky voice. With the last chord, the song ended. I kept my head down while looking around with my eyes.

"Okay," said Rennes. "Friday night." And that was it. I was in the band. I had made it. And they played "Southern Man" long into the night, while I sat on the couch and beamed. Not quite a rock star, but close.

Friday came. Bad things always happen when you least expect them, and from the source you're not expecting, because all I could think about was my thirty-second riff that night in the gym. Then came third-period English. I arrived, thinking about my big harmonica riff. I didn't care about Mr. Rock or his class or anything, and for once I had done the reading and turned in my paper. I was untouchable, I thought.

"And so we beat on, boats against the current, borne back ceaselessly into the past," read Mr. Rock. He put F. Scott down. "What do we think of that? Anyone?" No one spoke. You're a loser if you speak up when a teacher says, "Anyone?"

"How about you, Mr. Stafford?"

"How about me, what?" I replied.

"Who wrote that?" he said, trying to catch me.

"Fitzgerald."

"Ah, he's done the reading," said Mr. R.

"Sure, I did."

"What do you think about those lines, some of the most famous lines in twentieth-century literature?"

"I think they suck," I said.

"Really? Tell us why you think they suck, Mr. Stafford."

"Look, first 'we beat on.' *Beating* is a sailing term, meaning almost into the wind, so it has nothing whatsoever to do with the current, 'cause the current is one thing and the wind is another."

"Is that so?"

I was on a roll. "Next, we aren't 'borne back ceaselessly into the past.' No one cares a damn about the past, especially us, so we're not borne back, we're not beating into a current—that's stupid. We're not borne back anywhere, and anyone who thinks different is an ignoramus."

To make matters worse, Jamie yelled from the back of the room, "Take that, Mr. Rock."

Mr. Rock reddened, his eyes narrowing. "You don't know what you're talking about, Mr. Stafford."

"And you don't know anything about English," I said.

He lost his cool. "You're ignorant."

"And you're an asshole," I countered, *mano a mano*.

I knew right away I had gone too far. He turned quietly and wrote a note out and handed it to me. The silent killer. *The note.*

"Give that to Dean Harper," he said. I didn't move. "Now," he demanded.

After a pause I reluctantly got up, took the note, and walked out to utter and absolute silence. You knew it was bad when no one yelled anything after you. I walked down the empty hall, down the stairs and straight into Dean Harper's office.

"I need to see Dean Harper," I said to the Battleaxe. I said it in such a way that I didn't want to hear any bullshit. She buzzed him and he came out.

"Come in," he said. I marched past him into the office and handed over the note.

"You swore at him?"

"I might have. I don't know. I was upset and—"

"Mr. Stafford, as I've said, you can be your own worst enemy."

"He called me ignorant. I'm not ignorant."

"Ignorant doesn't mean stupid, my boy. It means you aren't aware of the meaning."

"He called me ignorant," I repeated hotly.

"That's not the point, my boy. You cannot swear at a teacher. What exactly did you say?"

I realized that Mr. Rock hadn't put it in the note.

"I don't remember," I said, turning away.

"That bad? Well, sit down and we'll sort this out."

I sat. He sat. He considered what to do.

"Mr. Stafford, you've been doing much better here, really much better. All your teachers say so. So, I'm not going to throw the book at you."

"Thank you."

"I'm just going to revoke weekend privileges. No going off campus."

"That's fine," I said.

"And no school activities," he said. "You are to remain in your room except for meals."

"Okay, that's—whoa, wait a second, Dean. I'm playing in a concert tonight and—"

"A concert?"

"Yes, I've been practicing and it's a big concert and I'm playing—"

"Sorry, out of the question."

"No, but I must play," I pleaded. "I'm in the band and they need me."

"Tommy, argue all you want, but no privileges means no privileges, so you must remain in your room, and if that means no concert, that means no concert—"

"But that's not fair," I yelled, standing up. "It's not fair."

"Tommy, you're lucky—I could do much much worse—"

"You can't," I yelled.

"Calm down, Tommy."

"Dean, listen, you can dock me, ground me, whatever you want, but let me play tonight please, because—"

"Tommy, let me be clear. Your privileges are revoked. That's final."

I steamed my way out of the office and straight over to Rennes's room.

"My privileges are revoked," I screamed.

"What?"

"I can't play tonight. Dean Harper revoked my privileges for the weekend."

"What did you do?"

"I called Mr. Rock an asshole."

"That was stupid."

"I know. Sorry."

I hung my head and walked back to my room. George came over and I told him about it. I went to dinner and ate practically none of the chicken tetrazzini, which we called chicken tetracycline.

"What's wrong with him?" asked Wugs.

"He fucked up," said George.

Returning to my room, I shut the door and sat in my chair, staring straight ahead. Every half hour I looked at my clock . . . 7:00 . . . 7:30. The band would be loading up to go to the gym. 8:00 . . . setting up. 8:30 . . . sound check. 9:00 . . . green room. At 9:30—they were going on.

A knock at my door. It was 9:37. I opened it and George came in.

"Why aren't you at the gig?" I demanded.

He threw some black clothes on the bed. "Get changed," he said. "Quickly."

"What?"

"Just fucking get changed, okay?"

I put on black pants, a black T-shirt, black felony cap, black socks, and a ratty pair of black sneakers.

"Okay, you ready to do this?" he asked. "If they catch you, you'll be thrown out. So are you okay with that?"

"Let's go," I said. I followed him out of my room, looking both ways, down the stairs, out the back, over the railing, down into the field, along the road, up the hill, and into the back door of the gym.

"George, if I go on, they'll see me and I'll get thrown out."

"You aren't going on," he said.

We entered the backstage area and came around the curtains, and looked out onto the stage, where Rennes and the band were between songs.

"Okay, we're on," said Rennes. " 'Bad Company.'"

George handed me a mic. "Here," he said. "You stay here, and I have this." He held up a harmonica. "Get it?"

"Okay."

George nodded, went on stage, and joined the others warming up. The first notes sounded. George played rhythm guitar. The song went on. Just before the harp part, George took off his guitar, took out his harmonica in a grand gesture so everyone in the audience, the wild, screaming audience, could see he had a harmonica, and put it to his lips. And I played. From behind the curtains. Into the microphone. At first, it was a bit weak and I saw George look over at me, so I amped it up. And then I really got into it and played my heart out, with George really getting into it on stage, jamming his harmonica. As soon as the song ended, George rushed offstage, grabbed the microphone from me, and yelled, "Go." And I went. I ran out the back of the gym, straight down the road, cut into my dorm, up the two flights of stairs, around the corner and back into my room. I threw off the black clothes and got into my other clothes and sat down in my chair. It wasn't a minute later there came a light tapping at my door. Light tapping meant only one thing: a teacher. I opened it. Dean Harper stood there.

"Yes?" I said.

"Hello, Tommy," he said.

"Hello." I wanted him to see me mad.

"I just wanted to say that you are showing a very mature attitude, accepting your punishment as you have," he said. "I'm very proud of you. I know the concert's going on and—"

"It's not fair," I wailed. "It's not."

"I know it's not fair. Or it doesn't feel fair. But there will be other concerts and other chances. I hope you know that."

"It's just not fair," I wailed again.

"All this is behind us now, isn't it?"

I came to terms with it, for his sake. "Yes, Dean, it's all behind us."

"You're doing quite well, Tommy. Keep it up."

I shut the door. His footsteps clattered on the linoleum as he walked the long hall. The door clanked open and then slammed shut. And I took out my harp and played "Bad Company, *'til the day I die.*"

Chapter Twenty-Eight
Oh, Mr. Rock

At four a.m. I heard a knock at the door, followed by a kick, the secret knock combination. George and I got up and opened the door quietly.

"Let's go," said Rennes. In the hallway were Jamie, Chart, and Winton. Everyone was dressed in black: black caps, black pants, black shirts. Black. I peered out into a darkened hallway. And we slipped out, carrying a bundle wrapped in a towel. The red exit light glowed at the end of the hallway. We took the stairs, dark and cold, with only a night light to guide us down.

"Hold on," George whispered, holding us back at the door. He opened it a crack. From across the Quad we saw three flashes of a flashlight.

"Now," said George. We were out of the dorm in an instant, running in that crouched way you always do in the movies, until we reached the arches on the other side. Rennes and Jamie shot into the shadows, and soon they led us down the long brick walk towards Founder's Hall. Winton and Charts came out of the bushes.

"All clear?" said Rennes.

"All clear," said Winton.

All six of us walked past the door to Founder's Hall, which we knew would be locked, to below the high-up window on the first floor.

Rennes gave Jamie a leg up, and he got a hold of the window ledge, pulling himself up onto it. With one arm on the ledge, he slowly, almost silently lifted the window. Giving us the thumbs-up sign, he crawled inside. We left the window, walking back to the door, which a few moments later Jamie opened for us. In a second we got in and fanned out. Winton took up his position at the stairs, Charts at the landing, and Jamie, Rennes, George, and I went up the staircase to the second floor. Jamie took up his post by the top of the stairs, and that left Rennes, George, and me to head down the hallway to Mr. Rock's classroom.

George bent down and removed the matchbook he had put in the door after our last class to keep it from locking—removing it slowly. Rennes held the door so it wouldn't close and lock. It swung open. In the glow from the security light they looked at me. I went in, turned a sharp right, and walked along the wall. At the back of the room was a row of lockers, the classic one-on-top, one-on-bottom metal type with a latch you pulled up and a hole for the lock. I put my towel-wrapped bundle down on a desk near the lockers and carefully unwrapped it. A tape recorder revealed itself in the dark.

"Time," I said.

George checked his watch. "4:07."

I threaded the tape through the recorder knobs and pulled it up at the end, so it caught. The reel was bulging full of tape.

"Battery check," said Rennes.

I turned the recorder over and checked the batteries to make sure they were securely in place; they were. With the plastic case closed, I righted it and looked up.

"Okay," said Rennes.

Opening one of the top lockers, I placed the towel in the bottom. The towel was from the gym, so it couldn't be traced. I then turned the tape recorder on its side and pushed it through the opening, then laid it flat onto the towel. I adjusted the towel. To make sure the tape recorder was secure, the reels free and clear and nothing in the way, I ran my hands over the tape recorder. To make sure it turned properly, I spun the reel to one side, then to the other.

I nodded.

"Let 'er rip," said George.

"Playback," said Rennes.

In the pitch dark, I felt to make sure I had the right button, then pressed down and heard the click; the red light came on. The reels started to turn. Nothing came out, just a semi-silent hiss of the reels going around.

"Flashlight," I said. George held it so I could see the tape player. Everything was turning properly, and the brown shiny tape wrapped around the empty reel as it turned.

"Close 'er up," Rennes said.

I closed the locker, silently letting the latch fall. I spun the combination lock from my pocket to seventeen, thirty-two, fourteen, and it snapped open. I put it through the hole in the locker latch, pushing it up, and heard it click.

"Okay," said Rennes. "Let's get the fuck out of here."

As we entered the hallway, we heard two guitar picks against each other. We heard it a millisecond before we saw the flashlight bouncing around. Security! With Rennes pressed against the wall, we pressed alongside him. The bouncing flashlight shone onto the floor, with footsteps behind it. We were fucked if we stayed there, and Rennes knew it. He moved swiftly but silently into the drinking-water alcove; the two of us followed, trying our best to disappear into the darkness. The bouncing flashlight went by, the footsteps receding. We slipped out down the stairs, where Charts, Winton, Jamie waited at the door. One by one we slipped out, Jamie going last, closing the door and hearing the lock click into place.

"Go," whispered Rennes, and everyone split, slipping into the moonlit shadows, crossing the Quad.

"What time is it?" I asked George as we got back to the room.

"4:19," he said. "Nineteen minutes, right on schedule."

I didn't sleep at all and at seven o'clock went off to breakfast. We all sat together, but nobody spoke much. I went back to my room, got my English book, met up with George, and walked into Founder's Hall through the open door and upstairs to Mr. Rock's class. Mr. Rock entered, as he always did, at precisely eight o'clock, went to this desk, opened his notes, and looked around.

"Good, everyone's here. We can begin."

He started some chatter about Dostoyevsky and *Crime and Punishment*, to which I didn't pay much attention, and when he called on me, I said something. It must have been okay, because he didn't follow up or send me to Dean Harper. He just moved on to torture somebody else. I checked my watch: 8:06. One minute to go. I watched my second hand go round, till it hit 8:07, the time it was to go off. And nothing happened. I waited. Rennes checked his watch. Nothing. We waited: 8:08. 8:09. 8:10. *Fuck, it must have malfunctioned.* I looked at my watch, and it was 8:11. I looked at George and Rennes, and we all shook our heads. What the hell had gone wrong?

Then came a loud hissing. My eyes rose but not my head. I wasn't sure about it, so I listened hard. It got louder. It was the beginning of the recording. But it wasn't loud enough. All we could hear was the hissing, and at least for now Mr. Rock didn't seem to notice. Then came the most sensuous female voice, moaning softly, from the playback on the tape recorder.

"*Oh, yes, yes, oh yes,*" she moaned.

"What's that?" asked a startled Mr. Rock. "What was that?"

I shrugged. We all shrugged. No idea. It got louder.

"Where's it coming from?"

"I think it's inside the locker," said Rennes.

And it was, the female voice. "*Oh, yes, take me baby, take me. Oh, take me harder.*"

Mr. Rock raised one eyebrow. "What is that?" he persisted.

"*Oh, yes, harder, harder. Yes, oh yes, baby, give it to me.*"

The class broke out laughing.

"Stop it," said Mr. Rock.

Jamie went to the locker, put his ear to it, then tried to open it. "It's locked," he said.

The recording got louder still.

"*Oh, Mr. Rock, Mr. Rock, take me, you brute. Take me with your wizard stick.*"

"Make it stop," demanded Mr. Rock.

"We can't," said Charts. "It's in there." He pointed to the locker. "And it's locked."

Mr. Rock walked over and pressed his ear to the locker.

"Oh, Mr. Rock," said the voice, *"you've got such a big... oh my god, you're so incredibly big."*

"Stop this right now," he spat out, his face full of rage.

"We can't," said Charts.

"Oh, Mr. Rock. Now I know why they call you Mr. Rock," she moaned, going all out.

"I insist. Stop this right now."

"Ram me, baby. Ram me, Mr. Rock," moaned the woman.

"Open this locker," shouted Mr. Rock. "Open it now."

"I can't," said Jamie. "It's locked."

The woman was now screaming out in passion. *"Oh, Mr. Rock, do me, do me. Yes, like that. Do me, yes, like that. Make me come. I'm commmmmmiinnnnnnng."*

"Out! out!" yelled Mr. Rock. "Class is over." We all grabbed our books and beat it. I looked back to see Mr. Rock hitting the locker with his fist, his face red as fire.

"Can they trace the tape recorder?" said a worried Charts as we got out into the Quad.

"Naw," said Rennes, "I bought it in Boston three years ago, and we wiped it clean."

At lunch I was sitting with George and Rennes, when Susan Carter came up to us.

"I heard what happened," she said, a smile creasing her face. "How did it go?"

"That voice certainly had some experience," I said.

"I'll bet." She winked. And she walked away, carrying her lunch tray, with a wicked smile.

Chapter Twenty-Nine
Battle Stations

This scandal could not go unpunished by Dean Harper, who chose to raise it in the daily bulletin. He published a notice:

A VERY UNTOWARD INCIDENT OCCURRED IN FIRST PERIOD ENGLISH TODAY. IF ANYONE HAS ANY INFORMATION CONCERNING THIS INCIDENT, PLEASE REPORT IT TO THE DEAN'S OFFICE IMMEDIATELY.

Untoward? That's what it was? That just made everybody freak out. Before lunch it was all over school what had happened, and of course the rumors ran wild. A bolt cutter was found and brought to the scene, and at four o'clock that afternoon a black car pulled up. Someone whisked the tape recorder away in a box.

Dean Harper published the notice for three straight days, to no avail, and finally gave up. Mr. Rock took a week off, and when he came back, he seemed, well, somewhat different, possibly less sure of himself. Behind his back everyone stopped calling him "Mr. Rock" and took to calling him "Oh Mr. Rock.".

"One down, one to go," said Rennes.

There were two things that Dean Harper liked. One was to sadistically torture students who were not classic Bashford men, and the second was flowers. Every year he held a flower show in the Quad, inviting the town of Windsor, and even some people from West Hartford, to show off the great varieties of roses, lilies, and whatever the fuck else he grew in his backyard there on campus. He, of course, won first place in the lily competition every year. The Quad was set up like a graduation, with rows of chairs, a podium, and a big banner that read FLOWER SHOW.

"Dean Harper even invited some students—his little pets," said Jamie—and some of them actually go. Like Ben Warden, who was expected to show up with Trixie, the Dean's daughter.

"Hmm," said Rennes, thinking about the flower show. "Hmm."

"They get a shitload of people up there in the Quad, who all wear suits and dresses and give each other flower awards," said Charts.

"Hmm," said Rennes.

So when the day came, we watched as the B&G guys set up the chairs, create a little path between the chairs, and set up the sound system for the speeches and the awards. They put out a dozen or so tables, and Dean Harper and all the other contestants produced their flowers to display on the tables with little cards with the flower names. From the balcony of Rennes's dorm room about a hundred yards away, we watched all this take place. And we were ready.

The first guests arrived in their sport jackets, with the patches on the elbows, and the women in yellow and white dresses. Some even brought their small children and a few dogs that ran freely.

"Anyone who hates kids and dogs can't be all bad," said George.

"Who said that?" said Charts.

"W.C. Fields," said George.

Dean Harper arrived, sporting a seersucker suit, red bowtie, white shirt, and of course conspicuous black shoes with a high shine.

"Now?" asked Charts, ready for action.

"Not yet." Rennes was observing carefully.

The flower show began, with people wandering from table to table, admiring the flowers—Dean Harper standing in the middle, with a flower in his lapel, greeting the guests, bursting with flower pride.

"Now?" asked Jamie.

"Not yet," said Rennes.

Every few moments came a burst of applause across the Quad, when someone had won something, and after a half-dozen bursts Dean Harper took to the stage to announce the winners.

"Now," signaled Rennes.

We all moved into action. The audience took their seats and Dean Harper got warm applause at the podium. He smiled and waved them off, like *please, no more.*

"Okay," said Rennes, "battle stations."

Charts lifted a blanket to reveal two two-by-fours with surgical tubing tied to the top of each. A ripped up T-shirt tied to the end of the surgical tubing made a nice little pocket. Together, it was a perfect five-foot-tall slingshot. Winton stood up, surveying the Quad like a general. He took up his position about ten feet back and assumed command of the operation.

"Positions," he said. We moved in. Me to the right side, holding a two-by-four. George took the other two-by-four.

"Up," he yelled.

We hoisted the two-by-fours up and pressed them against the balcony wall. The tubing hung down.

"Pull." Charts and Jamie grabbed the tubing and pulled it back. Rennes was waiting for it, grabbed it, and held it in position.

"Balloon," said Winton. Jamie placed a red water balloon into the pocket and stepped back.

Winton peered down, sited the angle, and called out, "Two to the right. Down one. Back one." At each command Rennes moved the angle of the tubing.

"FIRE!"

Rennes let loose, and the water balloon launched high in the air.

"Reload." Charts retrieved the tubing, while Jamie placed a blue water balloon in the pocket.

Winton sited again. "Over two. Down one. Ready. FIRE!" Rennes let go. It flung into space.

"Reload." Charts scrambled for the tubing, and Jamie placed a yellow balloon in the pocket. Winton sited again. "Two to the left, down one, back, back more, over one, FIRE!" The yellow balloon went flying.

"Okay, take 'er down," yelled Rennes. We pulled the two-by-fours down flat. I slapped them against the brick floor. "Move it out," yelled Rennes.

"Hit," yelled Winton. I turned to look in time to see the guests scurrying as the water balloon broke and sprayed the party; then the second balloon made a giant hit on the flower table, and the water flew up everywhere; people were scrambling. The last balloon, in its high arc, started down towards the party. I knew I should get out of there, to get rid of the slingshot, but I had to stay and watch.

The balloon plummeted towards the garden party, and I hoped it would hit Dean Harper right on the head, but it flew over his head and into the crowd. The last thing I saw, the very last thing, was the water balloon hitting someone right on the head, then exploding with water everywhere.

"Warden," yelled George. "You got the fucker."

"Get going," said Rennes. "Go!" I stuck the two-by-fours under my arm, with the surgical tubing flopping around, and headed down the hallway, down the stairs, and out onto the road behind the dorm. My plan (I did have a plan) was to run to the river and hide the slingshot among the trees. It was a good plan that on any other day, at any other time during the year, would have worked fine.

But not today. As I jumped the railing, I saw to my horror a giant pile of fresh dirt that had never been there before and a half-dozen workmen pulling out the water lines. I would surely be seen. So, I changed course. I ran down the dirt road. I'd ditch the slingshot in a streambed behind the building in the woods, I thought. But as I ran down the dirt road, a B&G truck came rumbling up the hill towards me.

I turned and ran back up the hill. Now I had no plan at all, except to run. I ran alongside the dorms and got to the gym, darting into the front door, still not seen, and came running out the back. And who should be there—who should be leading a posse of men in blue blazers—but Dean Harper, and I basically ran right into him.

Busted. I had careened out so fast, carrying this big slingshot, that I couldn't turn around fast enough, and the Dean settled his eyes on me. I mean, there I was, holding a four-foot slingshot, with surgical tubing now hanging with a pouch for the water balloons and I couldn't pass it off as a science project. Dean Harper calmly walked up to me.

"Mr. Stafford," he said, "come with me."

And hell, only four weeks till graduation.

Chapter Thirty
The Trial

As much as he would have liked to do it, Dean Harper could not just throw my ass out of school. He had to follow *Protocol. Procedure. Due process.* With some remnant of English common law from the Puritans or some such thing, that meant a trial or, as they called it, a Dean's Committee meeting. This august committee consisted of the Headmaster, the faculty, the Dean of the school, the defendant (me), character witnesses, and members of the public. But it was really a firing squad, a death panel, the gallows, because in the history of Bashford, in all such Dean's Committee meetings over the decades, not one student had survived. They were all thrown out, every one of them.

Dean Harper wasted no time in setting the Dean's Committee meeting for the following Tuesday, in Founder's Hall. Word got around school pretty quick.

"Tommy's going down," they said. "Tuesday night."

I'm not sure I liked the sound of "going down," and yet it was true, I was going down, and I knew it.

"It's a show trial," said Charts. "Like in the Soviet Union."

"Thanks, Charts," I said. I wasn't aware that he knew anything about the Soviet Union.

"This will lead to your utter ruination," said Winton, "unless we do something."

"But what?" I said.

Fuck it, I had already given up, wondering what would happen to a student like me (if you could even call me that) who got thrown out of school with only a month to go. What college would take me (not Yale!)? My parents were called, due to my pending dismissal, and my father called me that night and asked, "What happened?" When I told him, he said, "They're throwing you out for that?" I assured him that was their plan.

"What do they want, another wing for the library?" said my father.

"I don't think that would help," I replied. "I'm on my own this time."

"If they throw you out, I'll come up Wednesday morning and pick you up," said my father, which might have been one of the nicest things he ever said to me.

It was Friday. We went down by the river, where I spent the day watching the Farmington wend its way towards the Connecticut River—not far away, I didn't think, like a few miles to the east. I smoked a pack of Dunhill's, given to me by Charts, as a sort of last smoke before the firing squad. At sunset, the temps dropped quickly, and I went to the dining hall to tell Wugs.

"I been there," he said, and that was all he said. But he looked sad for me. I got my tray with a plate of spaghetti with meatballs and went to sit at our usual table. Wugs came out with a piece of German Chocolate Cake, only for special occasions. Warden sat nearby with his laughing morons, but I didn't even care. And that's when George showed up, accompanied by Charts, carrying a bunch of law books he'd taken out from the library.

"I'm representing you," he stated flat out.

"You're what?"

"I'm going to be your lawyer," he said.

"I don't get a lawyer. It's not a trial, George."

"I talked to Mr. Howe and he said it was okay."

"Do you have any idea what you're doing?" I asked.

"No, but I got four days to figure it out," said George, looking over his law books.

"Oh, fuck me," I said.

"I'll be a character witness," Charts offered.

"I'm not sure that will help either," I replied.

"Back to the room and let's get to work," said George. "Come on."

The books—*Law 101, Legal Eagles, Law for Those in A Hurry, Why Law Sucks*, and the best, *Don't Go to Law*

School, Just Read This Book—he just spread out on the bed and we looked them over. He spent that one night with his head in the books, then the next morning announced they were a waste of time.

"Fuck them," he said. "I'll just do it."

"Okay," I said, not very hopeful, "What are we going to do?"

Charts, Jamie, Winton, and Rennes piled into our room and sat quietly.

"Well, let's review the case."

"Okay."

"Here are the charges," said George. "Shooting water balloons into a garden party."

"Guilty," they all yelled.

"Thanks for that," I said.

"Swearing at a teacher."

"Guilty!"

"Being caught out after lights out."

"Guilty."

"Getting sucky grades."

"They're getting better," I protested.

"Suspected, but not convicted, of drinking."

"Guilty," everyone yelled.

"Every night," said Charts.

"Thank you, Mr. Charts," said George in a most lawyerly way.

"Leaving campus without permission."

"Only every weekend," concurred Winton.

"Suspicion but no evidence of putting a sex tape in Mr. Rock's classroom."

"Not proved," everyone yelled.

"Suspicion of using marijuana."

"Not proved."

"And that's it." George put the paper face down.

"Is that all?" Rennes yelled. "Fuck them."

"Yeah, fuck them," everyone yelled.

"Okay, okay, settle down," yelled George in a lawyerly way. "We all know that if they knew everything that Tommy has done, he'd be out of here."

"Right."

"But they don't. So, we have a chance."

"What do we do? Anybody got an idea?" Rennes thought about it, but nothing came to mind.

George considered for a long while as we waited for his great legal opinion. He sat, crossed his leg, lit a cigarette, looked up at the ceiling, and smoked.

"For fuck's sake, George, tell us," said Rennes.

"Fuck if I know," he finally conceded. Everyone groaned. "But don't worry. I got till Tuesday." And he laughed that heckling laugh that made everyone feel better, no matter what.

On Tuesday, Wugs made me my last meal: roast beef, mashed potatoes, asparagus, Yorkshire pudding, with chocolate mousse for dessert. He made it for everyone and stood by, watching, as we ate.

"You can cook," said Rennes to Wugs. We all nodded. Wugs could cook.

My father called after dinner, saying he'd wait for my call after it was over. He seemed very supportive, funny thing, when his son was about to get kicked out of school. I thanked him.

The Dean's Committee meeting was scheduled for 7:30 p.m., so I went to my room and changed into a blue Bashford blazer, grey flannel slacks, a white shirt, a red-and-black diagonally striped tie, and black wingtips. I arrived at the meeting at seven o'clock and sat on the long, shiny wooden bench outside the hearing room. Mr. Howe came over to me.

"You okay?" he said kindly.

"Yeah."

"Okay, good luck. I'm for you, you know."

"Thanks."

From down the hallway came a commotion—the posse arriving: George, Jamie, Rennes, Charts, Winton, and Susan Carter, who sat down next to me on the bench and gave me a kiss on the cheek. "You'll be okay," she said. George came scurrying down the hall, holding several folders with papers falling out.

"There he is," I said. "Clarence Darrow."

"Who?" said Charts.

"Leave us. I need to confer with my client," said George, and they all went inside the hearing room.

"Hey," said George.

"Hey."

"You okay?"

"Fuck, George, I'm about to get thrown out of school three weeks before graduation, I'm not okay. Okay?"

"Look, do me a favor."

"What?"

"Don't give up."

"Why not? Why fucking not?"

"'Cause you can't."

"And why can't I?"

"'Cause we need you here."

"Okay," I agreed half-heartedly.

Dean Harper, all dressed up for the execution, came out of the Dean's Committee room.

"Are you ready, Mr. Stafford?" he said perfunctorily.

I walked in, head held high. George, carrying his piles of paper like a good lawyer should, walked behind his client, me. The committee room was large, rectangular, set down low with the windows way off the ground, too far to reach. A pole stood in the corner to open the windows. In a horseshoe arrangement, tables were set up, with chairs now quickly filling with teachers, deans, and various other torturers. Looking presidential, the Headmaster, someone I'd never even seen before, sat at the center of things. His nameplate said Mr. Tonner, HEADMASTER. Dean Harper sat next to him, Mr. Howe on the other side. About fifty chairs had been set up, with an aisle in the middle, like it was a wedding or something. They were mostly occupied too.

Rennes, Charts, Jamie, and Winton sat in the front. Susan Carter sat behind them. And others were there, like actors from the play—hockey teammates, even some of my teachers so impressed with my improvement. Dean Harper nodded towards a chair in the center of the room, a wooden chair with the arms worn down, brown and shiny. It was the center of the horseshoe, and now all the deans, teachers, and the Headmaster looked directly at me.

"George here has asked to speak on Mr. Stafford's behalf," said Mr. Howe, addressing the body. "If that's all right, with you, Headmaster?"

Dean Harper made as if to speak, and the Headmaster shot him down.

"That's fine, Dean Harper," said he. "Makes it more interesting."

George took a seat next to me, and Mr. Howe pushed a table over for his books and papers. Dean Harper opened a massive file in front of him.

"He's the fucking prosecutor," whispered George.

"Did you say something?" asked the Headmaster.

"No, sir."

"Very well."

Ben Warden came in and sat in the back. George shot me a shut-up look, so I did. Dean Harper opened his file and started to read.

"On May second, Mr. Thomas Stafford disrupted a garden party—"

"Objection," yelled George, standing up. The Headmaster looked up in surprise.

"This is not a legal proceeding, George," he said. "Now sit down. Dean Harper has not finished reading the charges yet."

"But we are not challenging the charges," said George.

"We aren't?" I whispered to him, desperation in my voice.

"You aren't?" whispered a frantic Rennes.

George went blithely on, unperturbed by our opposition. "We wish to concede that on May second of this year the aforementioned student, Mr. Thomas J. Stafford, did launch three water balloons into a garden party in the Quad sponsored by Dean Harper and did upon this day hit the aforementioned party with the said water balloons, which splattered on several members of his party, including a direct hit on Mr. Benjamin F. Warden." The room bellowed with laughter, until after a while the Headmaster raised his hand for silence.

"You wish to concede this?" asked the Headmaster, somewhat incredulous.

"We do, your honor."

"This is not a court, young man," he repeated.

"Sorry, sir."

"Do you also concede to the other charges?" the Headmaster asked, reaching for his notes. "Absence from classes, caught out after lights out, abysmal grades, swearing at his teachers, disruption in class, and smoking cigarettes. Do you agree to all that?"

"We do," said George.

"Then what are we here for, may I ask?"

Dean Harper stood up. "In that case, Headmaster, I move for dismissal of Thomas Stafford from Bashford, effective immediately."

The Headmaster considered this and said to George, "Then, if this is the case, what exactly is your defense?"

"Our defense, sir, is this—Thomas J. Stafford is and always will be . . ." Everyone leaned forward in their chairs. "A BASHFORD MAN."

And the courtroom broke out laughing: the teachers in spite of themselves, several students in the gallery, even the Headmaster. But decidedly not Dean Harper or Mr. Rock, who scowled.

"Headmaster, since Mr. Stafford admits to these acts, then there is no reason to continue this hearing," said Dean Harper. "I, therefore, move that we dispense with testimony and move immediately to a motion to expel Thomas Stafford."

"Actually, I'd quite like to hear the defense. Wouldn't you?" said the Headmaster to the teachers around the horseshoe. And they all nodded yes, they would.

"You may proceed," said the Headmaster. Dean Harper reluctantly sat back down.

"Thank you, Your Honor. I mean Headmaster," said George. "I call Mr. Dexter Barnes to the stand."

"What?" yelled Dean Harper. "This has nothing whatsoever to do with—"

"Please, Dean, sit down," instructed the Headmaster.

The doors opened, and Mr. Barnes walked in to sit down in the witness chair.

"Could you please identify yourself for the, uh, committee?" said George.

"I am Dexter Barnes, a teacher here at Bashford."

"And what do you teach here?"

"I am the drama teacher."

"And can you tell me, were you in fact the director of the school play for this term?"

"I was."

"And would you tell us the circumstances?"

"I was unable to perform my duties."

"Can we say, Mr. Barnes, that your wife left you and you totally freaked out?" asked George. The crowd laughed.

"That would be accurate."

"And what happened to your play?"

"Well, my assistant director took over and directed the play and did quite a good job, it must be said," testified Mr. Barnes.

"Aha," said George. "And is this assistant director in the courtroom right now?"

"I remind you, this is not a courtroom," reminded the Headmaster.

"He is," said Mr. Barnes.

"Can you point him out?"

He pointed at me. "Tommy Stafford," he said.

"And are you still employed here at Bashford?" asked George.

"I am."

"And why is that?"

"Because Tommy Stafford saved my job."

"Saved your job?" asked George.

"Yes, if the drama teacher can't put on a play, he probably gets fired."

"And how are you doing now, Mr. Barnes?" asked George.

"Better, thanks."

"Is it true you have a new girlfriend, the French teacher, Mademoiselle Latarde?"

"Yes."

The Headmaster cut him off. "That will be all, thank you, Mr. Barnes."

He stepped down. George rose.

"We call Coach Muzzie to the stand," said George.

"Headmaster, please—" Dean Harper stammered, rising to his feet in protest.

"Sit down, Dean," instructed the Head. "This is very amusing."

Jamie jumped up, opened the door, and the hockey coach entered—and he led him to the witness chair.

"Coach Muzzie, I presume?" enquired George.

"Yeah, that's me."

"You are the hockey coach, are you not?"

"Yes, I am."

"And did you not have Tommy Stafford on your team this year?"

"We did."

"And did Tommy play hockey before you got him on your team?"

"He did not."

"Ah." George moved and sat on the edge of the table. "Did you have a game against Exeter this year?"

"We did."

"And have you beaten Exeter in the past few years?"

"We have not beaten Exeter in over *twenty* years."

"And did you beat Exeter this year?"

"We did."

"And was it true that one player scored two goals against Exeter to win the game?"

"That is correct."

"And who was that player, Coach Muzzie?"

"Tommy Stafford."

"Is that right? The boy we're talking about throwing out of school?"

"That's right."

"So Tommy Stafford helped you beat Exeter for the first time in twenty years?"

"That is correct."

"And without Tommy Stafford?"

"We would probably have lost to Exeter—again."

"Thank you, sir. You may step down. That is all."

Dean Harper rose to his feet. "I don't see why this has anything at all to do with—"

"Thank you, Dean," said the Headmaster. The dean sat back down.

Coach Muzzie and Dexter Barnes took seats next to Rennes and the others.

"We call Roger the Wrestler," said George.

Dean Harper jumped to his feet. "Enough! What is this all about, may I ask? Who is Roger the Wrestler?"

"Headmaster, Roger the Wrestler is a student at Kent," said George.

"And why are you calling him?" asked the Headmaster.

"Wait, just wait, Headmaster," said George.

"Very well, can't hurt," said the Headmaster, really enjoying this. "Bring him on."

The door opened and in came Roger, better known as Roger the Wrestler.

"Please state your name," said George.

"Roger Townsend."

"And where do you go to school, Mr. Townsend?"

"Kent," he said.

"And are you the wrestling champion for Western Connecticut?" asked George.

"No."

"No?" said George, his voice shaken for a moment.

"I *was* the wrestling champion for Western Connecticut, but I have since competed in the regionals, and now I'm the wrestling champion for all of New England," he qualified.

"Ah, very good," said George, regaining his form. "And do you know Tommy Stafford?"

"I do."

"And can you tell us how you know him?"

"During Christmas break, I had a party at my uncle's apartment in New York City. After the party got going, we had a little wrestling match on the floor in the living room."

"Really? And what happened?"

"I lost."

"You lost?"

"Yes, to him, right there," and he pointed at Winton, who waved.

"And what happened then?"

"I was very bummed out at losing," he said.

"And what did you do?"

"I had several drinks and then crawled out onto the balcony and almost jumped."

"You almost killed yourself?"

"Yes, and I might have done it, jumped I mean, but Tommy came along."

"And what did he do?"

"He told me not to do it, that I'd wrestle again, that it would be all right."

"And so is it all right?"

"It is."

"Do you feel you owe your life to Tommy Stafford?"

"I don't know about that," he said, "but without Tommy I wouldn't be sitting here today as the wrestling champion for the whole of New England."

"That will be all. You may step down."

He took his place in the row with the others.

"The defense would like to call Miss Trixie Harper."

Dean Harper went red and jumped to his feet. "This is outrageous. That's my daughter!"

"She is your daughter," said George calmly, "but she is also a senior at Chalmers and has important evidence to give. She would like to testify."

"Against me?" spat out Dean Harper.

"This proceeding is not against you," said the Headmaster.

When the door opened, Trixie Harper walked to the front of the room and sat in the witness chair.

"Miss Harper," said the Headmaster, "you are not required to be part of this proceedings if you do not want to."

"I'd like to," she said. Dean Harper went white, and he stepped back and almost fell into his chair.

"Can you tell us your name, please?" George addressed the witness.

"Patricia Harper. But everyone calls me Trixie."

"And you are a senior at Chalmers School?"

"I am."

"Have you ever gone out with Tommy Stafford?"

"I have. We dated in New York City during Christmas break."

"And what happened after you came back to school?"

"We broke up."

"Did you break up with him, or did he break up with you?"

"I broke up with him."

"And why?"

"I got back with my boyfriend."

"And this boyfriend's name?"

"Ben Warden."

"Ben Fucking Warden," whispered Rennes.

"Would you say you broke his heart?" said George.

"Yes, I'm sorry about that, but I may have."

"Did your father know about that?"

"He did not."

"When you broke his heart, what did he do?"

"He was in bad shape," she said.

"In what way?"

She shrugged and George let it go.

"Now, did you attend a party in West Hartford in April of this year?"

"I did."

"And who did you attend with?"

"Ben Warden. He was my boyfriend."

"And did he hit you that night?"

She hesitated.

"Please remember you are under oath, Miss Harper," said George.

"You are most definitely not under oath," said the Headmaster. "But please answer the question, anyway."

"He did. He hit me," said Trixie.

"And what happened next?"

Charts jumped up and yelled, "Tommy Stafford jumped Ben Warden and beat the crap out of him." This sent the room into a tizzy, which the Headmaster settled down with his hand in the air.

"And why did he go after your boyfriend?" asked George.

"Because he hit me."

"What happened next?"

"Tommy and his friends threw him out the front door."

"Are you still going out with Ben Warden?"

"No."

"And why not?"

"I dumped him." She turned to her father. "I know you like Ben, but he hit me and I'm not going out with him again."

"Thank you. You may step down," said George.

"Nice going, George," whispered Rennes.

"We call Wugs to the stand," George announced to the committee.

"Wugs?" asked the Headmaster.

"Wugs is William Galloway, sir. We call him Wugs."

"From the dining hall?" responded the Headmaster.

"Yes, he is the head cook at the dining hall," said George.

"And how does he bear on this case as head of the kitchen?"

"He was in charge of Tommy's work job, sir."

"Then let it be Wugs," said the Head.

The door opened, and Wugs entered, walking haltingly—looking very unsure of himself. He had taken off his white industrial kitchen shirt and his white pants, and now he was wearing a blue shirt and a tattered but respectable sport coat with patches on the elbows.

"Please, come in," said George. Wugs sat down. "Now, Wugs—may I call you that?"

"Everybody does."

"Now, can you tell us your job here?"

"I'm the head cook in the dining hall."

"And how long have you had this job?"

"Nineteen years. I was dishwasher, then line cook, then breakfast cook, and now head cook."

"And do you know Tommy Stafford?"

"I do."

"Can you point him out?"

"He's right there."

"And how do you know him?"

"He shines the best silverware in Connecticut." Everyone laughed, till the Head quieted them down.

"Really?"

"That's right. He works for me in the kitchen three days a week."

Dean Harper rose. "Headmaster, I must object. This man, this Wugs has served time in prison, which is well known, and so I don't think his word is good here."

A shocked room looked at the Headmaster, who said firmly, "We are all aware that Mr. Galloway spent time in prison, but that does not disqualify him from speaking here today. Please sit down, Dean. Mr. Galloway, you may continue."

"Well . . ." Wugs stopped and was silent for a moment. Then he raised his head and went on. "Yes, I spent some time in a correctional facility before I came here."

"You spent time in jail?" said George.

"That's right. It's no secret."

The room tensed.

"You paid your debt to society?" asked George.

"I did. I think I did, anyway."

"And what bearing does this have now?"

"Well, most of the boys all know and they won't talk to me."

"They won't?"

"No."

"Because you were in prison?"

"That's right. But Tommy here, he knew, and he didn't care."

"He talked to me," said Wugs. "We became friends. And he shined the best silver in all of New England."

"And can you tell us what happened on the night of February fifteenth of this year?"

"Sure. My sister had to go to the hospital."

"Yes?"

"She needed me to drive her there, but I had a dinner shift. I had to serve the dinner and get ready for breakfast, if you know what I mean."

"We do."

"Anyway, Tommy got a bunch of his friends together, and they took over and finished the dinner, so I got to take my sister to the hospital," said Wugs.

"And did they do a good job?"

"When I got in the next morning, you woulda thought I had done it all, it was so beautiful."

"And how is your sister doing?"

"Fine. Just heartburn."

"One more question, Mr. Wugs. While you were in prison, you must have heard about real transgressions."

"Uh . . . I think so."

"Crimes," said George.

"Yeah, I heard a lot."

"And these were real crimes, correct?"

"Oh, real as real," he said.

"What would you say if I told you about a really serious crime here at school. Would you be able to determine if it was a real crime?"

"I think I would."

"If someone threw a water balloon into a garden party, would you say that was a serious crime?"

"A water balloon? Naw, don't think so."

The room let out a laugh.

"You may step down, Mr. Wugs," said George, and Wugs got up. "Oh, just one more thing if I might?"

"Sure."

"Would you say, if you were asked, that Tommy Stafford is a Bashford man?"

"What's that?"

"It means someone who upholds the highest standards of honor at this school."

"Well, I can tell you this," said Wugs. "Most of the boys at this school walk by and throw their plates at me. It doesn't bother me. I'm glad to have a job. But one boy did not do that. He talked to me, got to know me, did his work job beside me, and didn't look away when we met outside the mess hall. That's Tommy. So, if that's what that means, he's the most Bashford man I've ever met."

"We rest our case," said George, to the cheers of the crowd.

But the Headmaster held up his hand.

"This has been very informative today, very informative, but the fact remains, Tommy Stafford has committed offenses that warrant expulsion," said the Head. "Isn't that right, Mr. Stafford?"

I stood up. "Yes, sir."

The Headmaster went on, "Tommy Stafford, after reviewing the evidence before me today, with the concurrence of the Dean's Committee, I am—"

Dean Harper stood up in such an abrupt manner that the Headmaster stopped and looked at him.

"Headmaster, may I?"

"Yes, of course, Dean Harper."

"In light of the witnesses coming forward today, and that he stood up for Trixie, er, my daughter, I might recommend that we could allow Mr. Stafford to stay at school."

"Really?" said the Head.

The crowd started to cheer, but Dean Harper held up his hand.

"Under one condition."

"And what is that?" said the Headmaster.

"Mr. Stafford could not have acted alone in the water balloon incident," said Dean Harper. "If he can give us the names of the other boys involved in the incident, we will drop the charges, if that's the right term after all."

Chapter Thirty-One
Tire Tracks

"What about it, Tommy?" said the Headmaster. "Are you willing to? If you do, Dean Harper will withdraw his recommendation of expulsion, you can graduate and go on to college. What do you say to that?"

Rennes nodded to me. *Go ahead, tell them, tell them it was us,* he was saying.

I stood. "Sir, I acted alone," I said.

"That is somewhat far-fetched," said the Headmaster. "That was quite an apparatus we found you with."

"I acted alone."

"That is impossible," said Dean Harper, losing it completely and lashing out. "He's lying."

"I'll show you," I said.

"You'll show us?" asked the incredulous Headmaster.

"Yes, sir, if you let me."

"Well, this is something," said the Head. "I'd like to see that."

My lawyer stepped in, that is, George. "Sir, if Mr. Stafford does succeed, if he can sling the shot without any help from anyone else, will you allow him to stay in school and graduate?"

"Why not?" said the Headmaster. "Who's got the slingshot?"

"I have it," said Dean Harper, "but there is no way one person could have shot that water balloon the length of the Quad."

"In that case, we have one request," said George.

"And what is that?" asked the Headmaster.

"That if Dean Harper says it is impossible, then let him stand in the target zone."

A buzz went through the courtroom.

"Would you be willing to do that, Dean Harper, if you think it is impossible?"

And at that moment, that very instant, I realized that the Headmaster didn't like Dean Harper very much.

"I . . . I would," said the Dean.

"Well, then, let's try it," said the Head.

The apparatus was located and brought to the Quad. Now it was a big event. Students gathered on the balconies and in the windows to check it out. It had turned dark, and the outside lights were on. But it was a beautiful May evening, warm and inviting. The faculty wandered out onto the brick patio in front of Founder's Hall. Jamie took the slingshot apparatus from Dean Harper and brought it to me.

"You can't do this by yourself—" he started.

I winked at him. I don't know why. I don't usually wink. Winking was weird. But I did it.

"I got this," I said.

"Just tell him it was us."

"I got this," I repeated. He backed off.

Jamie walked back into the crowd. Rennes, Winton, Charts, Jamie, Susan Carter, Trixie Harper, Mr. Barnes, Wugs, Roger the Wrestler, and George stood clumped together. The Quad filled, and every window and balcony teemed with students.

"Dean Harper," said the Headmaster, nodding towards the target zone.

I held the slingshot in my hand and looked around for something to brace it with. There was nothing except the short wall dividing the brick patio from the Quad lawn. I walked over and examined it. George joined me at the wall.

"If you get off a good shot, you can say you acted alone," said George. "If your shot sucks, they will want names."

"Thanks, Counselor."

"Good luck."

I had to think quick. I took the two-by-fours and looked them over. I stretched the surgical tubing. I checked the pocket to make sure it was still sewn tightly. All was as it should be.

Dean Harper put on his glasses, handed his portfolio case to a teacher, straightened his tie, and walked out onto the lawn. He walked halfway down the Quad, about forty yards, turned, looked directly at me, turned and walked another thirty yards, turned, looked at me, turned and walked another twenty yards. That put him about ninety yards away, almost the length of a football field. He stopped only when he reached the end of the Quad, standing on the brick patio in front of the dining hall.

"Mr. Stafford"— the Headmaster motioned for me to proceed.

I placed one two-by-four against the wall. The wall was short, almost too short, to support the slingshot, so getting down on the brick, I put one foot up against the wall. I then put the other two-by-four against it and my other foot against it too. Charts arrived with three water balloons. I weighed each one in my hand, selecting a large yellow balloon filled tight with water, almost to the point of bursting. I figured I needed the weight to make it fly far. With the water balloon in the pocket of the slingshot, I tested the tubing, pulling it back. Immediately I saw I had a problem. I could only pull back the surgical tubing as far as my stomach, which would not give it the blast it needed. Dean Harper was ninety yards away. I looked over at Rennes and the guys to see if they had any ideas, but just saw blank expressions. I was on my own.

So I lay down. I found that by getting down all the way on my back I could stretch the tubing all the way over my head. I moved my feet to press the two-by-fours against the wall. I put the water balloon into the pouch and pulled back. At the last moment I realized I needed more loft and pitched my head all the way back, looking straight up into the sky, and pulled the water balloon over my head, with the last little strength I had left, my arms stretched out fully, the surgical tubing straining. I closed my eyes and thought of, well, Jimi Hendrix.

> *I'm not the only soul who's accused of hit and run*
> *Tire tracks all across your back*
> *I can see you've had your fun*
> *But, darlin' can't you see my signals turn from green*
> *to red*
> *And with you I can see a traffic jam straight up ahead*

And let go.

Once I let it go, the whole slingshot apparatus came flying apart, clanking down, the two-by-fours clattering on the brick and hitting the wall, the surgical tubing slinging the two-by-fours off the wall, back onto my legs. I looked up—and high in the air, just a small spot very high up, I could see the balloon. For one slight second it paused in midair, then started down. It came down like a rocket plummeting to earth, and for a second I thought it would fall very short, like in the middle of the Quad. It was a blur now. Dean Harper stood watching the balloon on the brick patio. He didn't move. He just stared at it. And I lost sight of it for a moment.

It smacked against the brick. I heard it before I saw it. It smashed into the patio, and I followed the sound to the explosion. A giant waterfall of spray grew out of the explosion, washing over Dean Harper's head and dousing him.

And then came the sound. First it was low and rumbling, like something from the earth. Then it grew and grew some more. Before long, it was deafening: the sound of hundreds of students in the Quad, in the windows, on the balconies, cheering to see Dean Harper all wet, letting their lungs sing of every infraction, every disciplinary action, every weekend taken away, that Dean Harper had ever done to each and every one of them.

Tire tracks all across your back
I can, I can see you had your fun

In an instant I was surrounded by Bashford guys and Chalmers girls, by Winton and Charts and Jamie and George and Rennes, even by faculty, and even by the Headmaster himself; they all seemed delighted and slapped me on the back.

"And that, Headmaster," said George breathlessly, "I think you would agree, makes Tommy Stafford a Bashford man once and for all."

Chapter Thirty-Two
The Sword of Damocles

"Tommy, have you ever heard of the sword of Damocles?" asked the Headmaster.

I looked at George for a little help, but he just shrugged. It was the three of us—the Headmaster, George, and me—in his office the following day.

"I haven't."

"It's a parable from the Romans," said the Headmaster.

"Everything comes from the ancient times, doesn't it, Headmaster?" said George.

"Hardly," he replied blithely. "Anyway, King Dionysius was challenged one day by his number one-man, Damocles, who said the king had it pretty good and what was he complaining about all the time? Then the king agreed to change places for one day, so Damocles could see that it wasn't so great to be king. You know, you think it's so easy, you do it. And to drive home the point, the king hung a giant sword over

Damocles's head, dangled by a horsehair, so he would know that only a single hair was the difference between life and death. Do you get my drift?"

"Uh, not really," said I.

"You, Tommy, have a sword of Damocles hanging over your head."

"Oh," I said, "I get it."

Said the Headmaster, "If you do anything wrong, anything else, anything at all, one single infraction, one broken rule, one argument with a teacher, one single solitary thing that I or anyone else deems to be at all serious or inflammatory or even trivial, you will be summarily expelled. No talk, no discussion, just gone. Have I made myself clear?"

"Crystal," said George.

"Crystal," I said. "Thank you, Headmaster."

"Best damned Dean's Committee I've ever been to," he said, ushering us out.

George and I walked into the Quad.

"You got three weeks left," he said. "Think you can make it?"

"Sure, why not?" I was confident.

"You got some fucking sword hanging over your head."

"Yep."

"So you gonna stay out of trouble?"

"Sure."

"Okay, that's smart."

"Want to go smoke a joint?" I suggested.

"What did I just say?" objected George.

"Come on."

So we went down by the river and smoked a joint.

"Look," said George. "It's Susan."

She joined us in the trees and we skipped rocks on the river.

"I can see you've reformed," she observed as I passed her the joint.

"Oh, I've reformed all right," I said.

"Well, at least you didn't get kicked out." She seemed genuinely pleased.

"Let's go listen to music," I said.

"Where?" Susan asked.

"In my room."

"You gotta be fucking kidding me?" said George.

We snuck Susan up the back stairs, down the hall and into my room, with George trailing to make sure no one saw us. Once the door was closed, I put on "Sweet Melissa" by the Allman Bros. George put a rolled-up towel under the crack in the door, and we lit cigarettes.

"Rum and coke?" I asked, sliding the case from under my bed and pulling some cokes from my little square fridge. I fixed three, then three more, then three more. I put on the Jefferson Airplane. A knock and a kick at the door. George opened it.

"Harper is coming," said Jamie.

"Okay, we got to get you out of here," George said, turning to Susan.

"Let's go."

We shot out of my room, darting into the first stairwell on the left in the hallway. I went first, Susan in the middle, George in the back. We got halfway down the stairs when Rennes came bounding up.

"Harper's coming this way," he said. "Go back."

We turned quickly and started back up. Just at that moment Mr. Maroni came out of his faculty apartment across the hall and into the stairwell, walking smack into Susan. He stopped, looked at Susan, figured out what was happening, and had to make a decision. *To bust or not to bust?* That is the question. He looked away, like he hadn't seen her. But he must have been flustered, because he jumped the seven steps on the stairwell. Actually, he did this often, being young and athletic and not at all like the other teachers. He launched himself into the air, like an Olympics long jumper, with his feet out front so he could land on the landing, like always. But he must have had a shot of adrenaline, because he flew too high, striking his head on the top of the stairwell, landing in a crumpled heap.

"Oh, fuck," said George. We ran down. "Is he dead?"

"Take Susan," I said. "Get her out."

George and Susan ran up the stairs, disappearing into the hallway. Mr. Maroni was out of it, unconscious, totally not moving.

"Mr. Maroni . . . Mr. Maroni," I said. He moved. Not much, but a little. And opened his eyes.

"Stars," he said, holding his head.

"What?"

"I see stars."

"Oh, right, stars." Did people really see stars? I guess they did.

"What's happened here?" Dean Harper said, arriving at the landing at that moment.

"He hit his head," I said. I could have added, *He hit his head because I startled him with a Chalmers girl coming out of my room, and he panicked and jumped seven stairs and misjudged the jump because he was so rattled and almost killed himself —* but I didn't.

"Are you all right?" said Dean Harper, bending down to Mr. Maroni.

"I . . . I see stars," said Mr. Maroni, holding his head.

"How did this happen?"

The moment of truth. All Mr. Maroni had to say was, *I saw a girl*, and it would be over, done, finished. I would be totally gone.

"I don't know," he said. "I just hit my head."

Mr. Maroni, you are awesome, I thought. They carried him off to the infirmary, where I heard he was released soon thereafter with a bump on his head but no concussion.

Susan caught up to me in the Quad.

"That was stupid," she said.

"I know."

"You could have gotten kicked out."

"I know."

"And you could have gotten me kicked out too."

"I know."

"But it was fun," she said with a wicked smile.

"Yeah," I said. "It was."

"You aren't gonna make it to graduation at this rate," she warned.

Chapter Thirty-Three
Socks

S ocks. One of the ironclad rules at Bashford was about socks. That in the dining hall you had to wear socks. At least for dinner. Everyone had to wear socks to dinner, no matter what. And they checked. If you were running over straight from hockey practice and you forgot your socks, you just put your pants down on your hips and hoped no one noticed. They always did.

There were socks monitors when you lined up for dinner. Dean Harper or Mr. Rock would stand there, holding a cane, something old, wooden, and highly varnished. As boys came by, they would stick the cane on your leg to raise the pant legs and check on—socks.

And so it happened that on a warm May evening a few days before graduation, one of those evenings full of promise, we lined up for dinner at the usual time. Mr. Rock, at the front of the line, stood, cane at the ready, for socks check. I was discussing Senior Sneak Day with Jamie and Rennes when Mr. Rock came down the line.

"Mr. Stafford, do you have your socks on?" he said.

I dutifully lifted up my pants to reveal two blue New York Rangers socks—not, mind you, in the Bashford tradition, but certainly not illegal. He shook his head and continued down the line.

"Mr. Rennes," he said. Rennes stuck his leg out for Mr. Rock to use his cane to slide his pant leg up. "Very good, Mr. Rennes," he said approvingly. He moved on to Jamie, who lifted both his pants legs to reveal one red and one white sock.

"My God, what are we going to do with you boys?" exclaimed Mr. Rock, moving down the line.

"Ah, Mr. Rock," said Jamie. "What about your socks?"

Mr. Rock looked away quickly. But Jamie reached out and took told of his cane. Mr. Rock resisted for a moment, then realized it was useless. Jamie lifted a pant leg—and revealed a bare ankle.

"Oh, Mr. Rock," said Jamie. "No sock."

He lifted the other pant leg, and sure enough, no sock there either. Mr. Rock reddened, and we all burst out laughing as a small crowd formed around us.

"Sorry, but socks are mandatory," said Jamie and the crowd jeered.

Now Mr. Rock could have just ignored us, and frankly there wasn't much we could do about it. But he didn't, because after twenty years of living by the Bashford code, he could barely, in the midst of all these witnesses, just ditch it. Considering his next move, he paused. Then he handed his cane to Jamie and walked off. To his credit, maybe because he had a touch more humanity than we gave him credit for, he gave a backwards wave as he disappeared around the corner.

Trixie was waiting for me as I came out of dinner.

"Walk?" she said.

"Sure."

We walked out of the Quad, across the road, over the railing, down the hill and onto the playing field.

"I guess I should say thank you," I said.

"For what?"

"The Dean's Committee."

"Oh, that."

"You helped."

"Oh, they couldn't possibly throw out Tommy Stafford."

"They sure could." I laughed.

We walked along in silence for a while, and she bumped into my shoulder. Was it intentional? Then she did it again, and I knew.

"I'm not with Ben anymore."

"Really?"

"Oh, stop it. You know we aren't."

"And you're telling me this because . . ."

"Tommy Stafford," she snapped, her old self, "don't make me say it. You always do that. It's right there in front of your face, a very nice-looking face by the way, and you won't see it or you won't say it. You just sit there like a lump on a log."

"Say what?" I was enjoying this very much.

"That it's you," she said. "It's you I should be with . . . you."

"Really?" feigning surprised. " 'Cause I'm not the best-looking boy at school, you know."

"Tommy, it's the end of the year. Everyone looks at who you're with at the end of the year."

"So that's it?"

"Remember New York," she said.

"Yeah, that was fun."

"Oh, I hate you," she said. We walked on.

"This is about Susan Carter," she said finally. "Isn't it?"

I wasn't sure it was, or it wasn't. But Trixie knew.

"Sorry, I hate to lose."

I walked her back to the Quad, and right there, in front of everyone, she gave me a peck on the cheek.

"What are you going to do for Senior Sneak Day?" she asked.

"We're going camping," I replied.

Chapter Thirty-Four
Crossroads

Senior Sneak Day went way back. Hell, I don't know how long but a long time. It was a Bashford tradition, a day of cutting class and giving the finger to the school after many long years of the yoke. You were supposed to be bad, but only in the official way the school wanted you to be bad—you know, by cutting class, throwing toilet paper rolls across the Quad, singing dirty songs; that kind of thing, you know, official evildoing, very controlled, very managed. You weren't supposed to go off campus, drink, smoke, do drugs, drive illegal cars, stay out with Chalmers girls, or anything of the sort. But that's exactly what we were going to do.

On the picture-perfect May day, the day before graduation, we met in Rennes's room just after breakfast. When we got there, we discovered a heap of camping gear—tents, sleeping bags, pots and pans, knives, stoves, you name it—in a giant pyramid in the middle of his room. And there was a food stash, straight from Wugs in the dining hall. He had coolers stocked with food. *Magic happened sometimes.*

Besides the camping gear, we produced three guitars, one harmonica, a set of bongo drums, three ounces of pot, two cases of beer, a carton of cigarettes, and marshmallows and chocolate and graham crackers to round it out for s'mores. In one giant line, we walked all this stuff brazenly around the back of the school, down the road past B&G, and into the woods. Rennes, just like in the movies, looked both ways; then at his signal, we pulled the branches off his old, very illegal station wagon and shoved all the stuff in. But there was no way we could all get in with all this stuff; there was no room.

"What now?" I said.

"Wait," said Rennes. A moment later a VW van pulled up with George in the driver's seat.

"Where'd you get that?" I said.

"Just fucking get in," he said, so we piled in. Leading the way, with George following, Rennes drove off in the station wagon, a mad two-car caravan going fuck knows where. I surely didn't know. Nor did I care. Somehow, we always got where we were going. So I sat back and smoked a joint with Charts in his cutoff jeans, and Winton, who came to the camping trip dressed as Jimi Hendrix in swim trunks. We drove out of campus, officially crossing the line we weren't supposed to cross, and onto Route 159 headed north.

"Put that out," ordered Rennes and we put out the joint and sat up straight. "There's cops all over."

I saw the towns go by outside my window: Granby, East Granby, Bloomfield, Simsbury, and with each town the woods grew thicker, the lakes more remote, the forest denser. Rennes stopped at a general store in the middle of nowhere to ask directions when he got lost. And that added to the mystery, the great Rennes lost in the wilderness. He set out again in the station wagon, followed by George in the VW bus, not really caring where we went at that point. As we moved off the main roads, we found ourselves on narrower roads, where the trees almost extended over the road and branches hit the side. "Holy fuck," said George as the branches swept the side of the van.

Eventually, Rennes stopped at a turnoff with no sign and no way to know if it was the right road, but he turned down it and we followed.

"Where *are* we going?" asked a baffled Winton.

We all wondered the same thing. Rennes drove over a small State Parks bridge and came to a resting spot about fifty yards up a hill in a turnout used for vehicles to park. This was it. We got out. Rennes heard something and held up his hand to listen. A second later, clear but low, we identified the rumbling of water, perhaps running over rocks. Or tumbling down a steep drop. Rennes broke out into that great wide smile of his.

"Right the fuck on," he said, with a husky laugh.

We unloaded all the supplies and carried it all in backpacks and armfuls a half-mile up the trail—one Jimi Hendrix look-a-like, five guys with long hair, three guitars, several beat-up coolers. The trail took us deep into the woods, down a hill filled with oak and maple leaves still wet from winter snow, up another hill with patches of blue sneaking out between the trees ahead of us, and over a small, cleared ridge from which we could see a hundred miles of trees. Then we plunged back into the woods; the distinct sound of a waterfall grew louder, and louder still. We broke out into a clearing and found ourselves overlooking the waterfall, a deep pool below—and for about a mile below that the river winding into the woods.

We made camp on the hillside above the waterfall and collected rocks for a fire circle, then spread out our sleeping bags, tents, pots and pans, tarps, and backpacks.

"I wouldn't put your sleeping bag there," warned George.

"Why not?"

"Above the fire?"

Rennes and Jamie went back to the car for the water jugs, and when they returned, they had Susan Carter, Cindy, and several other Chalmers girls with them, all in cutoffs and tank tops.

"Right the fuck on," yelled Charts, letting out a holler. The echo rang in the canyon.

"Swim!"

At the bottom of the waterfall, there was a wonderful pool, pretty deep, with rock ledges all around so you could pull yourself out of the water and sun yourself on the rocks. We swam naked. Well, the boys went naked; the girls insisted on wearing bathing suits. But Susan took off her top halfway through, then put it back on a few moments later. The guys let it all hang out.

It wasn't the hottest part of the year, it being the end of May, but hot enough that when the sun slanted through the gorge it got really warm. George dove in, went under, and grabbed Cindy by the leg. She shrieked, then giggled. Jamie had something going with a new girl, Donna Frost.

"Why don't you at least take off your top?" he teased.

" 'Cause I don't want to, Jamie O'Connor," she said, playfully splashing him.

And Rennes moved off to the side of the pool with Camille Fortuna, who seemed to bask in his very large shadow, taking refuge there, looking out at the swimmers happily. As the sun slanted through the water Susan Carter and I swam to the bottom of the greenish pool. We were face-to-face, and she kissed me underwater. I took on water, and since we were both running out of air, we raced to the surface.

"Up here," yelled Charts—about forty feet up the rockface. He was standing on a ledge almost at the top of the waterfall, looking down on the pool. Disappearing for a second, he then jumped in a cannonball out over the water, landing with a gigantic splash, safely avoiding the rocks.

"Whoa," called out Rennes. "Cool."

When we climbed the rocks up to the ledge, I walked out and looked over with George, as Cindy and Susan Carter watched from below, shielding their eyes from the harsh rays. It was high up.

"Fuck," said George. But we weren't Bashford men for nothing, so after several palm-sweating moments, I retreated five paces, shook my head like *what the fuck am I doing?*—ran and jumped. As if I were coming down on a roller coaster, the world went by in a blur. I cut the water and sank like a rock till my feet hit bottom. I came up yelling and swam for the side.

"I'm gonna do it," Susan announced.

After mounting the hill, she stood intrepidly at the top, looking down in terror, rethinking the whole thing. Then without a word, she plummeted the whole fifty yards, fearless, making a somewhat smaller splash, and came up with utter joy on her face. Soon everybody was up there, peering over the edge. I jumped five, six times, or more. I lost count. Susan and I jumped, holding hands until they ripped apart halfway down and we made side-by-side splashes. Then Jamie and his girl and Rennes and his girl all held hands and jumped. We went up again and again, till the ledge got slick wet; we had to grip the rock with our toes.

Jamie and Charts stood at the peak, waiting to jump until we cleared. Jamie walked back not five or six steps this time, but twenty yards; he ran down the hillside, out onto the ledge, and jumped far out into the pool.

"Whoa, I gotta try that," Charts said,, running back.

Depositing his beer, he let out a war whoop from twenty yards up the hill – and ran. He made it down the hillside okay and out onto the ledge, but there he hit the slick part of the rock. His right leg slipped out from under him, and he fell with a thud. Bouncing towards the edge, he reached frantically out to stop himself from going over, but his hands found nothing but slick rock. They slid along it. He couldn't get a grip.

He went over. He cycled his legs against the air, trying to force himself out as far as he could, away from the rocks below. He was headed straight down when his last leg kick caught the cliff and propelled him out just a bit. I could see he was heading down towards an underwater rock ledge, about two feet out into the pool. He cycled his legs madly in the air to get out further. He hit the water right at the edge of the rock and went under. I couldn't see if he bashed his head on the rock or not, no way to tell. I waited, not daring to breathe. A moment later he came up, splashing around, and held up his arms in triumph.

"Holy fuck," said George, "that was close." Charts swam to shore, where Jamie pulled him out. They both lay there on their backs, breathing hard, laughing.

"You fucking idiot, Charts," yelled Rennes. "You're a fucking idiot, you know."

"Yeah," said Charts breathlessly, smiling up at the heavens, "I know."

His close brush with death didn't deter us, however. We jumped a dozen more times, making cannonballs and flying butterflies and double gainers into the water. Susan Carter jumped a half-dozen more times. Each time I couldn't help but admire her body in her bikini as she came down and slammed into the water. When she came up, she always looked at me first. When we were all tired and safe—bathing suits back on—Susan Carter put her head on my lap while I played with her hair on the rocks.

"Why do you always call me Susan Carter?" she said.

"What?"

"You never call me Susan. It's always Susan Carter. Why do you do that?"

"You've just always been . . . Susan Carter."

"I don't mind," she replied. "Just wondering." She closed her eyes.

"I guess it's because there's only one Susan Carter."

She hit me playfully, her eyes shut again. "You're crazy."

We didn't speak for a while.

"Will we see each other again, I mean, next year?"

"Sure we will."

"You don't get it, do you?" She sat up. She was mad, but I didn't know why.

"Get what?"

"You'll go off to Yale, I'll go to Cornell, and we'll see each other once or twice and then drift off and then that's it. That's what always happens."

We had hot dogs for dinner with a head of lettuce that everyone passed around, tearing off a giant leaf and rolling it up, eating it with mayonnaise. We had buns for the hot dogs, and ketchup, and little packets of relish sent by Wugs from the dining hall. George made a pot of baked beans, but somebody forgot the plates so we all dug into the pot, with pieces of wood for spoons, and ate the beans off the bark.

It was dark when we all crowded around the fire. Two new faces appeared in the dark, standing up, Trixie Harper and some friend she brought along. Trixie didn't say anything but looked at us, asking silently if she could stay. Everyone looked at me. When I nodded, Trixie sat down by the fire, and for once in her life Trixie didn't talk. Susan moved closer to me. I put my arm around her. Trixie smiled at me: she got it.

We built the fire up real high, and the sparks rose up into the trees like fireflies in the night sky. Trixie had brought more beer, which we drank, and Charts lit up two joints—one that went around one way and one the other. A noise sounded in the forest.

"Run," yelled Rennes, and all of us scattered, taking cover. A Forest Ranger ambled into our camp. He looked harmless enough in the firelight.

"At least it's not Harper," said George—showing himself in the firelight. I watched from about thirty yards away, then when I heard George laugh got up and joined him. The ranger was not much older than us, and he was just checking.

"Just make sure your fire is out," he said. "It's early in the year, but forest fires can still start."

We all gathered around him like he was a celebrity. His name plate said RANGER ARNOLD.

"You go, Arnie," yelled Charts.

Winton took a chance on this young ranger and handed him the joint.

"Want some?"

The ranger shook his head, smiled, turned his back to us, and disappeared into the dark.

"Bye, Arnie," we yelled.

Rennes got out his guitar. George grabbed his guitar. I grabbed my harmonica, and Jamie got the bongos. He hit the first chords and everyone sang . . .

Crossroads, seem to come and go . . .

"I didn't bring a sleeping bag," Susan whispered into my ear. The fire still raged.

"You can share mine," I said.

"Don't be long," she purred, heading off in the dark for my sleeping bag. She found it in the dark just up the hill and crawled inside. Rennes switched to The Grateful Dead.

What a lonnnnnng, strange trip it's been . . .

Susan was still awake in my sleeping bag when I got there. She moved over as much as possible, but it was a tight fit. She looked into my eyes. I could see her eyes shining in the firelight. There was sadness in them.

"Year of years," she said.

We kissed, and she pulled the sleeping bag over our heads. We could hear them at the fire.

"Where'd Tommy go?" asked Jamie.

"Shut up, Jamie," said George. "Just shut up."

Susan and I laughed and kissed and looked up at the stars and listened to the guitars from the fire circle.

"You can . . . " said Susan.

"But—"

"Oh, shut up," she said. And kissed me.

I woke at dawn. Susan was still asleep, but George was gathering firewood. I reached over and tried to unzip the sleeping bag but it wouldn't unzip.

"I moved you," said George.

"What?"

"I moved you. Or you could have burned up."

"Thanks."

"What happened?" said Susan, waking up.

"Nothing," said George. "Just Tommy."

I helped Susan out of the bag, and she reached for her clothes. A few moments later we were sitting by a roaring, George-built fire. Rennes woke up and made coffee. Jamie woke up and drank coffee. Trixie and her friend came to the fire, and Susan Carter smiled at her. Trixie smiled back. Winton—dressed as himself, not Jimi—took a rock to sit on. Charts poured a cup of coffee, and we all sat, in silence, drinking coffee and nursing our heads.

"We gotta get back," said Rennes. "Graduation is at two."

Nobody moved.

"So this may be the last time we're together," said Rennes. We all nodded.

"What a year," said George.

"It's not the end," I said. "We'll see each other next year."

"You'll be at Yale next year," said Susan.

"I'm not going to Yale," I said.

Everything stopped. I hadn't meant it to be an announcement, but it was.

"But you got in," said Susan. "To Yale."

"Yeah, I did because of my father . . . but I'm not going."

"Where are you going to go?"

"I'll find somewhere else," I said. "I got time."

That's all I said, and everyone nodded like *yeah, okay*, and we packed up the camp and got into the cars, drove back to school, this time driving right up to the dorm, it being the last day of school, since no one cared if we had illegal cars.

We made it to graduation, and our world slipped away in an instant. Dad in a sport coat, Mom in a dress, sisters, cousins, friends of the families, the Headmaster, even Dean Harper.

"You made it, Tommy," said the Headmaster. "I'm glad."

Music played—not Crosby Stills and Nash, but music from a flute player and a cello—and someone made a speech about the future, how we should never give up on our dreams. We looked at each other, like *who the fuck gives up on their dreams?* Winton, dressed like Jimi Hendrix to the end, even at graduation, wrapped in a yellow scarf around his Afro, threw his right arm in the air after he got his diploma.

Rennes and Jamie loaded up their family station wagon to head back to Virginia. Charts loaded up his ride to Wyoming to work for the Forest Service for the summer.

"See you," I said to each one. That's all I could think of to say.

George came over last, holding his duffle bag, dressed in a blazer.

"Look," he said, "no socks." He lifted his pants to show bare ankles.

"No socks," I said.

He helped me throw my duffle bags into the Rolls.

"What you doing this summer?" he said.

"Hanging out in the city, I guess. Why?"

"Well, I just got an offer to work at a summer stock theater."

"Really?"

"Yeah, somewhere in Massachusetts, building sets and running the shows. That kind of thing."

"Sounds cool."

"Want to come along?" he asked.

"What?" I said, truly shocked. "Me?"

"I told them I'd only go if you could go too," he said.

It took me only a moment. "Yeah. Count me in."

The year of years was over. Look, I know it's hard to understand, but it was beginning of the seventies, and as most people who lived back then know, the sixties didn't happen till the seventies. That's when the world changed for us. Everything changed. Ties were out. Jeans were in. Girls painted flowers on their faces. Soldiers fought the Vietnam War. Others protested it. Hair got longer, and not just for the hippies. There was love in a different way— the pill, free love, they called it. People did things they'd never even thought of before. Everything that could change *did* change. The world was a different place. And we didn't ask for it, it was just the place they put us. We just took it over.

Most people think it was about the drugs and the pill and the drinking and the fact that they handed the school over to us, and we didn't want to give it back. But it wasn't about any of that. We didn't create the world. They did. We just lived in it. We brought it to life. There was a flicker, and we made it into a flame. And in the middle of it all, we found something real, and alive, and great, and made it ours.

What a lonnnnnng, strange trip it's been . . .

But there's one thing we knew. There were no boats beating against the current, no being borne back into the past, no ceaseless anything. It was just us, and just the future, our future, and that's exactly where we planned to go.

THE END

Acknowledgments

Several people were instrumental in the publication of this book; the warmest thanks go out to Abbe Horsburgh, whose comments and encouragement helped get this project off the ground; George Blaxter, who read the early manuscript and blessed it; my editor Margaret Harrell, who managed to improve this book tremendously with her skill and perseverance; colleagues Jennifer DeGraaf and Andrea Brown for their advice and contributions; marketing assistant Sarah Groth; professor Ben LaFarge, my first and best mentor; my family for their support and encouragement, and Barbara Hartzler and SPS, which gave me valuable guidance.

About the Author

Thomas Louis Carroll is the author of the novels *The Colony* and *Young and Dumb: Year of Years*. He grew up in New York City and went west after graduating from Bard College in upstate New York. After several years in California, he now lives with his wife Sheri, a successful Educational Assistant, in Santa Fe, New Mexico, where he writes and runs a public relations company, Carroll Strategies. He has three incredible daughters who live in California. He has also written screenplays and produced and directed two films, *Big*

Bad Budget, seen on PBS stations all across the country, and *Who Stole the Tasmanian Devils?* When not writing, Tom is an avid skier, windsurfer, swimmer, and dogsledder, which he does most years in Northern Minnesota.

* * *

He can be reached at tc@ThomasLouisCarroll.com.

A Free Gift

Can You Help?

Thank You For Reading My Book

Write a review!

I really appreciate all of your feedback, and I love hearing what you have to say.

Please help and leave me an honest review on Amazon, letting me know what you thought of the book.

It means a lot for other readers to hear from those who have read the book.

Thanks so much!

Thomas Louis Carroll

And you can reach the author personally at tc@ThomasLouisCarroll.com.

Made in the USA
Coppell, TX
19 May 2021

55991358R00213